FALL

C.A. Allen

Novels of Arborand by C.A. Allen:

A Dewdrop Away

Dewdrop Prequel Trilogy:
Flight
Fall
Overworld

Dedicated to my Grandmother Gloria DeAngelis
to my Aunt Marge, and to my friend Chelsea Mitchell.
Because y'all always read every one of these things, and it
means so much to me :)

PROLOGUE

"I know why you've come."

The sunlight slanted down through the trees in a weak gesture nearly forgetful. Pinewood would always be a second thought in the realm of lighting. There was something in the air today, however, unrecognized by the motes of dust waking to the light, but real nonetheless. The pines whose branches the light traversed to the clearing below seemed to stand to listen to the strain of the two voices coming from the hollow in the base of one of their brethren. Time, as it usually seemed to do in this particular neck of the woods, held its breath.

"I'm getting really fed up with this," Edgar grumbled, pulling at his ears as he was wont to do in frustration. "Why can't you just give me straight answers? Are my cousins traitors or not? What was that twinge in my back this morning? Is it too many Dew Frosts? Because I can stop that. Just give me something I can look in the face, you know. I'm a direct squirrel."

The corners of the other's mouth turned upwards in what looked to the grizzled gray squirrel to be an unpleasantly private joke. He twitched in his seat. *Seers. I should have known!*

"Your concerns have a basis," the flyer seated across from him said after a time. "But you do not want to look outside yourself."

Edgar felt he was getting nauseated by the smoke in the room. *Flyers.* Why these crazy creatures had to use smoke and mirrors when they went into seer-mode was beyond him. He'd never met a seer he could trust, and never met a seer who wasn't a flyer. It wasn't that he was prejudiced, it was just facts. They all talked like this, too.

"Look outside yourself, look into the beyond, look past last month's crumpet". It was ridiculous, and he had the distinct impression that he was being taken for a fool.

"What do you mean by that?" he asked, letting the annoyance creep back into his voice as he involuntarily let his eyes drop to the cluttered floor beneath him. He focused on a pile of cards, then a red velvet something that looked like a smock of sorts. There were strange symbols on the cards; they made him nervous.

"I mean," there was a venomous edge to the seer's weak, raspy voice, and Edgar wondered if he had heard his thoughts. "That you are going to die. And in light of what is unfolding in Arborand of late," his laugh sounded like a sickness, "You may be getting the better part of the deal."

Edgar felt the tightness in his throat as though he were in a dream—and not a very nice one at that.

"You're not serious," he said, flicking his glance up to the seer's shadowy, gaunt features and back to the cards strewn out on the ground again, unable to keep his gaze. The symbol staring up at him from the nearest card was a jackrabbit etched in spiky black, wearing a manic grin. He wanted to throw up.

Perhaps it's only the Dew Frosts, his mind scrabbled frantically. *You had too many of them last night, and what's more, you'll get out of here and have too many again, and that ought to calm you down. Why be fatalistic? Most seers are fakes. By Astrippa, I could use a drink.*

"Can I go now?" he asked, mustering the ability to smile as though nothing had happened. Let that smug bastard take it however he wanted to. Most seers were fake. This was the truth.

"Why, of course," the seer smiled disarmingly back at him. It was a sharp-lined, insincere thing. From the floor, the jackrabbit on the playing card mirrored its master, leering up at him in obstinate silence.

CHAPTER I

"Cripes! Rotting tight rotted good for nothing spaces!"

More than a day's trek away from our former scene, these and many more colorful curses echoed from a rotting log wedged between two decrepit trees. This area of the woods was dark and continually damp, a last resort for those creatures who had had bad luck finding a home elsewhere, and more often than not, bad luck in general. The young, curiously dark-furred and scruffy being inhabiting the log was no exception to this rule.

It was not the first, or even the second time Lute had knocked over all of his earthly possessions upon waking. It was starting to get quite discouraging. Piled up haphazardly as everything was on the little ridges made by the decaying wood inside of the log, it was no wonder it all came raining down on him if he so much as moved the wrong way. Great for a wake-up call.

"Well I'm up now, huh," Lute muttered. A frightening thought seized him then, and he frantically began to dig through his belongings, throwing them roughly this way and that. "Oh," he said finally, letting out a great exhalation and clutching the reflecting glass to his chest. "Yer not out of luck yet, Lute-boy."

The mirror was a precious commission given to him by an elderly gray he guessed was living in the area, though the old guy hadn't given him much information on where to find him, just said he'd show up later. He'd confided to Lute shamefacedly that he'd traded his wife's antique looking glass for Dew Frosts and needed a reproduction to replace it with. He'd provided Lute with the reflecting glass and a description of how the fake must look; Lute had gathered some good wood and begun to create a frame around the glass. He needed to make some convincing carvings and weather it up a little for that authentic used look, something that was no small task, though Lute was a match for it certainly. He'd been promised payment for his services, and if he didn't get it, he had ways of making it so. His collection of knives, some freshly carved, others old and worn at the handle, made up a decent part of the pile back in the rotting log he was calling home.

Lute wasn't sure how the old gray had heard of him. The only thing he could think was that he'd been seen carving his mark on the old tree of the white squirrels and the word had spread.

Not too far from the dank part of the forest Lute lived in now there was a clearing full of ghosts. Full of memories and the burnt out shell of a tree, a lone wall on which he'd left the last mark. He could not remember anyone stumbling upon him at that time, but it was as possible as the day was young. Other squirrels were nosy and no one went into that clearing after all; he would have stood out to passersby. The clearing belonged to another time, and they were frightened of it. *He* was a bit frightened of it himself. Seasons ago now, he'd witnessed the extinction of a race, seen things that had eclipsed his understanding, and journeyed places his heart quailed at. It all seemed a dream now, whether a good one or bad one, Lute wasn't sure.

Lute went to work setting everything up in an orderly fashion again, grabbing his knives and arranging them delicately back on the ridge they had fallen from. Last, he picked up the reflecting glass again and considered it. His face as it appeared within seemed to him ridiculous, and he looked away from it, passing it downwards in embarrassment. He would work on the glass today, but to do that, he needed a good source of light, and immediately outside it was too gloomy. His mind flashed to the deserted clearing once more; it was cropping up in his thoughts more than he was comfortable with of late. It had been a while since he had been back to that place; the ghosts had become too much for him, the air too full of them, and they'd begun to influence his carving. It sounded so dumb when he thought it aloud, but, well, how else could he explain what had happened the last couple times he'd carved there? It had come out as the same thing, the same pattern, though each time he had set out to carve something different. Lute brushed his paws distractedly over his none-too-clean fur, stepping out his door. He'd walk until he found something, that was all. It shouldn't be too hard. He hadn't gone far when on second thought, he doubled back to take one of his knives, the oldest one with the bumblebees carved on the handle, as a precaution.

There was something wrong. He did not notice it immediately, but as Lute bounded smoothly across the pine-needled ground, a sense of unease spread through him. He stopped to listen but he could hear nothing except the usual sounds of rustling, chittering, animals calling to one another. Nothing seemed out of place, but as he kept going the feeling persisted, and he began to suspect. The object of his suspicion was so laughable that he thought maybe he really had been alone too long. *Yer losin it, Lute-boy.* He could imagine how Saecka, the chickaree whose band he'd been raised as a part of, would laugh at him, cocking an eyebrow, flicking her tail repeatedly in mirth. It was stupid maybe, but the more Lute walked along the ground, the greater his unrooted anxiety grew. *Roots, roots, roots,* he thought; the word tasted curiously warm. His suspicion seemed a lot more likely though no less dubious now. It was the ground.

To test this, Lute jumped to the nearest tree, clung to it, and waited for the feeling to fade. After some time, the turning in his gut lessened, though it did not go away. He began to climb, and when he got to the first good-sized branch on the tree, the feeling had completely subsided into nothingness.

What is this? Lute, completely bewildered, stared down at the ground from the dizzying height at which he'd positioned himself. *The instinct of the hunted?* The words popped into his mind through some invisible awning, and he recoiled at the idea. Who preyed on the squirrels? No one, really. There were fish, rabbits, even foxes, occasionally, but the squirrels were many and the squirrels were more, everywhere in Arborand. Was it another squirrel, a dangerous one? None of his confrontations thus far in life—and there had been many—had given him a feeling like this. Other squirrels, as dangerous as they could be, were a known factor. They couldn't produce this fear. Or so he thought. An unbidden image of that other, the tawny-furred monster in disguise from what seemed ages ago came into mind, and he pushed it back firmly.

Lute leaped to the next tree and then the next, surprised he hadn't bumped into someone already, screaming at him for invading their property. A silence had crowded in around his ears when he wasn't looking, like so many unpleasant cotton plant-ends. He looked down at the ground again. The ground looked back up at him. Lute went to meet it…and ran headlong into someone else.

At least, he thought it was a someone. It could have been a some*thing* the way it carried on, screaming and flailing and stumbling backwards on the branch they shared. For a second, he nearly panicked: the fur of this one was the same tawny color that had been troubling his mind mere seconds ago. It took only mere seconds more, however, to see that this was decidedly not the same squirrel. Lute, who had leapt back, hissing and brandishing his knife, stared at the being in front of him, lost for words. He nearly sheathed the knife and laughed, but contained himself just in time.

The squirrel he'd run into was absurdly plump, and festooned with the strangest articles, as though he'd taken to decorating himself like a wall of someone's home. Lute couldn't stop staring, though he sensed he was making the other squirrel extremely nervous by doing so. At least, he thought it was nervousness that made the other squirrel take to repeatedly slamming one meaty fist against his head, over and over. It might be a concussion.

"Uhm." Lute said, sheathing his knife, though he still kept his paw on the handle, just in case. "Are yew in need of any…assistance?"

The other looked up at him with round eyes, as though he'd just realized someone else was sharing this branch with him. The many necklaces hanging about his neck jingled with the movement. Lute raised a sardonic brow. Thankfully, at the sound of his voice, the other had stopped beating himself senseless and was now staring gape-mouthed at Lute as though he couldn't believe what he saw. When he finally spoke, his voice was thick and slavering in a way that should've been repellent but was somehow not.

"No no, not at all, not at all. Um. Bon't durry about it. I mean, don't worry about it." He winked one eye, and then the other, and then grinned apologetically at the nonplussed Lute. "Luck," he said by way of explanation, flushing a little. "Wink if you meet someone, and they'll stick by you until the end."

"I sincerely doubt that," Lute said. The other was unphased. He tapped the several hats on his head, the necklaces around his neck, the many belts straining against his girth. "All luck," he said. "My ma, she thinks I'm insane."

"I wonder why."

Lute, satisfied that the other squirrel wasn't dying of a concussion, had begun to walk away, but the other only followed, talking away at him.

"Well, it's just that she doesn't think I need all this to be going outside. She thinks I shouldn't go outside at all. It's a family tradition. She hasn't gone outside her whole life."

Lute turned and stared at him, feeling his brow twitch in irritation. "That is impossible," he told the fat fox squirrel, plainly and clearly. "She would need to eat."

"Oh, she does. She eats the walls."

Lute stared a second more and then briskly turned, bounding more quickly away to put some space between them. The other squirrel followed along, panting. Every once in a while, he would pause, bring one of his pendants up to his mouth and kiss it, before huffing and puffing onward. Finally, Lute decided to stop the madness. He turned around and waited, pointedly, for his unwanted companion to catch up to him, idly fingering his knife as he did so.

The other stopped, caught his breath, and, seeming to notice either Lute's unpleasant disposition or the knife at his side for the first time, paled. Lute suppressed a smirk.

"I don't know what else yer mother told yew while she was chewing on the walls of yer house, but not following armed strangers around talking yer fat bottom off would have been irreplaceable advice."

The other took a step backwards now, face dampened with sweat. He fiddled with one of the hats on his head-another ritual?—and said, "I was told today...I was supposed to meet someone who would be 'a friend to the end.' Sounds kind of corny, I guess, but that's what the card said! I keep a deck of cards, see, and I flip the three on top up every morning and see what they're telling me. So this morning there was a symbol for friend, and then a brick wall. It couldn't have been clearer." He bowed his head and rolled his eyes upward to look at Lute disarmingly, as though what he'd just said was extremely convincing.

"Yer cards are wrong," was all Lute said, turning to go. What sort of place was this that you couldn't run into someone by accident and go your separate way?

The big fox squirrel looked put-out. Lute thought this time he might get away—or so *help this fat idiot*, he thought privately—when the other said, "Don't go down there!" and made him pause.

Lute turned around and arched a brow, his heart racing despite himself. "Whyever not?"

For once he didn't preface it with an *you'll think I'm crazy* or a *I know how this sounds, but*. The other squirrel only said simply, "The ground is poisonous."

"Really..." Lute started to say, but the other came over to stand beside him, and for once he didn't put his paw on the hilt of his knife.

"You know it, too," the fox squirrel said brightly.

"Well, maybe I noticed something," Lute snapped, but his heart was not in it.

"My name is Kinder," the fox squirrel said in that same bright tone. "Just like the word 'kind', not the other way."

Lute gave up the fight. "Lute," he said.

"That's an instrument, you know."

"I know." He hated his name.

Kinder smiled wide, cheeks getting all puffed up like those ugly brown mushrooms that bloomed in the fall. "I like it."

***

"So what do you know about the ground being...poisonous?" Lute asked. He'd traversed into an area of sunlight and found a place atop a large, craggy rock to work on his carving. His back fit into one of the nooks perfectly and it was actually rather comfortable, for a rock. Naturally, Kinder had followed him, and Lute, feeling that he might have been a bit harsh on Kinder in the beginning, hadn't tried to stop him. He really wasn't a bad sort; perhaps Lute *had* just become too fond of solitude, though he was possessed of the perhaps irrational concern that after today, Kinder would follow him all over the woods raving about his superstitions for the rest of his life. Then he would have to knife him.

"Just what I told you," Kinder told him. He was shrugging off one of his many necklaces, one that looked suspiciously like it had a peanut dangling from the end of its chain. He placed it on the rock in front of him.

Lute could feel his hopes at getting any real information out of him plummeting. "So it's just because you *feel* it or something?"

"Well, yes, but my feelings are very formidable." Kinder squinted up at the sun, then looked back down at his peanut-necklace and adjusted it on the rock. He did this a couple more times before speaking again. "I know, for example, when someone I love is in danger. I know when it's going to storm, and I know when I'm going to have to take a pee."

"Everyone knows when they have to pee."

Kinder remained unperturbed by this news. "Some things you just know," he said simply, as though he were trying to impart some particularly sage wisdom to someone not so wise.

Lute couldn't manage to be irritated. He'd finished carving one whole side of the mirror frame; it was now covered in a design of interlocking, fearsome vines and predatory yet beautiful flowers. Lute found it an odd thing to have on one's looking glass, and it made him wonder what sort of squirrel that old imbecile had stolen from. Wife or not, he might be regretting his choice sooner or later.

"Hey, Kinder, care to answer a question for me? Why do yew think we can't feel it now?"

He'd been so absorbed in his carving that he hadn't noticed how the feelings of malaise he'd experienced so close to the ground before were now gone. They were not too far off the ground now, after all, he should be feeling it at least a little, shouldn't he?

"It's still there," Kinder said, almost disinterested. "What's that you're making?"

"It's something someone wants…made."

Kinder nodded like the vague answer explained everything. There was a moment of silence between them, and then he said, "It's really good."

"Yeah, well, I learned from a master of—

"I mean, it's really, really good."

Lute looked over at Kinder in some alarm. It looked like the fat squirrel might cry or something.

"…Thanks," he said awkwardly.

Kinder nodded like this was all he wanted to hear, and looped his peanut necklace over his head again. "I think it's time to go."

"Kinder? Can we not walk on the ground now? I mean, is it not safe or nothing?"

"When the feeling gets stronger, it's worse," he said solemnly. "It won't kill you to walk on it when it's weaker."

"But this is the first day I've felt it."

Kinder looked taken aback. "Really? It's been this way for quite some time—"

"Kinder, I can't feel it now. How am I supposed to know when to…go up a tree or something?"

Kinder considered this. "Today it was stronger than it's ever been," he said. "My cards told me that ahead of time, too, which is why I was taking the trees even though other squirrels yell at me sometimes when I do."

"So what yer saying is, when it gets really bad, I'll feel it?"

Kinder did that unfitting, radiant grin of his again. "Yeah, you got it! Lute, do you mind if I find you again?" He looked hesitant.

"Find me? What d'yew mean by that?"

"It's another of my skills."

"Sure, whatever." He paused before adding, "Just so long as yew don't, I don't know, 'find' me when I'm asleep or minding my own business or something."

Kinder beamed again and scampered away, although you really couldn't call the activity he was engaging in scampering, Lute thought—heavy bouncing was more like it.

When Kinder had gone, he was again provided with refreshing peace in which to work on his carving, but he found that an unwelcome nervousness kept stealing in while his head was bent over his work. Lute looked up two or three times, but there was never any physical sign that anything was amiss. It was enough to drive you crazy, he thought grumpily. He couldn't believe that he'd be missing that obnoxious slob so soon, but somehow the other's presence had taken his unease about the ground, or at least his focus on it, away. Finally, Lute stood up and, tucking his carving carefully into the threadbare sack he carried for such things, began to dart away. Half on, half off the rock he stopped, feeling angry with himself.

"This is ridiculous, Lute-boy," he muttered. "Afraid of yer own shadow, is what you'll be next." He made himself stay and finish his carving, thinking of things to soothe his mind and the tremors in his paws. It was then that he thought of Edelle.

"No," he said, getting up again abruptly, packing his things without looking at them, without care. He walked away, over the ground without thinking, and it turned out he needn't have feared anything.

He felt nothing.

CHAPTER II

The gray squirrel known simply as Edgar to his few acquaintances was treating himself to a Dew Frost or five, trying his best to wash away the bad taste the meeting with the seer earlier that morning had left in the back of his throat.

"Ten rengolds," the barkeep, a small, pointy, slit-eyed fox squirrel, said in a bored draw. He was accustomed to Edgar's service.

"Listen, but I only have five," Edgar said after a panicked moment of digging in the pockets of his sloppy tunic. Billum narrowed his already narrowed eyes much narrower. Going for a different tack, Edgar leaned close to him over the counter, sliding him the coins as he did so.

"Billum, I'm going to die," he whispered.

The barkeep's eyes remained narrowed, and Edgar realized he probably thought this was just drunk-talk, that the Dew Frosts had idled his mind.

"I mean it, Billum. I talked to this...this seer— a flyer, mind you, so he was the genuine article, and he said 'you're going to die, Edgar, and you're going to die this very night, so I'd get my pleasure while I can!'" So maybe the last part wasn't entirely true, but he felt he had the right to exaggeration. "Listen, I wouldn't lie to you. I'm just desperate to enjoy my last day on earth, with Astrippa's good grace. You wouldn't deny a chap that, would you?"

Billum remained immovable. "Ten rengolds, or what have you," he repeated.

Edgar went on the offensive. "I gave you my wife's mirror last week," he sputtered. He did not even need to fake indignation for this one. "Do you know how much that cost, for a what have you? More than ten rengolds, I can tell you that!"

"Ten rengolds, *or what have you*," Billum growled.

"Do you have any idea of the cost of my bodily harm if she found out? Why, she'd probably skin me and stick me on the wall—"

"If you don't hand over the rest of the payment, you're never coming back. Perhaps your wife will have less reason to skin you then," the barkeep snickered.

Everyone was looking at them now. There were a good deal of squirrels in here, too.

"Well," Edgar said, standing up unsteadily and trying to put some force into his words. "Since you always do such great business, I'm sure you won't miss me if I self my let- *let myself out.*"

"By all means." Billum gestured to the door at the same instant as a shriek roused the night beyond the walls of the bar.

Talk and laughter, drunken shouts, all died down immediately. One nervous gray knocked over the candle on the table he was sitting at, dousing his companions in hot wax. Edgar looked at Billum, who was staring wide-eyed at the door as though he suspected the source of the trouble outside was going to come crashing into his bar at any second.

Edgar turned to the door and back uneasily. His pleasant drunkenness had been eclipsed by what should have been fear but felt more like excitement. Billum brushed past him on his way to the door, turning to look at the rest of them distractedly as though he were going to say something, before going outside.

Everyone waited, the room a package of held breath, but no further noise came from the hollow space below their feet. Billum did not come back, however, and soon the sound of voices could be heard outside, a cacophony that grew louder and louder until one of the squirrels at the nervous gray's table stood up, brushing dried wax from his fur. "I'm going to see what this is about, who's with me?" His voice was loud and commanding, and several of the others seemed to gravitate toward his sudden leadership. Suddenly everyone was crowding for the door, and Edgar found himself caught up in the rush of bodies. The cool night air hit him and made his head pound and the gorge rise in his throat. Buffeted this way and that out on the branch outside, Edgar finally found purchase in the wood, leaned over, and threw up. A disgusted cry sounded from below, and he briefly wondered what unsuspecting target had fallen victim to his discharge. Once the other squirrels from inside the bar had all gone down the tree, Edgar sat a moment, head throbbing, watching the tiny milling shapes far below him.

When his headache had subsided a little, Edgar followed them down and was inundated by the surging, chattering crowd once more. This time he could weave through them, finding the cool gaps where no one tread, and looking ahead he could see that they weren't simply milling about as mindlessly as he'd thought. They were crowding towards *something* nearby. A large huddle of squirrels packed close against one another, straining to see over the shoulders of those in front of them, blocked Edgar's progress. He supposed he could have turned away, but that feeling that was not quite fear and queerly resembled excitement had come back to him, mounting slowly inside until it matched his rapidly beating pulse.

"Move aside!" Edgar screamed, on sudden inspiration. "I'm here to investigate, move aside!"

At first no one moved, and he was disappointed, then as he strained against the mass of bodies forcefully, they began to pry themselves apart, shifting and grumbling as they did so. Many of them gave Edgar suspicious glares as he passed, and one even dared to shove him before backing quickly away and fading into the anonymity of the crowd. He found himself walking through a parted sea of bodies—*all* of these squirrels could not have come from the bar—and to the center towards whatever was causing all the fuss.

When he saw the source of the panic, Edgar nearly threw up again.

If it had been a gray squirrel, it was only a deflated caricature of one now. It was as though all of the insides, the meat, the bones, everything, had been sucked out of the squirrel lying dead at his feet, turning it to a grotesque, deflated version of what it had been in life. It was surprisingly clean, except in the area of the eyes, now two holes like negative buttons, leaking a minimal amount of blood and something else, whitish and foreign and thick. The cleanliness of the thing somehow made it more repulsive to Edgar, who shielded his eyes and stepped backward into the crowd again.

"Hey," someone said from behind him, "I thought you were an inspector!"

"Yeah, where are you going?" someone else yelled.

A clamor of voices cried out, anxious and angry in turns, as he turned back and fled across the darkened ground, the spots of yellow light coming down from the open door of the bar up above. He did not pay them any mind; there was only one thing in his head.

I have to get home, I have to get home. If I can get home—

He didn't finish the thought, caught up in running and thinking and repeating the mantra he had made for himself. He was so busy running and thinking and repeating that he failed to notice as the air became hot around him, thick and musky. When he did notice, he turned, feeling as though he'd gone into some strange zone of slow motion, of stopping and starting, a zone he could not come back out of. At first he could see nothing behind him; it seemed as though the air had filled up with a steam so thick he could not see through it, and then what he saw was nothing he could make sense of. A mouth, teeth, and then...thick, plantlike tendrils forcing themselves, green and earthy and rotting, into his eyes.

Edgar couldn't scream. He'd been running too long.

**

The seer Absoulim sat in his twisted-backed chair in the flickering light of his small chamber and let the pin fall softly from his open paw to the scarred tabletop below.

"Twenty-two," he mused, voice soft and unpleasant against the solitude of the room. He considered the number, then slowly rose from where he was seated and walked to the window. Silhouetted for a moment between the sphere of the window and the dark room behind, his arms rose from his sides and the aching light from the moon punched its pale agony through the confusion of jagged holes rent through his wings, reflecting off scar tissue in a dully ominous glow. Absoulim moved forward and placed his paws on the window frame, staring out at the lights of the several hundred homes he could see glowing as miniature pinpricks off among the other trees.

"Now," he said, voice rasping on the word. He began to count them as they went out. "One. Two. Three. Goodnight. Oh, yes. Goodnight."

CHAPTER III

Lute was having a better day than he could justify to himself. He made himself rise early and finish his work on the looking glass's frame, which had shaped up to be beautiful, all interlocking leaves with thorny petals. It made him oddly reminiscent, in a way where he didn't know whether to cry, laugh, or to hide his face altogether.

It's good, he thought. *It is really* is *something good.*

It was only then that he realized how foreign this thought felt to him. True, at the end of every carving, he'd felt pride, but it was more in the time spent, the accomplishment of finishing. Perhaps it was the way his mentor Pember had once stood beside him when he made his things, critical eyes and a firm paw on the back of the chair on which he worked. He had never known those eyes to soften, but then he supposed they could have in observation. He hadn't quite dared to look up and see; all he did know was how those firm paws could hurt. And at the end, the magic would be gone, maybe for them both, and Pember would take whatever he was working on from his paws, utter a criticism, pass it back to him and walk away to attend to his own matters. If he was lucky. Was this why he couldn't ever let himself see his work as anything but accomplishment after accomplishment?

"I love it," he murmured, and allowed himself to know it was true. This was the thought that gilded his morning: of the things he'd loved, this could be his at least.

It was this feeling of contentment that accompanied him to the door of his log when he heard someone knocking with a forceful urgency. As soon as he confronted the old female fox squirrel outside he knew who she was despite the surprise of her color and kind, different from that of her gray husband. He also knew that this meeting was not likely to go very swimmingly.

She started talking the second he appeared in the entrance, looking him up and down as she talked, her eyes bright and keen—they were eyes that did not miss a thing, and Lute knew right away that lying wouldn't be getting him out of this one.

"So you're the young squaw my Edgar went to visit, hey? What did he give you for it?"

Lute was momentarily nonplussed, before it dawned upon him.

"Oh, no. No, see—he didn't sell yer looking glass to me, ma'am. He'd already sold it, I don't know to where, but—"

"You expect me to believe that?"

A hint of scorn crept into Lute's voice. "Lady, I don't care what yew believe, it's the truth."

"Right," she hissed, recovering quickly from his change of tone. "I'm sure that's what it is. How much did he pay you to say that? Usually when you types are caught out, you just throw those like my husband out to the wind. And I can tell you're one of those types, so don't bother lying to me about that either. What are you, an urchin, a clinger-on, a *thief*?"

"No," Lute blurted, aggravated even as he felt his color rise behind his dark fur. The truth was, he'd been all three of these things in his early days. Being raised by chickarees didn't generally cause other self-respecting squirrels to embrace your existence, as he'd found out soon enough. It was like they could smell the difference on him, like a curse.

The old hag at the door opened her mouth to say more, and Lute held up a paw. He ducked into the log, bumping his head on the ceiling and cursing, stumbling around in the suddenly green-tinged darkness as he searched for what he wanted.

"Here," he said, crossing back out into the blinding light and pressing the looking glass into her paws.

"I told you—"she began again, fiercely, but stopped, staring at the looking glass. "This isn't it."

"No."

"It…it looks a lot like it, though."

"That was the idea."

She jerked her head up and gave him a sort of glare, but her gaze softened again almost immediately. "It's very…" Whatever Lute was expecting, it was not the tears that began to slide from her eyes to the ground, trailing like pearlescent slugs among the dirt and the pine needles. He stood there awkwardly.

"Yew can take it," he said, after a moment of painful internal struggle. "Free of charge, like." He felt oddly ashamed of the knife lying a few feet behind him on the table, and the way his mind had gone to it as soon as the mirror was in the other's hands.

Edgar's wife looked up, showed him the mirror. "This is a very immoral thing to do," she said.

"I know." Lute was enthralled with her words, without knowing why. He watched his wavering reflection talk in the mirror, hating it from a calm distance he wasn't accustomed to.

"I wouldn't have bought it," she continued, utterly unaware of how weird he felt. "He would have come to me with it and I would have known, and he would have felt put-upon, and carried himself off again to that bar he's always going to, and I would probably have murdered him when he got back."

He didn't know whether she was joking. He felt as though she didn't, either. She shrugged.

"As it is, there's no need for that." Her eyes got teary again and she put her head down, embarrassed. "I don't know why I'm crying over it. We never really had anything going for us."

"Maybe once yew thought yew did."

Lute hadn't realized he was going to speak; the sound of his voice took him by surprise.

"Maybe."

With a pensive expression on her face, the old squirrel handed over the mirror. Lute felt something close between them as it changed paws again, no longer held up before him, but clutched to his chest and forgotten.

"Listen," Edgar's wife said to him. "Edgar's died, just last night, and no one will give me any information about it." If she were about to break at this, she gave no sign of it. Lute found himself thinking that if she had been younger, or he older, he could have fallen for her.

"The last place he was seen was the bar. Someone else died around there last night, on the grounds below. You may think me horrible, but I want to find the other mirror, the real one. It meant a lot to me, probably more than he did. Think whatever you want of me for that, but I have my reasons. The only places I ever knew him to go just before his death were here and that damned bar. I can't think what he would have done with the mirror."

"Does the bar take what have yew?" Lute asked, the cogs already turning in his head. If he was good at anything, it was knowing systems of barter down pat.

She looked at a loss.

"It's when yew can give 'em anything and they'll take it, usually for less than it's worth, in place of rengolds. Lots of places of the like do it. I'd try the bar. But, er, be careful." He felt foolish for adding the last bit, and hoped she didn't take him for being condescending.

She smiled at him. It was the first real smile he'd seen her give, and Lute couldn't remember how she'd appeared a hag to him. Well, aside from the furious temper.

"Do I know you?" she asked him, and for one wild second he wanted to say something besides the truth. He only shook his head.

Edgar's wife looked at him, puzzled only for a moment more before she drew herself up and got to business.

"Well, son, I'll go pay that bar a visit now," she said. "No sense wasting time, and I need to be doing something with myself."

She turned. He held the mirror out to her again.

"Are yew sure yew don't want to...?"

She smiled at him again. "No. You keep it. You need it, I think."

She walked away, leaping gracefully through the spots of sun, leaving him to stare at her retreating tail and wonder at her words. When she was out of sight, Lute turned and stared back inside at his things, his knives, his scanty food rations, his makeshift bed, all dimmed in his vision. The world had grown curiously bright outside his door and the day thus far felt unreal to him, a string of formless feeling that left a strange but not unpleasant taste in his throat.

***

Kinder was counting.

It was something he did every morning, to ensure that Bad Things, like rocks falling on his head, for instance, didn't happen. He counted the drool stains on his pillow, the fur he'd shed in bed, and recorded the numbers on a sheet he had tacked to the wall. Next, he looked in his book on number meanings, to see what it would tell him about this day's readings.

"Sixteen furs....trouble, possibly," he murmured. He had a charm for possible trouble. Certain trouble, on the other paw...

"Two new drool stains...or three, possibly three." It was hard to tell with one's drool. "Let's see....two is boredom, three is intrigue. Well, those are two completely different things!" He picked a bracelet that would allow him to become intrigued by the smallest things in order to make boredom more bearable, as a compromise. A sense of accomplishment was already beginning to wash over him. Only one more thing to do.

"Dreams," Kinder said, and with considerable gravity, pulled a different book from under his bed. This one was old, its pages yellowed and inexplicably torn in places. Kinder immediately began to page through it. "Floating...on...old...cheese...let's see...Old...cheese...old...acorns? No. Cheese. Ah! To meet up. Floating? Reliance. Hm. Reliance on meeting up? Meeting up with reliance? Doesn't make much sense..." These old editions were always so out of date! Kinder supposed he would just have to keep considering those words throughout the day. Maybe it would come to him, though it made him nervous not to have a charm. To compensate, when putting on his extra-good-luck items, he put on two extra hats and an earring that he felt made him look jaunty, even if his mother said it made him look like a chickaree. He wasn't sure how she knew this, since the last time she'd been out of the house was seasons ago, and he wasn't entirely sure she'd ever actually seen a chickaree.

After doing a double-check in front of his mirror to make sure he had everything, Kinder skirted down the winding wooden stairs to the downstairs of his home.

Kinder's aunt, who came to visit only when she had stories to tell about her own life, was always obnoxious about how small and ill-lit their home was—ill-lit all except for the extra bedroom, in which his mother had opened up some holes in the walls to the outside quite by accident.

He came upon her now, gnawing at the wall across from the foot of the stairs. Her chewing always made this *ccccrreeeapppppp creeeeeaaaaap* sound that he couldn't ever have done justice to if he were to explain it to anyone. It was a scary noise; or so he remembered thinking when he was very young, lying upstairs in the old cot that smelled of mothballs and Aunt Millie's memories, trying to go to sleep like they told him, his aunt screaming, screaming, his mother chewing, chewing, chewing, screaming, chewing.

Not now, of course. He had grown far too old to be afraid of such things. Now it was more of a nuisance and caused this kind of crumple-pang in his chest when he found her places, like yesterday when he was getting something to eat, and he found her in the way, chewing on the kitchen wall, blocking the watercress salad.

Now, as he went down the stairs, she looked up at him with a twitching sort of grin. "Going somewhere?"

"Outside, mother." He tried to slide past her, but she blocked his way. There were wood chips sticking to the sides of her mouth, and a patina of drool making its way down her jaw, catching flakes of wood up in its stream as it went. He stared at it, rather than at her eyes.

"You went outside yesterday. You're always going outside." The tendril of drool dropped to the floor in the midst of her brief silence. Kinder switched to looking at the destroyed wall behind her head.

"Well, I have friends out there. I do things. You should try it, you'd really like it." He said this last part wearily, out of habit. Every time he'd done so, some part of him hoped… but always the same response greeted his suggestions.

"What, and have them kill me? No thank you! They're just lying in wait out there, hoping to get the opportunity to take me! And you, Kinder. You better watch that they don't come for you."

"I'll be okay, mother," he said, distracted: she'd moved, and there was a good-sized gap he could slip through between the foot of the stairs and his mother's bulk, and he took the opportunity to squeeze through and make for the door. "I think they've given up, though," he told her, trying one last time. "It would be perfectly safe."

She stared back at him, bloodshot eyes narrowed.

"That's exactly what they want you to think, son," she said. "Don't let them get you on their side." She turned to the wall and bit a huge chunk off of it to emphasize her point. Kinder escaped out the door.

Once out in the cold morning air, surrounded by open spaces, Kinder's body relaxed in the way he was used to it doing when he didn't even know he was tensed. He was about to go down the tree as opposed to the treetop route when he remembered how the ground had been yesterday. The poison within could be felt radiating upwards, waiting for him to become idle or bold so it could…could…

Could what? Kinder wondered. Was it possible for the ground itself to up and snatch him, or was there something…underneath? The idea boggled his mind. The ground and the sky were the limits of the world, everyone knew that. There was nothing beyond a limit. His thoughts were starting to sound disturbingly like his mother's tirades, and the thought made him frightened.

But I'm not insane, another part of him reasoned. *Lute felt it too, remember?*

Yes, this was true. The squirrel he'd met yesterday by accident, the one his cards had told him was a 'friend to the end', even though Lute himself seemed vehemently to resist this title—he'd felt the wrongness in the ground, too. And though Lute was unkempt and scrawny and disagreeable and his fur was a weird color that made him look like a black squirrel and a grey had mated—despite all of this, Lute did not seem insane. Kinder would even have wagered he was saner than most.

Normally Kinder took a trip to Nadra and Skellan's tree to get himself some breakfast. They were an older couple; Skellan loved to cook and Nadra loved to talk, and, living nearby as they did, they'd somehow found out one day about Kinder's lack of consistent meals. It was horribly embarrassing at first, but seeing as one of Kinder's favorite things in life was constant food, he got over it the moment Skellan placed a warm elderberry pie in front of him and said, "Have at it, my boy."

Kinder paused near the base of his tree, thinking. He *was* hungry, but the thought of Lute had made him urgent to see whether his friend was doing all right. Plus, he thought, he ought to 'meet up'. Wasn't that what his dream interpretation book had suggested?

Kinder's stomach growled. There was a sense of uneasiness all too familiar coming back to him. Somehow, he didn't feel like Nadra and Skellan's was the right place to be this morning. Kinder could have counted the times he'd overruled his stomach on one paw, but it looked like this was one of them. The urge to see what Lute was up to, where he lived, if he was okay, all crowded in. Despite what he told his mother, Lute was the first other squirrel he'd had the nerve to attempt a friendship with. Most of them laughed him off for his charms or his size, or worse yet, knew of his mother. He knew he couldn't exactly call what he and Lute had formed a friendship, since Lute seemed more than a little unwilling, but he would persist. What was in the cards, was in the cards.

Kinder was well aware that Lute had never told him where he lived, but he was certain that the cards hadn't told him that thing about being connected for nothing. Perhaps he could just follow his intuition.

After an hour or so of wandering around the forest, Kinder was growing more panicked by the growing sensation of the poison in the ground, roaring incessantly under his feet, and he still hadn't found Lute. He began to think perhaps his intuition was no good after all. He was probably going in circles, and though he'd had a whole turnip pie and a loaf of walnut bread the night before, courtesy of Skellan, he now felt as though he might faint from lack of food. The problem with pine trees was that they all looked the same.

"Lute!" he called in a last-ditch attempt, "Halllllooooooo! Uh!"

In turning around in circles and not watching where he was going, Kinder backed into something large and painful on the ground and came crashing through a thorny layer of undergrowth to land solidly on top of whatever it was he'd tripped on in the first place.

Crack.

Kinder jumped up again quickly at the sound of shouting coming from below him. *The thing in the ground?* his mind scrabbled, terrified, but what he saw come rocketing out of the undergrowth was infinitely more familiar and welcome than any monster he could conjure up.

"Lute!"

"What in the name of rotten, filthy, hailing acorns are yew doing, yew blasted idiot?!" Lute shrieked. His fur was sticking up in more directions than Kinder thought possible. He saw Lute stop, taking him in. Kinder's spirits took a dip when his expression remained just as furious. "Oh. *Yew.* Same question!"

"I was looking for your house."

"Yew found it." Lute gestured in back of him, and Kinder stared with sudden comprehension at the dilapidated log hidden in the shrubbery.

"Oh," he said in a small voice. Then, because he couldn't help it, (*Kinder keep your big fat mouth shut* his aunt's voice berated him), "You live in a log?"

Lute was still glaring daggers at him. "I did. Nowhere else to go, is there, the forest all claimed nice and tidy like it was? Popular neighborhood," he sneered.

"Sorry," Kinder said in a small voice. "You...you told me I could find you."

Lute pocketed his knife. Kinder, who hadn't even noticed he'd had it out, jumped.

"What was I thinking," he moaned. Then, "Fine. Yew found me, yew did some renovations on my home, what else? What did yer cards tell yew this morning, Kinder?"

Kinder flushed. "I didn't do the cards this morning, actually," he said, slightly defensive. "But my dreams told me to meet up with you, and I'm having weird feelings about the ground, and I know you do too only you can't sense them, so you need me."

It all came out in a sudden rush, and Lute was taken aback for an instant. He opened his mouth then closed it again as though thinking better of it.

"The ground bad now?" he said, after a period of awkward silence.

Kinder shrugged. "Not at a danger level, I would say."

He squinted at him. "Why're yew here then?"

"To visit you." Kinder was astounded at how suspiciously Lute was regarding him.

"Why're yew wearing an earring?"

"Oh, erm…luck."

"Figures. It's been highly successful so far, yeah?"

Kinder studiously ignored him. "Did you finish that mirror you were making?"

"Yeah. Except it turns out the guy who commissioned it is dead."

"I guess we've both had good luck so far," Kinder smiled shyly, and Lute barked out a laugh, his mouth cracking in a slight grin.

"There's another that died too," Lute said, remembering what his visitor had told him. "They both died at some bar the one guy's always going to. Are yew thinking the same place I am?"

"Old Cut Up Leaves? Is there another one?"

"Yeah, that's what I thought. The weird thing is, the wife of this guy told me they wouldn't even tell her how he died. They have two squirrels, dead on their grounds, and they're not going to offer an explanation for it?"

"On the grounds…" Kinder muttered.

"What?"

"Never mind. I think we should go there."

"It's none of our business."

"So?" Kinder wasn't having it. Upon hearing of the two deaths, his breath had become shallow. No doubt the thoughts he was thinking were untrue, they couldn't be true, such preposterous notions, but he must see for himself. He still felt guilty about walking away and leaving Lute- what if he couldn't tell if the ground got bad, if it got bad? He lived in a *log*! "Come on! Don't you want to know what's going on?"

"No," Lute said. He ducked into his house, and Kinder felt a sinking in his gut before he came back out with his knife, stuck it in the ill-fitting belt about his waist and said, "But maybe I can get some money out of someone."

***

The real reason Lute went with the clumsy, superstitious fool was the old squirrel's wife. If he could find out what happened to her husband...well, he didn't know what, then. Someone at the bar had to have known where she lived, what with her husband being such a regular. The more he thought about that idiot, the more he was glad he was dead. No one deserved to live with someone who would trade their most treasured possession for a few damned Dew Frosts. Though the young squirrel knew full well he would be giving the mirror back to the bastard in exchange for payment if things went their normal course, he let himself think he would have done otherwise without being prompted. Still, the more he thought, the more he felt guilty about his part with the mirror. He switched his eyes to Kinder, walking up ahead of him. His walk was odd, a kind of half-waddle, and every now and then, he would shuffle through the charms around his neck as though he were reminding himself of what they were. He did this almost subconsciously; once he almost ran into a tree while doing so.

Cut Up Leaves was dead silent that morning, as sure a sign as any that something wasn't right. Nothing looked amiss on the ground below, but when they climbed the tree to get to the little gap-boarded mess of a bar, neither squirrel could fail to notice the lack of sound coming from beneath the slanted crack at the bottom of the door. Lute pushed the door in, and it swung back creakily, then slowly pivoted back to nearly close in their faces again. A voice shouted, "Here, who is that?" and Lute immediately took note of the quaver in those words. Yes, they had the right bar. Something had happened here, no doubt about that.

"Just coming for a drink. You know I like my misters in the morning."

Kinder was staring at Lute perplexedly.

"I don't know anyone who does, no." The voice sounded defensive and frightened. *New,* Lute thought, *That's just too rich. They got a new guy to handle the morning after.* He could have laughed at his luck.

"Just come in, why don't you!" the voice squawked, getting higher pitched by the second.

Lute pushed open the door, stepped through, and let it close with a bang behind him. He heard Kinder complain loudly, and a second later, his companion trailed on in, rubbing his nose and giving the bar at large dark looks.

Behind the bar stood a young gray, wearing a scarf and looking scared out of his mind.

Lute trailed up to the bar slowly, going for a languorous, comfortable look. He lidded his eyes a bit and sat down across from the unfortunate. Kinder plunked himself down next to him, gave the young squirrel a smile. For being the one who'd come up with this plan in the first place, Lute thought, he was being very thick.

"One mister?" the gray asked, tugging on his scarf and staring between the two of them.

"Don't be dense," Lute said. The gray flinched.

"We're here on behalf of one 'Edgar'," he continued. "Died here a night ago, yew know him?"

"Uhm," he could see in that instant the young squirrel making a valiant attempt at looking as though he didn't know what Lute was talking about, and failing. "I'm not, you'll understand, authorized to talk about that."

"But, you see, Herman, we are authorized to hear about it, so one of us is going to have to back down." The other squirrel flinched again at hearing his name, as though he'd forgotten how neatly it was printed on his square of a name tag.

"Listen," Kinder said, voice apologetic, and Lute wanted to punch him for a moment, or tell him to shut him up before he stuck his foot in the whole thing. "What we want is not unreasonable. We cared for Edgar, and if you told us what happened the night he died, we'd be eternally grateful. We're not going to tell anyone else, and we certainly won't mention that you told us."

Herman stared at him. "Okay," he said, finally. "I was waiting tables that night. I...don't know much."

"Tell us what yew do know," Lute said, impatience seeping into his voice. He glanced over at Kinder, expecting to see him looking smug, but he was busy fiddling with his single earring, a slight smile on his face.

"Well, Edgar—he's a bit of a—" He seemed to be casting about for a polite word to use. "He comes here a lot," Herman decided. "He and Billum, that's my manager, got into some sort of fight over payment. Anyway, it got really loud after a while, or Edgar did, anyway, from all the dew content, and he was talking about how he was going to die, or how someone *said* he was going to die."

"What?" This hadn't been what Lute had expected at all. "Are yew trying to tell me he *knew* he would die that night?"

Herman shook his head. "I don't know. Billum seems to think not. He thinks it's a load of rot, actually. I don't know personally, but it seemed like he was just doing it for a rise at the time. To try and get out of paying. Told Billum a seer told him that, and that he should get his Dew Frosts for free because he gave him something of great value the last time he was in."

Lute felt a shock of excitement. He dug into his bag and pulled out the replica mirror.

"Something like this?"

He did not get the reaction he was hoping for. Herman only blinked and said, "I don't really know, to tell you the truth. I've only been on the job since last night, but the other servers tell me Billum likes to keep shut up about the what have you he gets. We never really see any of it after the customers hand it over."

Lute felt a sinking disappointment. He felt as though he'd come so close only to be turned aside.

"Where can I find this Billum?" he asked without thinking. Kinder made a distressed sound next to him.

"You said you wouldn't tell anyone!" Herman said, fixing Lute with a panicked, accusatory stare. "And anyway, he hasn't been back since last night. He seemed very…upset about Edgar's death, said squirrels would start blaming him for not giving the slosher what he wanted." He broke off, then amended, "Those are his words, not mine."

"Yeah, all right." Lute slumped over in his chair, tracing the knife at his waist unconsciously. He stopped when he realized Herman had noticed and was on the verge of having a heart attack.

"We're still missing one very important piece of information that yew've somehow avoided telling us until now," Lute continued, leaning forward in what he hoped was an imposing manner and lidding his eyes again. "How did this 'slosher' die?"

Herman was getting more uncomfortable by the minute. "Would you believe me if I said I really *don't* know?" He had picked up a glass and was polishing it with the end of his scarf. Kinder was watching this display with a glazed expression, but Lute suspected he was still listening to everything they were saying. He was beginning to feel like he had underestimated the fat fox squirrel.

"I might," Lute said, pretending to think it over, "If yew told me how the hell yew don't."

"Well. The bar was full of noise and all, the loudest of which was when Edgar and Billum got into a fight, like I told you. I felt like Billum was going to kick Edgar out because that's what he does when they get like that, and then Edgar said the things about dying, and then…then we heard this screaming. That was the other one."

Herman broke off and looked around at them both. He looked apprehensive as though he thought it might be bad luck to talk about such things, like they'd start up again if he described them too accurately.

"The other one?" Lute asked, momentarily forgetting.

"Name of Nadra," Herman said, nodding. "Yeah, apparently she was either out on a walk or on her way to the bar or—

They both turned to look at Kinder. He was sitting bolt upright, no longer staring at the glass in Herman's paws. "Nadra?" He looked around weakly, as though he'd just been sentenced to some horrible punishment and was waiting for someone, anyone, to appeal for him.

"Yeah." Herman put the glass down. "What's wrong? You know her?"

Kinder stood up, knocking over his stool as he did so. For a minute he looked as though he might scream or burst out crying. Then he took a measured breath and said, "I'll be back."

They heard the door swing shut in the resounding silence that followed. After a time he judged appropriate, Lute addressed Herman again.

"Do you know what happened to this...Nadra?"

"No. Well, and yes. We found her skin."

"Her skin?" Lute looked over in the direction of the door, all too aware that Kinder was standing right outside, listening. He could see his shadow moving out there, an obstruction to the line of light coming in underneath.

"She had no..." Herman hesitated, too. "No insides," he finished, picking up his glass once more and rubbing at a nonexistent spot. "By Astrippa, it was the worst thing I've ever seen."

Disgust welled up in Lute's stomach in small, choppy waves. "Who...Then, what..."

Herman shrugged. "We don't know. The same thing, that's what happened to Edgar. By the time we got to them, no one was around. There was no sign of anything amiss. Well, except for the obvious. There was...very little blood. That I remember." He gave a sort of shudder and stared somewhere to the left of him.

Lute sat in contemplation, or what tried to be contemplation at any rate. Every time he tried to visualize what Herman had told him about, he felt ill. He stared at the miniscule crumbs caught in the cracks of the stained wood of the table in front of him. It might have occurred to him that Herman was playing with his mind, but he knew the difference between contrived fear and real, primordial terror, and there were traces of the latter in Herman's voice and in his manner. At the same time Lute realized, in the silence broken only by the cottony squeaking of Herman's scarf on the glass, that he could go home from here. He could go back to his log, dilapidated as it now was thanks to Kinder's bottom, and think about this no longer. He had no obligations, he did not know any of these squirrels. There would be some discomfort, some memory at first, but things would inevitably settle down to how they always had been, how they *should* be right now. Just he and his carving knife and some wood, a peaceful silence devoid of the talk of others, and eternity. That was the way he liked it. He was sure of it.

Then why, in the silence broken only by the squeak of Herman's scarf against the glass, was he less than happy with this scenario? Kinder's shadow moved outside the door. When Lute spoke, it wasn't to leave.

"Yew said something about a seer?"

Herman fidgeted some more. "Did I?"

Lute was suddenly extremely impatient with the whole thing. "Yes," he snapped, pleased to note that he made the other squirrel jump. "The whole part where yew said yew overheard Edgar talking about how he was going to die. Yew said something about a seer."

To Lute's surprise, Herman now looked even more nervous than when he'd been digging for information on how the drunk fool was killed.

"I...don't think I did..."

"Yew did. Are we going to have some trouble remembering?"

"No! No..." Herman stared at the knife at Lute's hip and bit his lip. "It's just...I shouldn't have said that, probably. Certain things are better not—I mean—surely you're not thinking of—"

"Who is it?" Lute pressed. "This seer? Apparently her predictions are quite apt."

"Yes, well." The discomfort was more than evident now. "You're not going to..."

"To what? Go and see her? Yeah, I might."

"Not a…her," Herman said in a constricted voice.

"Yeah, well…hey, whatever, yew can't even pretend you don't know what I'm talking about. It's all over yer face."

He was a bit surprised that Herman looked just as sad as he was frightened by the idea. "I don't want to be responsible for whatever you two," he cast a look over at the door at this last word, "do with what I just told you. That's all."

Lute snorted to cover up just how spooked he was actually getting by the gray's fatalistic attitude. "No problem. Do you know where this seer lives, by any chance?"

Herman sighed. He was no longer playing with the glass, but turning it around in his paws, staring down at the simple pattern on its sides.

"It's three clearings east of here," he said.

"Very vague."

"No, you'll find it. It's the only tree in the middle of the last one. It's dead."

The way he said this last gave Lute pause, but only for a moment. "Okay, thanks a lot Herman, we won't breathe a word of this, yew got my promise."

"Absoulim."

"What?"

Herman was still staring down, but his words were unmistakable. "That's his name."

"Oh. Okay, great. Look, I've got to go now. Thanks for…telling us everything. Sorry if I made yew piss yourself or something, but I've got to go find this seer-fellow. Don't tell anyone about us and we won't tell anyone about yew." He turned and headed for the door.

Herman looked up from his inspection of the glass like he might say something more, but instead he only watched Lute go.

***

Kinder was outside, leaning against the side of the bar and rolling a leaf around between his fingers. He did not look up when Lute came to join him, the bar door pushing warm, stale-drink smelling air out around them both.

Lute stared at his downward tilting face, trying to figure how to talk to him now. There was no need, as Kinder spoke up seconds later.

"You're coming."

Lute blinked. He should have known Kinder had been eavesdropping. He just stood there, biting his tongue hard and fast against anything stupid that might want to come floating up from the coil of mismatched words like snakes in his intestines, so many wrongs and so few rights to expend. He knew. *Few squirrels are not burned by their own words,* those were Pember's drunken words on one of the few nights he'd gone philosophical-drunk. The night they were both seated at that table and Lute kept trying to get up and he couldn't get up because Pember kept staring at him, talking to him, and he didn't want to upset the fine balance. That, he believed to this day, despite all he'd experienced with Saecka's band of chickarees, was what real terror was: being trapped at a table with a potentially violent philosopher and nowhere to go but listen to nonsensical phrases that frightened you—shouldn't have, but did.

Kinder spoke again, breaking the mad rush of his desperate thoughts. "You don't need to go. You didn't know her."

"Yeah, I'm coming," Lute grinned at him, then stopped and fixed him with a glare. "Don't think I don't have my own reasons."

"Do you?" Kinder looked genuinely interested.

"If it helps yew to knock that sick thankful look off yer face."

Kinder continued to stare at him like he was his savior.

"Okay, follow me or don't, I'm off," Lute pronounced, effectively putting an end to that. *Burned by yer own words should be yer middle name, Lute-boy,* Saecka's voice teased in the back of his mind. He didn't have the wherewithal to argue.

CHAPTER IV

Mariyen was more than a little frustrated. It was the second time the chief sage had told her to clean the corridors, and evidently, she was still lacking something. In between dipping her sopping rag into the clear water and up again, she stole glances at the recorder. He gave nothing away, merely looking up from his papers now and then, nodding and writing a thing or two, then dipping his head back down as though in sleep. Probably meditating. Every time he caught her looking at him, he would take his paws, trail them up to his eyes, and make a downward motion, smiling serenely.

This made her angrier than anything else, she thought, because she tried, she really *tried*. When her friends Ruby and Hontem had talked about cleaning the hallways as discipline, she'd laughed at them. How hard could it be? She knew all the categories: care, diligence, silence and restfulness, she was capable of every one of them, and yet here she was, scrubbing floors a second time. Ruby had told her *she* had had to do it four times before she got it right, and then the recorder had only remarked her mediocre. Mariyen had blown it off in her mind, attributing her friend's troubles to the fact that Ruby was a little slow, a little clumsy, a little indiscreet, but now she wondered whether these unkind thoughts had not cursed her to the same mistakes in some way.

They had moved into a cavernous room which possessed an echoing stillness that belied the humility of its unadorned state. The only movement in the whole of the dark cavern was that of another squirrel, seated in the middle of the vast space, moving his mouth very slightly and holding a basin of what she assumed was water cradled between his haunches.

The recorder gestured at the expanse of the listening room and she thought, unable to stop it, Oh *no*. The recorder turned his head sharply toward her and considered, before writing what looked like a very short note on his paper. She felt nervous. Had he picked up that thought? The recorder scribbled something else. *Not again.* Mariyen then did what she had not the last time, and forced herself to turn her worry lightly away. She crept a few inches forward and reached for the trough of water, dipping her rag in. Small flecks of shining perspiration hit the floorboards with the droplets, staining the wood a darker brown, an almost-black. Making random patterns, begging to be swept together as was the way. She swept them, guiding them into one thicker blackness, deeper she guessed than any one drop would have dared to imagine alone. Rubbed the rag back and forth, passing over every crag and crevice. Drawing it upwards, more flecks of black, this time on the perfect black she'd left behind, already drying into its original state. Inching forward more, stopping. More water. The most natural thing in the world. Part of her, in back of her mind, scoffed at the young squirrel who'd quivered at this splendid simplicity, but that part was far off, like speaking through fog, and Mariyen continued on.

When she got to the squirrel in the middle of the room, she paused. She had to go around him so as not to disturb him. She realized then that she was covered in sweat, so that it was falling from her equal to the water from her rag, so that she did not know which she was using to clean. She did not look up, so that when she came to the other squirrel, the first thing she saw was his basin, pointing upwards at her face. She was right, it was filled with water. The water rippled, the ripples flooding eagerly out to the sides of the basin and back inward again, disappearing at the center until the water was completely smooth, a sheen of mirror-quality. There was another pause, and then the water rippled again. Her eyes went upwards a bit to the squirrel's muttering mouth, though she couldn't hear any words, and she knew what he was saying anyhow. *Okay.* The ripples were his heartbeat.

Slowly, Mariyen reached forward and picked up the basin from between the other squirrel's haunches. She set to work again, and he must have moved to get out of her way each time she did, though the corners of her eyes never caught him shifting. She was sure he moved because there were new spots of unblackened wood beside him every time she looked up. The ripples in the bowl continued at their usual slow speed. She wondered if it was now her heartbeat that moved the water, or still his, and decided the question was trivial. When she was finished, she placed the basin back where it belonged and

(Okay, Okay, Okay)

made her way to the end of the room, inches at a time. When she noticed there was no ground left to blacken, Mariyen rose to her feet and was stunned, like waking from a dream, to realize the recorder was standing inches from her. He was not writing on his paper. Mariyen waited.

The recorder reached up, touched his eyes in the way he had before, only this time it did not aggravate her. He smiled.

So it was that Mariyen Edgewood finally mastered the discipline of washing a floor.

***

The dreams still terrified her. That was the only thing that could keep her from enjoying her accomplishment as she walked down the summer passageway that night for bed. She could see Hontem studying her, confused as they went together to their quarters; Ruby had parted for the spring passageway a while back, and Mariyen was thankful, at least, that she hadn't noticed a thing.

Hontem, the more perceptive of her friends, was not so easily put off.

"What's troubling you, Mariyen?" she asked as they walked with the other female flyers who bedded in the summer chambers. She spoke in a low voice, for which Mariyen was grateful; the procession was supposed to be entirely silent, and she did not want to be called by one of the recorders positioned along the walls, especially after her victory today. She shook her head at her friend but Hontem was not convinced. She remained silent the rest of the way into their chambers, even to the beds with the plain white sheets, arranged as they were at random throughout the candlelit room. No sooner had they prepped for bed and the hustle of others' feet had ceased to run about around them, then Hontem turned over in bed and hissed at her to wake up.

Mariyen had closed the gauzy hangings around her bed and was hoping this would dissuade her friend from questioning. She didn't even like to think about the dreams, how was she to go about explaining that they were the cause of such unhappiness? Especially when—and she did not even want to admit this last to herself—she had never had a real vision before. Not that she thought her dreams were visions, there was no proof for that, and all that the elder seers had told her about the sensations involved with a vision did not fit her experiences, but there was still something about them—

A pillow came flying through the curtains and hit her soundly on the side of the head. She tried to breath out steadily, and remembered her experience earlier today with the cleaning of the passageways discipline. Though she had lost any real memory of how it had felt already, it comforted her to think about.

"Mariyen! Please talk to me!"

She sighed and ripped open the hangings. "Can't you be satisfied with the fact that it's nothing? Or is that too boring for you?"

She felt bad almost as soon as the words were out of her mouth. Hontem regarded her, slightly hurt. "I just want to make sure you're okay. I won't tell Ruby."

"You mean you won't tell her as long as you think I'm fine."

"Well..." She didn't know what to say to this, and Mariyen moved beyond it in any case, deciding to take her friend at face value so she could have out and done with it.

"I'm having dreams. They're not exactly nightmares, but ...I'm afraid of them. I get anxious when we are all about to go to bed, because sleep is starting to mean I have to have the dreams again. It's been so long since I haven't."

"Mariyen, you know you're supposed to tell the elders about any uncomfortable dreams!"

Mariyen winced. She'd known it would get to that. "I can't."

Hontem appraised her critically. "Well, why not?"

She was silent. She did not want to say why it really was she wouldn't tell the elders. The idea had crossed her mind before, and it was undoubtedly the smart thing to do, but it also meant admitting that she was still dreaming. To still be dreaming at her stage of life was not a good thing, and as afraid as she was of the dreams, Mariyen thought she might be more afraid of what the elder seers might tell her if she told them.

"What are the dreams about?" Hontem asked, persistent as ever. "Is it one recurring dream, or what?"

"No, not recurring." She thought. "They're similar, though." There *was* one similar element, or squirrel, rather, who seemed to feature in them. She wanted this conversation to be over, and it must have shown on her face.

"Fine, I won't press. I still think you should tell the elders, though."

Mariyen drew the hangings on her bed again. "I'm going to sleep now."

Hontem heaved a sigh of frustration. "Throw me my pillow, then."

Mariyen laid with arms stretched out to either side of her, unblinking, long after her friend had gone to sleep. She stared down blankly at her wings for a moment, the thin membranous skin coated thinly with fine dust-gray fur. *Like the lining of clouds,* her mother would say about her wings, and she would get embarrassed, fold them as much she could out of sight, arms at her sides. Her mother with her soft, dreamy voice, her mother upstairs with the elders even now. Attending. She had had so much hope for Mariyen as a seer, the first, possibly, in the family, though no one could be certain of these things. Family lines were extremely blurred intentionally, symbolized by everyone's taking of the same name, Edgewood. It was the name of the tree they inhabited, the founder had said, and everyone had believed her. Everyone knew that trees spoke, their breath and voices calling out in the autumn air more than any other time, and Flora Gelbragis had possessed not only the sight but the power to listen, a skill rarer still.

Mariyen's mother's face kept coming back to her as she crept toward slumber. It had been so long since she'd really seen, really talked to her—they'd both had other things to do, other duties. No one could blame either of them, but now in sleep she was vulnerable, and as Mariyen dreamed, the first thing she dreamed was her mother.

It had her mother's face, at least, and at first she was convinced.

She was standing in the middle of a chamber so brightly lit it hurt her eyes. It was nothing like any room she had known, and made her grasp about for some sign of her location, but all she thought she could see were some bookshelves to one side, indistinct. When the figure across from her called her by name, she forgot any such efforts.

It was shrouded in a white, gauzy veil not unlike the shroud hanging around the bed in which she slept, the bed she could still, oddly, feel under her, though the power to open her eyes was so lost to her that she believed the room in front of her more real.

"Mariyen," the figure said again, its breath making the veil in front of its face ease outwards and back. It was holding something in its paws, stroking it fervently, and though the figure under the sheet looked exactly like her mother, whatever she was holding made Mariyen uneasy, and she felt the first trickle of doubt run through her, all the way down to her gut where it settled uncomfortably.

"Mother?" It was a question.

The thing smiled. It continued to pat the bundle cradled in its arms.

Though all her tendons and bones seemed to be screaming at her not to go any closer, Mariyen took a step towards the figure that so resembled her mother.

"Please," she said, "Who are you?"

The figure smiled. It was somehow an unpleasant sight, though the smile was as beautiful as she remembered it.

"Come closer, and I can show you."

Mariyen had ceased to feel the bed underneath her. She had no choice, and she needed to know, she needed to know so terribly...

She closed the distance between herself and her mother, and her mother tore off her veil.

The thing underneath had her mother's face, all except for the eyes: it had none. Where they should have been, there were only gaping holes ringed with red, with torn, irritated flesh and dried chunks of blood and fur. The thing in its arms squalled, and she looked down at it, trepidation and gorge rising simultaneously even as she did so. It was a baby, but it was not really a baby, it couldn't be. It was pure, ghastly white just like the robes the mother-thing wore, its eyes a roiling red that no fire, however greedily it burned, could have attained. The baby squirrel thing reached out its arms towards her, mouth agape to reveal pointed layers of teeth that should have had no rights to have grown yet. Its wings were shot through with several bulging veins, red and blue and pink, that made her feel ill. She backed up, or tried to back up, but no matter how fast she attempted to retreat, the mother-thing followed. She could no longer see its face, only the baby in its arms, which had some sort of weird hold on her. She attempted to turn around, couldn't, and panicked; when she turned back to face her tormentor it was no longer there. Instead, a young, tawny heavyset squirrel that seemed to belong to a strain she'd never seen in her life appeared before her. She might have been frightened, but instead she was just sad, fear fallen to the dust at his arrival.

The tawny squirrel looked at her, toying with several things hanging on thongs or chains around his neck. He seemed to be trying to speak to her, but his voice was faint and he was squinting as though he were constantly about to lose sight of her. She could only catch snatches of what she thought she heard him say,

"Coming...ground...when..." He looked across at her desperately, as though he knew she couldn't hear.

"What...?" she spoke, reaching out for his flickering form.

She woke up then, a thin sheen of sweat coating her face. She quickly registered where she was again, giving her breathing a chance to slow, though it would never match the contented rise and fall of the non-dreamers sharing the room with her. The dim lighting calmed her down more than anything else, the sense that she was no longer in the glaringly lit chamber, no longer at the mercy of mother-wraiths or demon-children.

That tawny squirrel, though, he was the common strand. Every single dream she had, he'd been there at the end, her waking image, leaving her with a sadness and a feeling that she'd missed something terribly important.

Mariyen turned over in bed. The room around her was completely undisturbed, meaning that she probably hadn't cried out in her sleep at least. Once, she had done so and it had taken her forever and a day to convince Hontem there was nothing wrong. She did not want to know what that scream had sounded like, as she remembered the dream that had preceded it all too well.

For several long minutes she lay there, unsure if she would ever feel tired again and knowing she did not want to. She needed an image, any image. And then it came to her: a cavernous, airy darkness, the ripples spreading in the basin and *okay okay okay* until she- miraculously- drifted off to sleep again.

This time there were no dreams to greet her return, and that was good, better than good.

Okay.

The dawn was still several hours in coming.

CHAPTER V

When Lute first broached the topic of Nadra, Kinder hadn't been expecting it, and he flinched when his companion remembered her name. When he'd gone outside the bar, he'd shed his tears and then stood in a kind of trance, picturing the warm kitchen, smells of spices and pies and what he imagined home smelled like in an ideal world. It was not real. Squirrels like Nadra, who sat talking to you about anything and everything and listened to everything you had to say, didn't die, and squirrels like Skellan, who always remembered to put pumpkin flavor in your tea, should not ever have to live without them. He knew that the thing in the ground, whatever it was, had disrupted the order of things forever. If he ever went back to that house one morning...but he wouldn't. That was over for him; he didn't know how to face Skellan, and he knew he would see Nadra in every exchange they made, even the innocence of tea.

Part of him thought that it might be his fault. He knew it was ridiculous—how could it be? But it worried at him all the same. Was there some sort of good luck charm he could have worn, some ritual he could have performed, something in the cards he had overlooked yesterday that would have made all the difference, would have caused Nadra to turn that night from wherever she was going and think better of it, decide to go another night or not at all? But Kinder knew better, or told himself he should. For some things there were no charms. No charms to keep Nadra from dying, no charms to keep his father from leaving, his mother from her insanity, from the *creeeappp creeeeap creeeeeeaaapp* sound of her chewing and the looking under couch cushions for food, squeezing around the cracks of a house that had grown too drafty.

There were no charms, perhaps, for the most important things, the *only* important things, in the world. But he liked to believe. He had to believe. If there was anything the drafts, and the screaming and the leaving had taught him, it was this.

"I can't really talk about it right now," he told Lute.

Kinder was apprehensive about this seer business; but then, what wasn't he apprehensive about? The only sensible thing for him to do now, he knew, was to find out what had killed Nadra.

And put a stop to it.

Could he do that? He was one squirrel, surely he couldn't, though it was nice to believe...

The voice which had delivered this ultimatum to him did not speak again, did not argue with this unfortunate fact. It did not agree either. It simply waited in the back of his mind.

"This is it," Lute said, stopping so abruptly that Kinder tripped trying to stop himself from running into him.

Kinder looked, but all he saw was a clearing like the rest—until he trained his eyes where Lute was looking.

The tree was enormous, a monstrosity rising up out of the ground like a tormented patient rising from a death-sleep, some of its limbs crawling outwards to grab onto others around it, twining around their branches with the dry husks of its own, choking them in the places it touched. It was the most horrible tree Kinder thought he'd ever seen in his life, and yes, as Herman had said, it was dead. Kinder could not understand how it was still standing, for not only was this tree dead, it looked as though it had been dead for a very, very long time. Yet it stood, its dry grip still twisted around its neighbors like some giant parasite, its body twisted and rotting as though it had been frozen in the moment of its final contortions.

They both stared for a moment, before Lute turned to Kinder with his eyebrows raised. "He lives..."

"In that," Kinder finished.

"You know, I think I'm beginning to understand why Herman back there was jumping out of his fur when I tried to ask him about this," Lute said, a nervous smile flitting across his face.

"Should we...go in?" Kinder was uncomfortable just standing in front of the tree, so vulnerable in the clearing. As they began to move closer, creeping under its branches and rustling up the autumn leaves, Kinder began to feel watched. It was a sharp, strong sensation like someone had opened him up and was perusing through his insides, and it stopped him in his tracks.

"What is it?" Lute was impatient, but Kinder could tell it was fear-impatience that Lute didn't want to move forward any more than he did.

"Do you feel like...someone's watching you?" His voice gradated to a whisper in his fear that the watcher might also be a listener.

Lute thought, shrugged uncomfortably. "No. Yer probably just feeling the typical side effects of being thoroughly creeped out." He moved for the base of the tree, eyes searching out the place where a door should be, an opening, anything. Kinder followed. They circled the tree once, but no logical entrance appeared to them.

"Who doesn't have a front door?" Lute groused. "It's *weird* is what it is." Kinder noticed he was trying to keep his voice from shaking. He searched the tree frantically himself, anything to rid him of the sensation of eyes on his back, and was rewarded by the sight of a knob and what looked like a door handle of some sort. He could not see the door, if there was in fact a door, from where he stood, but he nudged Lute and pointed.

"Kinder, what're yew...oh. Why's it up so high, blast it?"

Kinder shrugged and began to climb the tree. The bark was wet and spongy beneath his paws. He could not understand, once again, how the tree could still be standing; the fact that it was seemed a violation of nature. As he got within a clear viewing range of the place he was climbing toward, he saw that it was indeed a door, set inside a small alcove made possible by a knot in the tree. Lute puffed up to stand beside him, and they both stood on the landing before the door, hesitance clouding over any conversation, before Kinder stepped forward and knocked on the small, rounded door. The two squirrels sat back and waited, and Kinder tried to remind himself that the house did not necessarily reflect the inhabitant.

The squirrel who opened the door would make him rethink this comforting notion.

For a long time, however, no one *did* answer the door, and Lute said, "Let's go back, okay? We can come back again—

It was at this time that the door moved fluidly open, almost cracking Lute across the face, as though the seer had been standing just inside and heard everything they were saying. The thought did not make Kinder feel any more comfortable.

"And what would two *very* impatient squirrels like yourselves be doing at my doorstep?"

The first thing Kinder noticed about the seer was how incredibly gaunt and un-squirrel-like he appeared. He was a flyer, though awkwardly shaped for one, flyers typically being small and round, and there was something odd about the wings crumpled beneath his arms—held as they were by his sides in the dim light of the tree, Kinder could not tell what it was. His eyes were curiously pale for a squirrel, and when they travelled over the two of them, Kinder had no doubt anymore that these were the same eyes he had felt on his back ever since he caught sight of the tree.

Steeling himself with the thought of Nadra and his real reasons for being here, he said, "A squirrel came by here earlier. His name was Edgar."

Absoulim only stared at him. It unnerved him and he lost the threads of what he was going to say.

"We knew him," Lute thankfully broke in. "And he died last night. We want to know why." Then, realizing how accusing he must have sounded, "Yew know. Because he told me yew told him he was going to die, and I laughed it off then, but now...yew can imagine how I feel about that now."

"Yes, how sad," Absoulim said, not appearing so in the slightest. Lute was not dissuaded, and Kinder found himself exceedingly glad for the other's presence. That bit about being Edgar's friend! Small as it was, he would not have thought of it. Kinder had never been a very gifted liar, so he was surprised at how naturally it seemed to come to Lute.

"Yew told him he was going to die, and he did, and we figure since yer a seer and all, and apparently a good one, yew'd know how he died. Or..." he trailed off at Absoulim's gaze.

"You want to know about the ground."

Kinder and Lute exchanged a quick glance of astonishment.

"Er, yes. The squirrel at—someone, that is, told us that Edgar was found without insides. And he— he pointed to Kinder, "he can feel something wrong with the ground sometimes, so yeah, we did think there might be something linking the two but we weren't certain and—

"Come."

Absoulim turned and started back into the tree. He did not wait to see if Lute and Kinder would follow, and the two, with one last glance at each other, fell into step behind him.

A smell of dampness greeted them in the dark, a smell of mold and rot like forgotten things that are best forgotten after all, and it took a while for their eyes to adjust. When they did, it was to rest upon the craggy, pulpy ceiling lit up as it was in deeply contrasting shadows by the one firefly lantern standing on a rickety table by the door.

"Shut the door," Absoulim's voice drifted up to them from somewhere apparently close by, and they both jumped. It was an unpleasant voice, rasping and low like the seer had lost his voice by way of sickness and it was just now being returned to him, uncertain and damaged. Lute stepped to the door and did as he was bid, causing the entrance to fall into nearly complete darkness. Kinder's belly did a flip and then a flop, and he reasoned with himself that he was just over-reacting. They'd come here, and they would do what they had intended to do, then they would leave. There was no reason to doubt that, either. *The sounds of closing doors only sound like finality to the paranoid.* He couldn't remember who had said that to him, or if anyone had at all. It could have just as easily been one of his books. He clutched his charm for possible bad things and followed Lute, who began to walk into the dim tunnel in front of them.

The passageway was uneven and soft and occasionally dripped with water or perhaps something more unpleasant. Some of it fell on Lute's head and he swore in an unnaturally high-pitched tone. Kinder forgot to watch his feet and tripped over something lying on the uneven floor beneath him. He fell, still clutching his charm, and staggered, regaining balance against the wall and looking down with foreboding. It was only a book.

In fact, as Kinder continued down the sloping passageway, which was clearly headed downward, he noticed several other books scattered at random throughout the hall, some closed and propped up against the walls, others open and splayed in disarray on the floor. The titles were too small for him to read in the darkness, but he caught part of one: *Ancient Magics Moste Perverse: A…*

Kinder clutched his charm tighter.

Just when he was beginning to think that he would never stop walking, that the tunnel would go down, down into the earth itself, that the seer was perhaps planning to offer them up to whatever malevolent thing that made the ground feel so unsafe, they came to a set of crudely constructed steps. The steps themselves appeared to be made of stone, rocks piled one on top of another, so that Kinder expected them to wobble or fall as he was going down them. They were sturdy, and he was reminded of how the very tree they were inside of should have fallen long ago. These steps were more of the same. He knew just from looking at Lute's rigid back descending in front of him that his friend was experiencing similar misgivings.

The stairs opened up into a room that was lighter than any single bit of the seer's dwelling had been so far, and Kinder's eyes followed the shaft of drowsy autumn sunlight up to a crack in the wood near the ceiling. He at first rejoiced in the idea that at least here, where it seemed they would stay, there was some ventilation, scanty though it was: then he saw something move and looked again.

The edges of the opening were crawling with maggots.

Kinder looked away, his throat making a dry clicking sound as he did so, and glanced around, trying to clear the image from his mind. The rest of the room was tame in appearance, cluttered as it was with more books like the ones he'd seen in the hallways, piles of cards, scraps of velvety cloth that could have been clothing, and burnt out candles. There were empty tea cups with the crusty remains of the drink still clinging to their egg-shell innards, and odd vials and crystal balls of varying sizes lined the rotting shelves on the rotting walls. The air smelled sweetly pungent as though someone had left a piece of fruit somewhere and forgotten about it.

Absoulim turned around to face them, and Kinder's attention was immediately drawn back to him nervously. He could see now when the seer stepped into the single ray of musty light, paws clasped in front of him, what was wrong with his wings. They were tattered nearly to pieces as though he'd fallen from a high place and had his wings pierced by every single branch on his way down. It was the only explanation Kinder could think of for the way the skin was torn, skin hanging down in flaps from some of the long-healed wounds. He realized he was staring, and that the seer was also aware of this. He looked away, averting his eyes to the wall behind him, but Absoulim only smiled thinly.

"Would the guests like some tea?" he asked in that raspy, recovering voice.

Lute shook his head, but Kinder, his mind on his lack of breakfast and the fact that tea was in fact a lucky thing in frightful situations, nodded. "Yes, please."

Lute gave him a queer, panicked look. Absoulim had already turned to a shelf behind a battered wooden table draped with more strange objects. On the shelf were two cups, and as he took them down (Lute stared openly at his wings in the process) Kinder noticed the trail of steam smoking upwards from them both, disappearing in the air above. Kinder thought nervously, *That's not right. I saw those two cups earlier and I could have sworn they were empty.* But this wasn't entirely true. His eyes had passed over the cups, true enough, but he supposed he hadn't looked at them long enough to see the steam, considering how many other strange things there were to focus on in here. Still, he thought, hot tea. How did he keep it hot if it *was* there all this time? *Don't think about it, not now. We just need to get the answers, and leave.*

Kinder could smell the steam coming from the tea cups now, and it was pleasant: mint tea. He turned to Lute, who gave him a withering look. He was looking oddly drained, and Kinder guessed he was wondering about the cups as well. He wished he could communicate to his friend that the tea wasn't poisoned or anything—how he knew this, he wasn't sure, but it was in much the same way that he knew when the ground was dangerous to walk on: just a feeling, but a completely trustable one at that.

"Sit down, sit down," Absoulim murmured, his pale eyes moving over them and back almost nervously.

Kinder noticed a few worn out stools and poufs scattered at random throughout the cluttered room. Some had things completely obscuring them, draped over them so that they looked more like mountains of stuff than chairs. He chose a stool close to the table at which Absoulim stood, and Lute flopped into the pouf next to it. The rotting-fruit smell was more intense closer to the ground, and Kinder was glad for the tea the seer handed to him. His paws brushed the bony knuckles of the seer's own when he took the cup and he felt himself shudder inwardly. He hoped Absoulim hadn't noticed. If he had, he gave no indication, but sank down in the faded red armchair –now an ill shade of pink—on the other side of the table and watched them for an uncomfortable moment, taking a sip of his own tea as he did so.

"Um," Lute said.

Absoulim smiled again. There was nothing more unpleasant than that smile, Kinder thought. It seemed to serve the opposite purpose of what a smile should.

"Yes, you're here about the ground."

Lute nodded, but it was Kinder whose eyes those of the seer fastened upon next. Those eyes were so washed out, like a drowned thing's, and there was a deadness to them that made him hard pressed not to squirm.

"You feel the approach, then?" he mused quietly. Kinder didn't know whether he was supposed to answer. "That's…different."

"The approach of what?" Lute blurted. Absoulim switched his gaze to him, and he quieted.

"Suffice to say that they are…unfriendly, the guardians of the nether realm."

Kinder blinked. He sipped some more of his tea to steady himself. What did one say to this? Lute once again got there first.

"Nether world?" he asked, and there was skepticism in his voice. "What's that supposed to mean? Are yew trying to scare us? Because—"

Once again, the seer's gaze moved back to Lute, and that sickening smile that was not a smile came back to his face. It never touched those blank eyes. "Do I need to try?…Lute?"

Lute recoiled, and Kinder could see him frantically running over whether or not they had given him their names. They had not.

Absoulim pulled something towards him across his desk of sorts, and Kinder received another shock. It was a skull, and not just any skull.

"Is that..." his voice shook and he couldn't finish. Absoulim turned to him, that stomach-turning smile on his face still.

"Do you remember the white squirrels?"

"They're dead!" Lute spoke up, abruptly and shakily. Kinder looked over at Lute, a little surprised, and saw a strange expression fighting with his friend's features.

"Oh? Do you *know* that?"

"Yes," Lute said, and there was something like anger in his tone now, coursing through his words, anger and a single thread of an emotion Kinder couldn't identify. "There was a colony around here—the last. The tree burnt. They're all gone."

Absoulim had one long paw on the top of the squirrel skull's head, and was stroking it, watching Lute dispassionately. "Believe me," Lute said, then, his voice still heavy with something foreign.

"I believe you," the seer said. "But you're wrong."

Lute jerked his head around. He looked so frightening in that instant that Kinder flinched. "Yeah? Where's that skull from? Yew got one of 'em captive or something?"

Absoulim seemed completely unphased by Lute's sudden flare of temper, as though he had expected it. He continued to stroke the skull, and when he answered, that weak, scratchy voice of his hadn't grown any stronger or louder. He looked nearly amused.

"The skull is from one of them, yes. I know the colony you speak of; it is the one from which I attained this lovely...addition." He gave the skull a look that made Kinder, with all of his charms and trinkets, feel positively sane. "I do not have a 'captive', as you put it." Lute started to speak, but Absoulim held up a paw. "You are right in assuming that one of their number survived, though he is not truly of them."

Lute did not say anything immediately. Kinder turned to him and saw that he was staring at the skull, again with that expression Kinder couldn't place.

"Surely you must have heard the tale in which the white squirrels are the guardians of Astrippa?" Absoulim said. "Your kind is adamant on that sort of thing."

Kinder couldn't bother to be offended at this last statement, though he sensed Lute tense beside him.

"Yes, I have," he said. Then, knowing he must sound like an idiot, "Is it…true?"

"It is only true of one of them. I imagine they never corrected the misconceptions due to the feelings of power it gave them." He paused. They waited.

"The story goes that this one squirrel was sent by Astrippa to live among the other whites and to act as a silent guardian over our world. This squirrel possessed magic given to him by Astrippa, magic much stronger than that some of the other whites were born with. All that was required of him was to retain his purity as one of Astrippa's own. By his living in the guise of a mortal, we would all be safe."

"Something happened, didn't it?"

"Yes," the seer answered Kinder. "Something happened." He paused and stroked the skull some more, as though pondering how to proceed. "He made too much ruckus when he lived with the other white squirrels. He appeared to them an orphan and they were none too fond of the mischief he stirred up. They tended to keep him out of the way as he grew older and more energetic, more entranced by his own mortality. He was forgetting already.

When the tree burned, most assumed everyone had died. But he did not."

Absoulim halted, and Kinder hesitantly spoke up. "Well, that's a good thing, isn't it?" he asked.

"It would have been, if he hadn't gone on to thoroughly lose his purity. As it was, he went on to break one of the main pacts he'd made with Astrippa."

"What was that?" Lute said. His face still looked a little sick, and he sounded as though he wanted badly to be cynical.

"He fell in love," Absoulim said. "Or he thought he did, and he pursued it. This severed his bond with Astrippa, and left Arborand vulnerable to all he was guarding against. And now it seems that the effects of his negligence are making themselves evident." The seer looked oddly self-satisfied for having just predicted the downfall of their very world.

There was a silence, in which Kinder tried to swallow all of this information. He had heard tales of the whites squirrels, of course, that they possessed a link to Astrippa, that they all had access to extremely powerful magics, and even that they were immortal. These ideas had to have come from *somewhere*, didn't they?

Lute wasn't so convinced. "How do *yew* know all of this, then? And don't say it's because yer a seer, because I don't think even seers have that much power!"

Kinder shrunk in his seat, and even Lute seemed to notice he'd probably stepped beyond his bounds. Still, he didn't take his words back, and Kinder felt the anger coming from him again, coursing in slow waves. Lute's eyes kept going to the squirrel skull under Absoulim's spider-like paw and jerking away again; they repeated the action once more as he waited for the seer to speak.

Absoulim smiled. After a moment, he spoke and his voice was exceedingly calm and flat.

"Whether you believe me or not is really of no concern to me. You came to me, not the other way around."

"But yew didn't answer our question!" Lute burst out. "Our question was what happened to Edgar—"

"Oh, yes. Your *friend*," Absoulim smirked.

"Yes, our friend!" Lute shouted, though he'd faltered for a moment in the realization that Absoulim already knew this for a complete lie. "We didn't ask why weird stuff might be happening with the ground, but why our friends died. Only their skin was left behind. What kind of a monster would do that? But yew didn't answer that question, didyer, instead yew told us some fairy-tale about a white squirrel still bein' alive and I know they're not alive, they're dead, because I was *there* and no one survived! No one!" Kinder realized with a jolt that Lute was fighting tears. His words were opening up a new part of his companion, and a part of his history that Kinder found fascinating. He also could not help but notice that as Lute went on in his fury, his words became more and more vulgar and abbreviated, lapsing into a strange accent that Kinder hadn't particularly noticed before. When he'd looked at his cards and they told him Lute would be important to him as a friend, he hadn't thought of much else, as though this new squirrel were to be an extension of himself. Now he saw that he didn't know his 'friend to the end' at all.

Absoulim looked angry now, a gleam set into his pale eyes that Kinder did not like. He seemed to consider before speaking, pushing the skull to the side and leaning forward, paws clasped together in front of him. Kinder fell to studying the tea leaves in the bottom of his empty cup, avoiding that spark of something dangerous and praying Lute wouldn't have anything else to say.

"I suggest," he said, but Lute overrode him and Kinder's prayers went unanswered.

"Yer leadin' us off course on purpose! You want us to assume this is the fault of some mythical pact bein' broken and there's nothin' we can do about it! How can yew *divine* all that and not know what's happenin' with the ground?! Either yew don't know anythin' at all, or you do know what's happenin' with the ground and yew won't tell us because yew have some personal stake in it!"

The seer was saying something, but Kinder found it almost impossible to hear his weak, raspy voice over Lute's diatribe. Kinder was beginning to get a bad feeling about this.

"Lute?" Kinder said, leaning over and touching Lute's shoulder, but the other squirrel only brushed him away and continued.

"I mean, we must be pretty close to the ground now, huh? The floor here's all dirt. Why aren't yew afraid of whatever it is killed those others? Yew can't be immune just because yew got some sixth sense or whatever."

Suddenly, Kinder felt a hard, cold claw close around his arm. Absoulim had reached out and grabbed hold of him while Lute was talking, and as soon as Lute noticed, his words faded on the damp air.

"Hey," he said, but now the fear had come back to his voice. "Hey, let him go."

The seer gave another of his smiles that were not, and with his other paw, pried the tea cup from Kinder's loose grip. "Your friend," he said, after staring into the cup for mere seconds, "Is going to die."

Kinder stiffened.

"Resorting to trying to scare us?" Lute asked in what was supposed to be a mocking tone but fell short. Outside, the light momentarily deepened as the sun was obscured by a cloud.

The seer ignored him. "Believe whatever you like. My predictions fall at random. Only fate can decide what I know or do not know. As for fear," He smiled, this time with his teeth, "I have none."

"Let him go," Lute said again. Absoulim did so. Not breaking his gaze with either of them, he sat back down in the armchair behind his table and stared at them again.

"Well, then. Is there anything else you have come to know?"

Lute, who had risen to a standing position in his fury, said, "No. We're done. Come on, Kinder."

But Kinder remained where he was, staring at the tea cup on the table in front of him and feeling the imagined burn where Absoulim's cold paw had touched him.

"I want to know," he said after a time, "About the white squirrel, the one you were talking about. The survivor. Astrippa's messenger, whoever he was. Where did he go?"

Absoulim kept that thin, false smile on his face, as though he'd known it would come to this all along.

"He hid," the seer said. "It is the only rational thing to do for someone as rash and as arrogant as he. He hid after the burning of the last colony of whites, after the unfortunate love affair. He hid, but not well enough."

"Y-you know where he is then?" Kinder, like Lute, had thought perhaps Absoulim was only telling them tales to throw them off. The idea that there might actually be a squirrel connected to a goddess, one whose protection was needed in order for their world to be safe, was a little strange, both comforting and frightening at once.

"Yes, I know where he is. It may...cost you something."

To Kinder's chagrin, the seer's eyes lingered on the charms about his neck.

Kinder did some quick thinking. One of his charms was purely good luck, while the other was for possible trouble. He told Absoulim what they were, switching them around and hoping the seer couldn't see through the lie. He had other good luck charms, but there was no replacement for the possible trouble one. He'd got it from a crazy old gray who'd survived a lightning strike five times.

"Hm. I don't want to burden you with taking your best charm. How about the other one?"

Kinder's heart sunk. The seer's dead eyes revealed nothing of whether or not he'd known this was really Kinder's most important good luck item. Seeing no way to get out of it, Kinder slowly removed the charm from around his neck, clasping it hard in his palm. Absoulim reached for it and for a breathless moment Kinder didn't know whether he could let the charm drop. He did in the end, and it lay coiled in the seer's paw, looking absurdly small and innocuous. Absoulim's long-clawed fingers closed over it and he stowed it somewhere in the depths of the moldy looking robe he was wearing. Kinder had a panicked moment when he thought the seer wouldn't tell them after all, would only keep his charm and send them on their way, but Absoulim gave them another of his horrible smiles and said, "He lives in Firwood now, south of here. Aspen Forest, to be exact. You will have to search him out, but I don't see as it will be too hard. He's the only white squirrel there, and it's hard to stay hidden even if one has...considerable power."

Kinder stared at the seer, the skull, the cluttered room. All of them stared back at him. There was something about this that made him uneasy, aside from all of the obvious. *Your friend is going to die.* He shook his mind clean, grabbed for his charms, then remembered there was only one and felt in its solidity what he lacked.

"I will show you out," said Absoulim.

CHAPTER VI

"Mariyen!"

Mariyen turned over in her sleep. It wasn't morning meditation yet, it couldn't be...

"Mariyen!" Someone began to shake her, speaking in a fierce whisper. "I know you're awake!"

She peered out of the cracks of her eyelids and saw Ashby, a quiet squirrel she hardly talked to, waiting nervously at her bedside.

"What's wrong?" she asked, sitting up slowly, rubbing the sleep from her eyes. All of the other flyers in the room were still asleep. She turned questioningly to Ashby. She'd been right: too early for morning meditation. What was this, then?

"You have to...that is, Horus wants to..."

"*What?*" she jumped out of bed so quickly that she pulled a bunch of her pillows and all of her sheets off with her. Her mind was buzzing with anger. Hontem had told! She should have known!

Ashby looked sympathetic. "I'm sorry. I'd be terrified, too."

Mariyen paused. She was pretty sure Ashby didn't know the real reason she was being sent to see the elders—the average flyer would be frightened at a summons from them, after all—but she wanted to make sure.

"Ashby, do you know why he wants to speak to me?" Her voice sounded hesitant and forced to her own ears.

Ashby shrugged. "Sorry, Mariyen. I was doing the early morning tea ceremony discipline, and Horus broke in. Said it couldn't wait." She paused, apparently considering the implications for herself, "I hope I pass. They'll probably reschedule now, though."

"Sorry," Mariyen mumbled, not really paying attention. Her mind was in a whirl of destruction. Any way she sliced it, seeing the elders was not a good thing. If they'd heard of her dreams, it was probably the worst. But the only alternative reason she could think of was far worse. *You haven't had a vision. You're not a true seer.* Mariyen didn't want to consider. It was better not to think, just to go: so it was that she followed Ashby out of the Summer Chambers, down the Summer Hallway, to the intersection where the male and female hallways split into Summer and Spring for females, Winter and Autumn for males. Her eyes travelled with foreboding to a passageway further up in the wall, above the Autumn Hallway. They had to scale the wall to get to this opening, and when they were inside the sound of their footfalls effectively diminished until Mariyen could really forget she was walking rather than gliding down this completely circular passage, its sides so worn that they gleamed dully in the light of the lanterns hanging every dozen feet or so. She tried, in that quiet moment of gliding along, to imagine she was going somewhere else, but it didn't last long. They reached the end of the passage all too soon, a round, glowing pocket of warm yellow light, and she thought vaguely that if she hadn't been so frightened it probably would have been beautiful.

"Mariyen Edgewood, welcome," a pleasantly deep voice sounded from somewhere beyond her vision. Then she had come fully into the room, and from behind Ashby's tail, she could see the speaker. If possible, she became even more nervous at the sound of the familiar voice.

Horus, the chief elder, stepped fully into her line of vision and smiled gravely at her. It was a smile she found hard to return.

"Thank you, Ashby Edgewood. You may return to your ceremony."

Ashby bobbed her head and scampered off, leaving Mariyen alone with Horus, and her fears.

The chief elder was the type of squirrel whose presence immediately claimed your attention when he entered any room. He was large for a flying squirrel, his fur thick and glossy and of a brown hue that was uncommon, and therefore envied, among the colony. His eyes were stern, but there was a kindness behind them that, when he directed his gaze at you, made you want to tell the truth and nothing but. This was the gaze he leveled on Mariyen now.

"Please do sit down," he told her, and she took the nearest seat available. Only too late, she realized it was Horus's chair, and got up as though it had burnt her.

"Sorry."

"No, no. Go ahead. The seat is very appealing, after all." Horus's dark eyes twinkled and she realized he found her slip-up funny rather than offensive. She let out the air she was holding in and watched in amazement as Horus seated himself instead at one of the smaller leaf-covered chairs clearly intended for visitors and miscreants. "Now," he said, expression going stern again, "Do you know why you are here?"

Mariyen hesitated. She was almost certain that it was her dreams that had brought her here, but if she said so and it was not, it would only make things worse for her. "I'm not...sure," she said, a compromise.

"Mariyen," Horus said gently. "I know you have not been doing well in the realm of prescience and visions."

Mariyen flinched.

"But—and let me finish," Horus smiled. "We accept that sometimes, information can come to us in different ways."

Mariyen looked up at him sharply. Was he saying what she thought he was?

"I've been having dreams," she confessed to the silence. She hadn't intended to do it, it had just slipped out into the space between them. The warm, sparsely decorated room seemed to grow small and crowded around her then, and she wondered if Horus would get up and tell her to leave, to pack her things and go up to the chambers of service, leave behind the Summer Chambers and her chances at the seer's life forever. He did not say any one of these things. He merely sat and stared at Mariyen as though he were going to smile, and said, "I know you have."

Mariyen's racing thoughts were extinguished at his words. "You do?"

"Yes," he smiled at the shock on her face. "We elders have ways of knowing these things."

Mariyen's chest filled with foreboding. Did Horus know the content of her dreams? Could he—and all the other elders, for that matter—look into her sleeping mind and see all she dreamed? The thought robbed her of a certain security. If they could see her dreams, what *couldn't* they see?

Horus was studying her carefully. "You are very concerned."

"You know all about my dreams?" She didn't want Horus to think she had anything to hide, but she couldn't stop the question from bubbling up.

He smiled again, that winking light coming back into his eyes.

"No, I cannot see the content of your dreams—or your thoughts, for that matter," he said, answering the unspoken question. "I can only read the emotions, the sensations you are getting from them, and from there it is guesswork."

"Then how…?"

"How did I know you were dreaming at all? Yes, that's a reasonable question. When most squirrels are sleeping here, they are without dreams, and their emotions read blank, as close to the non-emotion of calm as they can get. When one dreams, emotions spike extremely far up, so that it is impossible for me not to catch them. The night is usually silent in terms of reading anyone's thought-color. Consistently, night after night, yours has been extremely…alive, and not in a positive way, I must say. At first, we thought you were awake during the night, that you weren't sleeping well, but upon studying your thought-color more closely, we have determined that you were in fact asleep when all of this was going on. Therefore, you dream."

Mariyen hoped he couldn't see how relieved she was at the fact that he could not see her thoughts, only feel them, before realizing that he must already know. No wonder at all of his secret smiles! It must be very amusing for him to be able to feel her immediate emotional reaction to anything he said. Granted, it was still a little scary for her, that he could feel her thoughts, but she supposed it beat the alternative. No one, she thought, could be *that* powerful and not abuse it. A question fluttered through her mind, and she grabbed onto it.

"Am I the only one?"

Horus got up and crossed over to a small, circular window she could see cut into the side of the wall. She had never noticed this aspect of the room before, and was surprised. Windows were usually against common practice, as they distracted one from one's internal workings and from focusing on the here and now. Windows were like soul-capturers, made to spirit one away on a glance. These were all things Mariyen had been told, but here, in the *chief elder's* chamber, there was a window. It had two thick, dark dyed curtains hanging over it, which may have been how it had escaped her notice until now. Horus saw her looking, and smiled.

"A travesty, I know," he said, as though he were humoring her.

"But—

"One day, Mariyen, if you are to become a seer, you may realize that there are several strictures in place for a reason."

She didn't know what to say to this. He'd never answered her question. Was he avoiding it? She opened her mouth to ask him again, but Horus cut her off just as gently as he'd spoken to her earlier.

"Yes-- that is the answer to your question. For now, at least."

"So there *were* others?"

Horus's expression grew grave. "Of course there have been. Edgewood has been around for a long, long time, Mariyen. Longer, perhaps, then you were told."

There was another long silence as Horus stared out the window some more, eyes narrowing as though he were attempting to focus on something that was becoming increasingly more distant.

"But you, er…I mean."

He turned to look at her.

"What happened to them? The others who dreamed? Did they become seers?"

Horus paused, a paw to his mouth as though he were considering something. "No," he said, with an air of deliberation. "All in all, it is not a good thing to have dreams. Usually dreams are unreliable as a mode of prediction or of foresight and are usually only tampering with the fears and hopes of the dreamer. Someone has expressed an interest in you, Mariyen, from a young age." She opened her mouth, startled, but one look bade her not to interrupt. "That is why we need to see the value in these dreams you have been having, to know whether they carry potential for you or not. The fact that they are recurring gives us some hope, though when paired with their turbulence, it suggests that you've merely been through some sort of trauma, which is counterproductive in the extreme."

Mariyen, in spite of this distressing information, had a moment where she almost laughed. The idea of calling trauma counterproductive was kind of funny in a way that was also sort of sad. Horus did not seem to pick up on this, focused as he was on other things, and she caught a spark of something from him, some thought or emotion that slipped away before she could be certain she wasn't just hallucinating. It left her stunned and confused.

"Mariyen," Horus said, leaning close to her, a gesture that was absurd, seated again as he was in the smaller of the two chairs. "I need you to tell me about your dreams. This is absolutely important to us, and by us, I do not only mean the colony as a whole. I mean you and I."

This was getting stranger and stranger. They were not encouraged to make statements like this, that separated the colony at such a large extent from one another, and hearing this from an elder, the chief elder nonetheless, in such a secretive tone…Mariyen felt a thrill of something that was either excitement or fear. Horus was waiting. Mariyen tried to explain.

"My dreams are…they're not all the same. But there are common elements. I mean, there's always this one part with the same squirrel…" Mariyen trailed off. Mentioning the squirrel who always featured at the endings of her dreams made her sad. She wasn't sure she wanted to continue down this road, but she'd already started, so she kept on. "He was a fox squirrel, a male. Large. Not really big, just kind of fat. He's always trying to tell me something, I think, but I can never hear it. It's like there's some kind of invisible wall separating us and he's trying to speak around that to me."

"Mmm..." Horus's eyes were gleaming, she noticed. "What is the rest like?"

"The rest..."

A nightmare cacophony.

"Unpleasant, usually. A lot of images that frighten me, usually not the same."

She prayed he wouldn't ask her for more detail on that score. Her prayer was, surprisingly enough, answered.

"Nightmares," Horus said, "on their own are not promising. But this one squirrel, the one you keep seeing at the end, *that* could be a promising sign. Have you ever heard of a messenger?"

"Of Astrippa?" Her brow creased. That was something other squirrels believed in, a laughable myth to the rest of them. She was surprised when he reacted so violently.

"No!" Horus nearly snapped, before subsiding, looking a bit ashamed of his sudden flare. "No," he said more quietly. "Mariyen, Mariyen. Where did you hear about that?"

"Nothing. No one." She wished she'd never brought it up.

The astounding thing, she would think later, was that Horus had to have known she was lying. He had to have known, but he let it go.

"A messenger in the course of dreams, Mariyen," Horus explained to her, "is someone who appears, usually at the beginning or the end, or even throughout a dream, attempting to speak in order to deliver some sort of message in which the import of the dream is usually made clear."

Mariyen blinked. Slowly, she was beginning to see what he was getting at. "So do you mean…"

"It's a form of divination, yes. I must give you some advice." He got up and went across the room to some carved wooden cabinets in the walls, another oddity in the room: most rooms she was accustomed to only had simple niches carved in the walls. Horus fussed around with something inside the cabinets; she could hear whatever it was clunking against the wood walls, and when he turned around he was holding a round-bottomed bottle of nearly opaque glass. Around the top of it was a pink ribbon, faded almost to white.

"This," Horus said, coming back to her and setting the bottle down on the chair he'd recently vacated, "Is a sleep serum. It puts special emphasis on clarity. I need you to put this somewhere safe, out of sight and nicely cushioned, and use it once a night. Take one swallow. Within a week, without a doubt, whatever is trying to emerge through your recent dreams should become clear. Do you understand?"

Mariyen nodded. Horus gave her the bottle and she clutched it to her chest. It was cool and surprisingly heavy, given the size of the thing, hardly more than a paw's width. She sat waiting to see if Horus would say anything more.

"You may go now." Horus's eyes drifted back to the window, and Mariyen wished she could be there with him. What did he see? When she didn't move for a moment, he started to turn back to her and she sensed something of his impatience surge at her. She hadn't been expecting it, and it made her a bit scared. Getting hurriedly to her feet, she stumbled rather ungracefully over to the door, daring only to look over her shoulder once as she left. Horus was right where she'd left him, though there was a distant look to the sharp sideways-angled plane of his face and from the stance of his body she knew that to him, she was already long gone.

***

Horus Edgewood the Elder stood by the window, looking down at the labyrinthine garden his wife had planted weeks that seemed days ago now. The ferns and ivy and ragweed all pulsed beautifully, tragically tangled, from the ground, winding around one another in a fierce medley he knew Sarina would have enjoyed. A tempest of weeds, but she could hardly appreciate it now, now that she was somewhere deep in that very ground. She was probably sick of it, probably hated the thought of roots and dirt and spiders that clung to her skin, earthworms rudely pushing into her orifices…it was so much easier to imagine she'd simply reintegrated, which was of course what he'd thought before. *Before* was so long ago though, a season and a half that felt like twelve. He didn't know if he could feel her in the great meditation now or not; sometimes, he thought he could—a breath, a smile, a nuzzle, the way she used to press her nose up against his tail and hold it there until she sneezed, just for the hell of it. That kind of thing. Horus was the chief elder only because he was the most accomplished. This he knew. He was also the youngest, though by no means young. If they knew his thoughts, if anyone was *able* to know his thoughts, he thought they might feel differently about him. They might even reconsider.

But they did not.

So he was Horus, chief elder extroadinaire, and Sarina had reintegrated with the great soul of things, as did all squirrels upon death.

A creaking sounded from the corner of the room. Horus did not turn around, or give any sign that he heard anything. He continued to stare at the garden until the top of one dandelion appeared to him a field of a thousand other dandelions—was this reintegrating? This he could believe.

"You didn't tell her about me," the voice, soft, mournful, accusing, said behind him. He turned around at last, taking his time, to face Llewellyn Edgewood, her velvet gray fur, her large sad eyes.

"What did you expect me to say to her?" he asked absently. He wasn't in the mood. "She knows all she needs to know."

"I'm her mother," the other squirrel said, indignantly. She took her time stepping around him to his other side. "You could have let *me* talk to her."

"You heard she's a seer, I presume."

"I know she's a seer," Llewellyn snapped. "Of course she's a seer. I'm a seer."

"You mean you were."

She gave him a very cold glare. "You know as well as I do that I could not have known."

He opened his mouth, but she turned to face the wall. He could see her scanning the walls around the door to cover her upset. He softened, coming up behind her and placing a paw on her shoulder. Under the warm fur, the still pounding, *living* blood, she remained tense. For one beat, two beats. Slowly her shoulder came back down again, and the sadness was back at her, choking her next words.

"You didn't let me talk to her."

"Llewellyn, you know—

"It's been eight seasons. Do you think I care about the reason?"

In the ensuing silence there were only the sounds of the shorter squirrel breathing, short, heated little gasps, keeping control, a dust mote falling on the two empty chairs and what had once been a kitchen table shoved up against a wall.

"We're all coming apart," he told her in a moment of honesty he hadn't known he was capable of anymore.

She stared up at him, wide-eyed. A single tear clung to the rim of one perfectly rounded eye.

"You really don't know," she said, an awful wonderment clouding her tone.

He looked, really looked at her in one confused second and then, suddenly the suspicion pushed in on him, crowded the rational self out of the confines of his brain.

"No." The word was like a question.

"I'm with child," she said, and before he could think to answer, before he could think at all, she left the room as she'd entered.

Horus spent the next two hours pacing his room, thinking, eyes closed, attempting to divine. He passed the window outside of which Sarina's garden waited, once, twice, three times.

"What do I do?" he asked, finally turning and resting his paws on the window sill. "What do I do?"

There were too many secrets to hold, too little time and propensity for holding them. He felt like his sides were made of wet paper and the next time it rained he'd simply burst, exposing everything he held for better or for worse.

He watched a small beetle crawl up the stem of a particularly curly fern. When it reached the top, tremulous, it stretched its wings so they caught the unnaturally bright autumn sun, sending it off in several sunlit directions. Messengers.

"Sarina. What do I do?"

There was no answer from the surrounding garden. The dirt into which he was sure his wife had been dragged was silent.

He was Horus the chief elder. He was Horus the wise. He was Horus the lost.

The beetle took flight, leaving behind no sign of its passage except for the quivering fern, which soon stilled.

If he hadn't seen it, no one would have ever known it was there.

CHAPTER VII

"I don't trust him," Lute grumbled for the sixth time since they'd set out the next morning in pursuit of the Aspen Woods and the last white squirrel. Kinder knew it was six because he was counting, a thing he did when he was nervous. The numbers were like a tonic in their reliability: over five rocks, two logs, up one tree with four branches on one side, down again when the ground had ceased to alienate him. Six times for Lute talking, period. Six times for Lute's distrust.

Kinder was nervous for the obvious reason that they were starting out on a journey of sorts where he didn't know what to expect (or as Lute called it sarcastically, "a royal quest and a half") but also because he was recovering from two experiences he'd always hoped he wouldn't have to have. The first was that he'd shown Lute his home.

They had agreed to rest a night before setting out the next morning to find the white squirrel—there was something about the mention of white squirrels that made Lute sort of...*jumpy*, but he wouldn't say what it was. Kinder never pushed it. He was still so relieved that he was not going to be in this alone that he did not press anything. In any case, he hadn't wanted to leave Lute to sleep in his log, close as it was to the ground and demolished as it had become upon Kinder's last visit. Lute had gone back to retrieve any special items he kept there, and Kinder realized only later that within that action there was the assumption that they might never come back.

When they'd come to his home, Kinder's mother had been blocking the door. It took a while to wean her away from the wall beside it, which it turned out she was working on with a hearty appetite that night.

"Who is *that*?" she'd asked, staring at Lute. "It's one of them, isn't it? Oh Astrippa, we're doomed! It's one of them!"

Kinder had to step in, and quickly. "It's just a friend of mine, mother."

She dragged her teeth along the wall. "You don't have any friends," she said, but she let them in reluctantly.

"Come on, my room's upstairs," Kinder said, not looking back at Lute. He finally turned around when he got to the top of the last landing and saw that Lute was looking at him with a mix of shock and—was that pity or was it sympathy? He felt his face go red.

"At least I don't live in a log," he said, his words sounding lame and defensive even to his own ears.

The morning was worse, and not only because his mother kept ranting at them not to 'walk on the bugs'. Kinder also had to count the furs on his pillow, the drool stains, and look up his dreams while Lute looked on, grinning not-so-secretly. Finally, he scooped up all his charms, all of his hats and all of his bracelets, rings and earrings and stuffed them into the bag he was bringing. He didn't look at Lute when he said, "I think we'll just need all of it." He didn't need to. Lute was howling with laughter by that time.

The worst was not any of this; in fact, he'd even been able to grudgingly laugh along at the charms.

The worst was when they went to Skellan's to get food for their trip. It felt very strange, very *wrong* to be coming to Skellan for food as though nothing had changed, but he hadn't known what else to do, and Skellan might want to know what they were about to undertake, and where he'd be. The last thing he wanted was for the elderly squirrel to think he'd stopped visiting because of Nadra's death. They already had *some* things when they started over:

Lute had some oat bread in his sack and they'd both scoured Kinder's house for anything that they could use, only successful in uprooting a moldy piece of cheese lodged in the sofa and a few walnuts hidden behind picture frames.

"Don't forget your rain jacket, Torven!" his mother screamed after them as they departed for Skellan's.

"Who's Torven?"

"No one." Kinder felt his face heat up again.

Skellan lived in a small abode made entirely from sticks and dried mud, resting in the nook of a pine five trees down.

"Ouch," Lute grumped as they dismounted the tree next to Skellan's—the branch had come up and hit him in the rear as a parting gift. Kinder was glad for the distraction. Perhaps he just needed this moment to himself. As he began to walk down the branch that would lead him to Skellan, Lute, rubbing his bottom and looking put out, called "Do yew want me to come or should I just stay here, like?"

Kinder shrugged distractedly. Lute got the message.

Mostly what he was surprised about was how everything was the same. Skellan and Nadra's door, the way it was wood hatched over wood, the dried mud in between, the familiar place he put his paw to knock, worn from the knocking. Skellan came to the door at the same time as usual, too, just softer, his paw more silent on the knob, all the stuff Kinder would've sworn no one could really notice before this.

"Kinder," he said. His face looked more lined than usual, but just as kind. "I'm afraid the house is a lot quieter now," he cracked a bit of a smile, and then Kinder came in and they began to talk.

He left with wet eyes but a full package of food, an amount he'd protested at. Apparently, Skellan still cooked to ease the pain of his loss, and he claimed it was only accidental that he found himself making double portions of everything. "It needs somewhere to go," Skellan had said, looking away as he took over the packing of Kinder's bag.

"Skellan," he'd said, and the old squirrel had looked up, wiping at his eyes.

"I know I'm weepy today, but don't you worry, okay?"

Easier said than done, Kinder thought. What did you say when someone who'd not only been your friend but fed you, counseled you, even clothed you at times—*like a parent*— was grieving? Was there anything you *could* say? Kinder felt this distance now, and the distance hurt. So he dried his own eyes, looked at Skellan squarely, and said, "I'm going to find whatever it is that did this. And when I do, I'll make sure it won't happen to anyone else."

He couldn't imagine this being any consolation for Skellan, but the old gray had smiled and said, "Be careful, my son."

It echoed in Kinder's head as he wandered back down the branch toward Lute, carrying a much heavier burden than he had started with. *My son, my son, my son.*

Now they were on their way, and Kinder was counting. They passed three crooked trees in a row, five gadflies, then came to one stream at which Lute cursed exactly once, then said, for the seventh time, "I don't trust him."

Kinder, slow to anger, was surprised to find that he was getting a little annoyed with his companion. Sure, he did not exactly trust the seer either, but what choice did they have?

"What do you want me to say to that?" he asked Lute, "You're the one who wants to come." Then, because he finally felt driven to ask, "Is it because of the white squirrel?"

Lute, who was in the process of crossing the river, stopped, two feet balancing on two slime-covered rocks, bag clenched in his teeth. He made some muffled sounds before spitting his bag out in front of him, and craning around to look at Kinder.

"Look," he said, "Yew know all yew need to know. Nothing else is really important. I was there, I knew some of them...briefly. There was this curse..." He shook his head. "Nothing. It's gone. I was stupid then. Maybe one of them is alive, but what's that to me? Truth is, I'm just a little bored, okay?"

Kinder nodded. Lute's feet looked dangerously close to slipping off the sides of the rocks, but he straightened himself out just in time. Somehow he didn't entirely believe Lute when he said seeing the white squirrel wasn't important to him. It might be a lot like seeing ghosts—everyone went after the phantom sounds around the corner, but for what? To relive the past, or to simply be sure what they felt, what they saw at one point was real?

Kinder, unsteady on his feet, slipped and fell into the river with a splash, just managing to salvage his bag from being soaked. Lute smirked from the other bank.

They developed a way of travelling, a pattern after a matter of days. Sometimes the 'bad feeling', as Kinder simply dubbed it, would spread out over the ground beneath them, and they would scale a tree and continue up high. They stopped for breaks as little as they could manage, which was hard for Kinder because his stomach always wanted more than they could afford to eat at once, and hard for Lute because his paws kept itching to hold a knife and a piece of wood. Sometimes when they rested in the trees having a bite to eat, Lute would take his knife to the tree itself, carving fascinating images they left behind in their wake for some other traveler to find.

Once, as Kinder sat eating an entire spinach pie and Lute carved something in a small length of wood, they heard the cracking of a branch not far off. Lute froze, looking up for a moment, and Kinder happened to glance at his carving.

"Who is that?" he asked, sound momentarily forgotten in lieu of curiosity. He could see the curve of a female's body, her eyelashes, the tufts on her ears...

Lute covered up the carving quickly, throwing it into his bag. "No one."

"Excuse *me*," a voice sounded behind them and Kinder spun around. Lute fumbled with the knife in his paws before turning it on their guest. When he did, the squirrel behind them eyed it only for an instant before saying, "There are more of us, you know. I would not try anything."

"What kind of squirrel are you supposed to be anyway?" chirped another voice, and a smaller, runty looking squirrel appeared beside the first, a stoic gray.

"Why don't yew come over here and find out?" Lute bit out

Kinder was nonplussed. "Why...?"

"This is our territory, big foxy and strange dark one. We have to, regrettably, arrest you."

The smaller of the two squirrels, the one who'd spoken, did not look as though he regretted a thing.

"I am Engelwaithe," said his companion, "The guardian of Northern Firwood."

"We're in Firwood, then. Guess that answers our question," Lute muttered to Kinder. They'd noticed the trees getting more unfamiliar as they went, larger and more spaced out, with a good deal more sun filtering through and a whole lot less rocky terrain, to Kinder's chagrin (he figured that if the ground became a bad place to be, rock was second to a tree in terms of their relative safety. Lute had shaken his head at this, which Kinder didn't know if he should take to mean Lute didn't believe it or just thought he was an idiot.)

"Last time I checked, there was no guardian of any part of anywhere," Lute snarled. He was getting really sick of the term 'guardian.' This white squirrel better be worth their grief.

"You are wrong, my friend," Engelwaithe said, shrugging a bit as though it really didn't matter. "Sycamore, where are the bonds?"

The runty squirrel disappeared for a moment and came back with a great length of twine.

"Yer kidding me," Lute muttered, gripping his knife tighter as Sycamore came towards him. Kinder's mind was racing. There was the snap of branches at his back and sides now, and he knew they were indeed not alone. He hoped Lute wouldn't do anything stupid.

No sooner had he thought this when they were swept up in a mass of rushing bodies, all crowding towards them. There had to be at least twenty grays in the surrounding entourage, all pinning them to the middle of the crowd so that they were unable to move. Kinder struggled against them, and for a moment, his mass freed him a little, knocking a gray off balance, but they were all too soon up again, and he felt someone grab his arm. When he thrashed, someone else bit him, and a mass of paws pulled his own behind him. It was quite the hopeless situation, he thought with dismay, as over the heads of several of the grays he surveyed a patch of darkness he was sure was Lute.

Suddenly someone screamed and there was a ripple in the crowd, spreading out from the place he had been looking. Kinder craned his neck, fear rushing through him. Had they done something to Lute? Was he in this alone? But as the crowd cleared off, he saw what was causing the commotion. A gray lay thrashing on the ground, a knife stuck hilt-deep into his neck. His mouth was foaming and he was making loud, pained panting noises as he struck out at the empty air around him. One of his fellows came forward finally, and leaning over him, pinned him to the branch below. They examined him closely, but somewhere in the process the injured squirrel stopped moving altogether, and the squirrel examining him rose to his feet, gesturing to two others behind him who came to take their companion with them and do whatever it was these squirrels did with their dead.

Everyone was slowly turning from the procession leading their companion away to look at Lute, a whole mass of glaring eyes and flattened ears. Engelwaithe came from beside where Lute was being tied up, holding the knife they'd wrested from his grip and held it up for the crowd to see. It was slick with their companion's blood.

"You see this?" Engelwaithe said, his voice still deadly calm, and Kinder realized, thought momentarily overcoming the sick feeling in his gut, that Engelwaithe could not have cared less about what had just happened to his fellow; he was only grateful for the chance to make a point with her death. "This," Engelwaithe said, waving the knife in little circles in front of him, "Is why we don't let strangers into our territory."

Lute's stare was hard and cold, uncompromising, unapologetic.

"He has more of them," another squirrel called from where he was going through Lute's pack. He whistled.

"*Five* more, as a matter of fact. What a sicko." Another squirrel somewhere laughed appreciatively.

"Practically all this one's got is food," another squirrel said from beside Kinder. "Predictable." He poked Kinder's gut and snickered. His paw was hard and cruel, like one big angle.

Some other grays began to laugh at this, and Engelwaithe shot a look into the crowd. He threw the knife he was holding off of the tree—out of the corner of his eye, Kinder saw Lute make a movement as if to dive after it— and then beckoned to his squirrels.

Kinder felt himself manhandled first one way, then the other as the crowd of grays started to move as one over a network of tree branches that, jostled as he was in front and back and with such limited visibility, made him feel sicker than the sight of the thrashing squirrel Lute had stabbed. He tried not to think about that brand of sickness, and concentrated on the new one. What did he expect Lute to do? They were in danger, after all. He thought wistfully of the things in his pack, the food and the charms, all unlikely ever to meet his eyes again. Had they been stupid to go off on this journey? He hadn't even bothered to think, in all his greenness, that they would come upon other *squirrels* who'd be bent upon hurting them this bad. It seemed wrong, a betrayal. They'd had squirrels come and tell them to get off of their trees before in times when they were resting, but that had been a simple matter of moving to a new spot. These grays actively wanted to arrest them even before Lute slid a knife into the throat of one of their number. The thought of the knife made him feel cold inside, and he wondered what his first words to Lute would be when they stopped moving, whether he could hide his brimming fear and…was it disappointment?

They were marched across the trees without rest for such a long time that Kinder wondered whether the grays were not lying about the area being theirs. If they weren't, their territory was extremely large, and he couldn't help but think how many guardians that would entail, how many Engelwaithes, and how many captures just like theirs.

They stopped outside of a gigantic fir, rising up above them for a dizzying number of yards. Its rough, scaly bark put Kinder in the mind of a fortress: impenetrable.

Inescapable.

Kinder could not see the door from where he was positioned, but Engelwaithe's haughty voice drifted back to him over the heads of those in front.

"Yes, I know, I know. Let us in before you have to do any more thinking, Simeon."

There was a pause in which whoever was talking to Engelwaithe had their say, though Kinder could not hear this part of the dialogue, and then the line started moving again. The squirrels in back of Kinder kept jabbing their paws into his back, and he felt his anger fluttering helplessly under the surface. He could see the door now, a great wooden thing with iron spikes protruding from the front, honed into fine points. There were windows in the place, he saw, looking up in a rush of vertigo, but they were all barred off, like a prison. He struggled to break free in one last desperate bid, but the squirrels around him bit and kicked him into submission.

"Forward, fat one," one of them sneered, and he realized with a jolt that it was Sycamore, the tiny runt who'd been with Engelwaithe when this whole nightmare started. "You don't want to be *late*."

Kinder did not want to gratify him by asking what he was late for, and in any case he wasn't sure he wanted to know.

Seconds later, he was thrust into a place where the air was more chill than it was outside, and had none of the fall briskness that made that cold all right. He could not see Lute, but deduced that he was in front of him from the immense amount of shuffling and jeering coming from up ahead. *Don't do anything worse*, he thought, though he didn't think Lute could, tied up as he was. Kinder was hustled into what appeared to be a large, cavernous room but which turned out to only be a widening of a particularly impressive hallway. Some squirrels were walking about in the hall, but stopped when they saw the large group enter with the strangers in its midst. A couple of them looked no older than a few seasons, and one of them pointed, excited, before his mother or older sister standing next to him lowered his paw hastily, casting a fearful glance their way. There were two slightly smaller tunnels leading off of this great hall, one going downwards and the other up. *It's not really a matter of wondering where we're going.* Sure enough, they were headed for the downward-sloping hallway. Kinder's mind flashed back to the seer's lair—if there were maggots down here too he didn't know that he could make it.

Calling back to mind the seer's lair had brought other unwelcome thoughts—the feel of bony claws on his arm, the tea cup being wrested from him. *Your friend is going to die*, those words in that scratchy, strangely weak voice. It could not be true, of course; it was merely to get their attention, and he should not bother himself thinking over it.

But—Kinder couldn't read tea leaves, and the seer's pale eyes kept regarding him over and over in his head, that washed-out stare attempting to communicate something thoroughly unpleasant with him. Something better off unknown.

And so he kept wondering, worrying.

This could be it.

The crowd of grays with their limbs full of hostility and their minds bent on punishment were shoving Kinder down the hallway. There were bright lights on either side of him at great intervals, impressing upon him the idea that this place might be grandiose and even festive, if it weren't for their predicament or the mind-numbing cold.

"Stop!" came Engelwaithe's voice from up in front of the queue, and everyone bustled into one another in an attempt to halt quickly. The squirrels directly in front of him began to squish up against the walls on either side of the passageway, and at first Kinder didn't understand what for. Then the squirrels holding him from behind tightened their grip on him, and the confusion melted away none-too-mercifully.

This is our stop.

The squirrels holding him pushed forwards, and Kinder walked with them, attempting to keep to their pace, though they seemed determined to make him stumble. They'd reached another door, this one smaller than the front door to the place by a good number of squirrel-lengths, but also studded with the long spikes in the same fashion. Now Kinder could see Lute and his captors parting the crowd ahead of him. The gray-black squirrel was swearing up a storm, and Kinder saw one of his guards reach out and hit him across the face, fed up to the brim at whatever the last thing Lute said was. Engelwaithe turned sharply to this guard and Kinder could hear what he said only faintly above the clamor of the others. "...are not to do that...unspoiled..."

With a lump in his throat, Kinder was walked through the smaller door after Lute and his guards and into something that was not even a room at all, but an oblong rectangle of space. There were two doors in the wall directly in front of them, to either side, and below them, there was also a door hidden in the ground. This one, Kinder had overlooked, and it was this one, rather than one of the two normal, larger doors that he was led through. One of the grays bent and heaved the trap door up from its hinges, setting it on the ground beside the newly uncovered opening and stood back to usher their captors in.

The space that Kinder found himself descending into was tighter than that above them. At first he was concerned that they were heading straight for the ground itself, but when they stopped descending down the steep slope of the tunnel, there was still wood beneath their feet. The guards in front of Kinder turned for an instant, making a gap with their bodies, and Kinder was able to make eye contact with Lute. Lute's teeth were chattering subtly, as he cast a dark glance back at his companion. He mouthed something that had the word 'cold' in it, but Kinder couldn't get the rest.

Kinder had noticed it too, of course. Despite the fact that cold temperatures rarely bothered him—*extra insulation*, his aunt would have said sneeringly—the cold in here seemed unnatural for a well-lit tree, as though it were winter and there were drafts coming through everywhere. But it was only early fall, and the tree was so strong and youthful that there was hardly a gap in the walls. It should be boiling in here, as a matter of fact. He didn't understand it.

"Come on now, get in there," the guards in front of Kinder and his escorts were saying. There was the sound of scraping metal against wood, and as Kinder and his guards entered the archway set into the middle of this small, dim, strangely cold room, Kinder saw their destination.

It wasn't so bad as the images his mind had been conjuring up for him as they marched, but a prison was a prison, and there was no disguising the fact that this was where they'd ended up.

The walls were lined with small barred cells, all facing out to the center of the room. The insides of the cells were also barred, but with solid panels of wood behind them so that, Kinder guessed, you could not talk to or see the prisoners on either side of you. The amount of room not taken up by cells was small and plain, covered in some of the dried grass clippings which also lined the bottoms of the cells. Kinder rightly guessed that the effect of being inside one of those obscure little rooms would be claustrophobia-inducing, not to mention mind-numbingly boring. There didn't appear to be anything to sleep on, aside from the grass, and this was so scantily spread that this could not have been its purpose. Lute was being locked into a cell next to the one other prisoner who appeared to be down here, a black squirrel who looked a good four seasons younger than Kinder, perhaps eight younger than Lute. Kinder, who'd never seen a black squirrel until this point, stared into this cell with interest. The squirrel's fur was a sooty yet exotic ebony, and he was shivering, wide frightened eyes staring back and forth between Lute and Kinder and the guards.

Kinder's shoulder was grasped by the gray behind him and he was steered into a cell of his own, on Lute's right side, two over from the black squirrel, and he lost view of anything but the wall behind him as they turned him around and untied his paws. Kinder thought, for a split second that if he acted quickly—if he were to make a move now, when he was untied, then maybe—but the gate had already closed behind him and when he turned around again it was to see their retreating backs headed for the door from behind which he thought he heard Engelwaithe's voice give a curt mutter, before the retreating sounds of a dozen feet made their way up the passage away from them, and they were eclipsed by total silence.

For a while, no one spoke. Kinder didn't even know where to begin. He and Lute hadn't got a chance to speak the whole time they were being herded around this place like lesser beings, and he still remembered the sight of the slain gray squirrel with the knife stuck in its neck, like its neck were a piece of wood or fruit or something. The image stuck stubbornly in his mind, even though he thought the predicament they were in should be more important as a matter of contemplation. Still, he felt completely robbed of speech, and the black squirrel two cells over made him hesitate to say anything about anything, even though he might not have even been present except for the fact that Kinder could hear his teeth chattering.

Lute was the one to break the silence.

"What the *hell* was that about?"

Kinder found it strange that he couldn't see Lute while he talked, and then another voice came from further away, and he knew it was the third prisoner.

"They're crazy," the black squirrel said simply.

"No, but what's it all about? Yew know…why are we all locked up? I didn't commit a crime last I remember 'cept for apparently walking on their property. That can't happen to everyone who passes their way. It's too dumb. What's it about?"

"They do, though!" the black squirrel was already saying. "That's exactly what they do! I'm Cainus. From Oakwood, just over the northwestern border. My family is always saying to me not to go into Firwood because everyone's heard about these nutters. Anyway, once they capture you it's all over. I was trying to find ragwort for my sister…she's ill…and then…well, you can see where my luck led me. I hope no one came after me."

His voice shrunk on his last words. He sounded even younger than Kinder had estimated him to be. Kinder was going to offer some sort of comfort when Lute butted in again, voice desperate with incredulity and fear he could not keep out. "So do we just *stay* here?"

"No," said the black squirrel, and Kinder felt a shiver at that word, as though he knew already what was coming next, in that child's voice.

"They sacrifice you to their faceless god."

CHAPTER VIII

Before all havoc broke loose, Mariyen was starting to hear.

She'd been taking the clarity potion that Horus had bid her to take every night, and it must have been working, because the fox squirrel who appeared at the end of her dreams was becoming clearer in shape as well as sound. She could almost hear the words his mouth shaped when he stood beckoning to her after the edges of a nightmare had just receded from the screen of her mind. She was close, she felt. So close.

The clarity potion worked in a way she had not expected. It didn't seem to her that there were any drastic or even unnatural changes in her dreams. It was not as though a wall were suddenly torn down in her consciousness. Instead, it merely seemed to her as though she had learned to listen.

Which was why Mariyen panicked when she woke one day to realize the potion was gone.

She'd just come out of a dream that had, for once, only consisted of her and the fox squirrel. They were standing on opposite sides of a pine tree, feet on the ground, and they kept glancing around the tree at one another. Mariyen would look around the trunk at the fox squirrel, then he would look around at her, but neither of them really managed to be looking at each other at the same time, which she remembered feeling was important. Coming around the tree to stand together was somehow impossible, she knew it without trying it. There was a quiet urgency to their lack of unison, so they'd kept trying, peering around at one another, and the fox squirrel had started to speak.

"He's coming. I think you need to know."

It was the longest phrase she'd ever understood from him, and her dream-self felt a thrill. She looked around the tree, the rough bark chafing her cheek, pushing her fur back. The tree was somehow large enough that she could only catch a glimpse of him, but it was enough. Their eyes met for a full second, and in that moment she knew that whatever he was trying to tell her, it was not good, for there was a sadness to those eyes that she had never seen before. The form of the other squirrel was wavering, as though he were not real, as though he really was only a fragment of a dream, a ghost.

"My friend—" the other squirrel started to say, but there was the sound of a rumbling in the distance, like a thunderstorm whose approach was imminent, and the other looked up at the sky, breaking their eye contact, and his physical form began to fade away.

"Wait!" Mariyen said; she'd been distracted for an instant too long by the realization that they had no surroundings—the tree seemed to be floating in a gap of white space. She just had time to wonder how thunder could occur when there was no sky, how a storm could come without a source, before she was driven back to the waking world.

Mariyen sat up in bed feeling lost and like she'd made an improvement at once. She didn't know how two such emotions could coexist, but there it was.

Mainly, she felt the sadness, as though it had trickled out of the other squirrel's eyes and into her chest, leaving a spot like something missed. Even the knowledge that she'd gotten more out of her dream-visitor—or messenger, as Horus would say—than ever before wasn't enough to put off the disappointment she woke with, the disappointment that she wasn't able to stay longer.

Well, nothing I can do, she thought, and reached over to the wooden table at her bedside to see how much more of the draught she would have to take. It wasn't that she minded it much: in fact it was practically tasteless apart from a lingering sensation on her tongue like mint. It was only that she wanted to make sure she had enough swallows left to be confident that she would understand her dreams by the time she was done. Lying back, she let her paw trail over the wood of the bedside table, and when it met with nothing, she merely reached further, thinking the bottle had been pushed to the opposite end. Nothing but a film of dust came back with the sweep of her paw. Mariyen looked over at the table, already knowing what she'd see. The bottle of pearly liquid was nowhere in evidence.

"Hontem!" Mariyen yelped, jumping up and searching frantically through her drawers and under her bedding.

Her friend stirred in the bed next to her, and she wasn't the only one. Most of the other squirrels in the Summer Chambers were rudely awakened by the noise, and were rustling around in waking duties, thinking it was time for morning meditation, or glaring in her direction.

"What is it?" Hontem moaned, staring at her through slitted eyes.

"I—my—have you seen my potion?"

Hontem sat up, rubbing her eyes rapidly. "It's gone? But Horus told you—"

"I know! I don't know how it's possible. Who would have done this?"

It was a good question. No one slept on the other side of Mariyen's bedside table, and she couldn't think of any reason anyone else in the room would want to take her potion. No one else had dreams—to admit to having dreams was not a favorable thing, and besides, Horus would have detected something. It made no sense to her. Undesirably bidden to her mind came a snatch of something Horus had said, *Keep this somewhere safe*, and she flushed at the reminder. She hadn't taken it particularly seriously, because really, who would have motive to take something of the sort from her? Well, now she was paying for her carelessness.

The lump in her chest moved into her throat and her head, and she had to lie down again. She knew the chief elder would have to ask her again how her dreams were turning out, and then it would have to come to light that she was no longer having them, at least any she could comprehend.

"I need to see the chief elder," she heard herself say to Hontem, staring up at the underside of the canopy over her bed.

"What do you think he'll do?" Hontem asked. Mariyen felt oddly grateful over the fact that Hontem was acting concerned on her behalf. Most of the others in the Summer Chambers were only glad they weren't her.

Mariyen shrugged, trying to convince herself that she meant every ounce of the careless gesture.

"I don't know. I guess I'll have to find out."

But Mariyen did not find out what Horus had to say on the topic of her negligence, because she did not go to Horus that day, or the next, or the next. She knew that she had resolved otherwise, and felt a clench of guilt in her gut whenever she thought about it, whenever she passed an elder in the hall or overheard another squirrel mention Horus's name. She never saw Horus at all during those days, which was perhaps a good thing. Her face would have betrayed her utterly. Her meditation at dawn and dusk was bespoiled by thoughts of going to Horus, what he would say—she went through several different reactions in her mind. She went through this hell of distraction for days, until the choice was taken away from her, and she was almost glad for it.

"Mariyen, the chief elder wants to see you," Ruby told her one bored evening, coming upon her in one of the divination rooms as she sifted through several sets of tarot cards, trying to put the decks together again. She dropped the cards she was holding, ruining all of her hard work.

My fate is sealed. So dramatic. So true?

So Mariyen found herself going once more down the corridor that led to her bed chambers, only to veer off and go up through the now familiar tunnel above the autumn hall. Ruby puffed along after her, under the excuse of wanting to see the chief elder's quarters. When they reached the door, it was closed, and Mariyen raised a paw to knock, extra conscious of Ruby standing right beside her.

For a while, nothing happened. The door remained shut, and Mariyen thought for a minute that it might be a mistake. Maybe the chief elder didn't want to see her; maybe he was not even in today. She turned to her friend.

"Well..."

The door came open so fast that it nearly hit her in the face, so little time did she have to jump back or to register the movement. Standing there was Horus, but he was not alone. Another flyer, a female with large, dark eyes and mist-gray fur stood behind and to the right of him.

"Mother?" Mariyen blinked.

It had been ages since she'd seen her own mother, and at first she felt awkward at the sight of her. Potential seers in training were not allowed to see their parents, for fear all of the emotion from such a meeting, whether regular or intermittent, would mess with their fine-tuning. What would her mother be doing here?

Llewellyn smiled at her daughter, but her eyes were sad and her paws kept fiddling with the red twine about her neck, which indicated her as a server.

"Come in, Mariyen," Horus said. His face was impossible to read.

Mariyen came in and sat in the smaller seat this time, the one closest to the window. Horus remained standing, and so did Ruby, in the doorway, until he gave her a look and she scurried away, giving Mariyen wide eyes before she left.

Horus circled to stand in front of her, and Mariyen felt it was best if she just said the truth and got it out there before everything fell down around her.

"I lost the potion," she blurted.

Horus raised an eyebrow. "I know, Mariyen."

"Oh."

Horus looked sharply back at her mother, who had situated herself up against the wall behind them, under the cabinet from which Horus had retrieved the potion. She was smiling now.

"You seem to forget too easily that I can read your emotions. Lately, I have been reading your dream emotions, too. I read them before you lost the potion, and after. After that, it was very easy to deduce what had happened. You are no longer dreaming."

Mariyen wallowed for a moment, stunned. That wasn't true...was it?

But it was. She'd been so concerned with what would happen when she finally told Horus about losing the potion, that she hadn't even registered the fact that for the first time in a long time, she'd stopped having dreams altogether.

Mariyen didn't know what to say. She put her head down, and began slowly, "I'm sure that if I had it back—

"You can't be sure of any such thing, and in any case, it hardly matters."

In comparison to the last time she'd talked to him, Horus was a different squirrel. A more frightening one, with his strong frame and authoritarian tone. She supposed this was what the other elders saw all of the time, and she wished he would smile just once, give her that knowing yet kindly gaze she remembered. She wished her mother would interfere for her, but she only leaned against the far wall, surveying their interactions. She looked as though she were elsewhere entirely.

"Your dreams are full of emotions that I do not relate to a seer's. They have become extremely personal, which is a danger. We do not feel, even though you have not been dreaming at all lately, that they have stopped. Your stress readings have been unnaturally high this week in your waking hours. This is barring your way as a seer, and we feel it is a sign."

Mariyen felt her heart plummet all the way down to the level of her feet. She knew what was coming before Horus spoke the words.

"Mariyen, you are not a seer."

Through the tears forming in her eyes, she saw the blurry image of her mother make a sudden movement and grasp the wall behind her. She had turned her eyes away from Mariyen, and when Horus spoke again, Mariyen had forgot he was in the room for a second, so concentrated was she on her mother's profile. She realized this was someone she hardly knew, standing across the room from her.

"Mariyen, look at *me*," Horus ordered, and she did as she was told, casting one last lingering look at her mother, who still would not turn to meet her eyes.

"It is not all for the worse that you are not to become a seer, and I will not have you be melodramatic about it. There is no less honor in serving around Edgewood, as I am sure your mother could testify. As I am sure she could also testify, sometimes being a seer has more negative than positive outcomes. I am sure you have heard about—

"Don't blame me for that," Llewellyn butted in with a surprising amount of venom.

Mariyen's eyes flew to her mother once more. She was leaning forward from the wall, her face heated and a flush showing under her fur.

"Of course, of course, you couldn't have known," Horus soothed. He looked to Mariyen. "You have heard of Absoulim Edgewood, no?"

Mariyen started at the name. "The exile?"

"Yes, the very same. He was a very promising seer as a young one, we all thought so—

"What you really thought is that he was odd," said Llewellyn. She sounded almost accusing.

"Yes, well," Horus looked annoyed at the interruption. "Your mother knew him better than the rest of us. Perhaps she can take over for me, if she knows so much." He turned to Llewellyn. Mariyen was surprised at how bold her mother was for a server. She felt a strange leap of pride at the idea that maybe she too, could be the server who spoke her mind and drove others mad with her dark eyes, as she had heard of her mother too many times in her life. Not until now did she believe Llewellyn truly held that sort of power.

Llewellyn stared at them both, giving Horus a long hard look before shrugging.

"As you wish. A non-biased perspective, then."

Horus narrowed his eyes, but did not break in.

"Absoulim was another squirrel in my set: that is, my group of would-be seers. I lived in the Summer Chambers, like you, Mariyen, and he lived in the autumn, so we would have ran into each other often. He was a little...strange, both in actions and looks, and so no one much wanted to hang around him. He made us all a little nervous. I knew the elders didn't want him to be a seer..." She looked over at Horus for a second as though she were daring him to interrupt. "They were trying to get rid of him for some time."

Horus stiffened. "That is untrue," he said, voice like a sheathed knife, and all Mariyen could do was look between this squirrel she'd hardly known as a mother and the chief elder as they stared across at each other.

"Your mother is biased," Horus said, in a way that suggested he was trying to keep his breathing under control. He smoothed out his fur and walked purposefully to his own chair, seating himself behind his desk in front of Mariyen and staring over the his folded paws past her, at Llewellyn. Daring her.

"She just does not want to believe that someone she was *friends* with would do what he did."

"We were not friends," Llewellyn said, only this time it was she who seemed to be struggling to keep her cool. "Just because I don't approve of what you did to him—

"What did he do?" Mariyen asked, tentatively. Her mother smiled at her, glad for an excuse to ignore Horus.

"Absoulim did one of the forbidden types of divination," she explained. "It was a very dark thing, one of the few for which immediate exile is the only rational solution."

Mariyen was intrigued. "There are forbidden types of divination?" she asked. She'd always considered divination as a fairly neutral, harmless practice of seeing into the future.

"Just as there are forbidden types of anything," Horus said. "When Absoulim reached into the future, he placed a *push*, a wish of his own into it. The wish was not good, and it had a way of coming true."

"How did you know he was doing this?" Mariyen tried to ignore the throb in the back of her mind reminding her that *she* would never do any kind of divination, good or bad.

"Well, I could feel his thoughts, as always. They weren't always worrying in nature, though they always had a flavor of their own. The pulse of one's thoughts is different when one is divining. Usually, it is very calm, with few 'spikes' of excitement. Absoulim's pulse was in this calm mode one afternoon, and then…an extremely large spike, the likes of which I've never experienced on my radar since. It was like an attack…yes, that was how it felt. An attack."

Horus wasn't talking to Mariyen anymore, though he was looking in her direction. He seemed caught up in the past, reliving the moment of the aforementioned spike. His brow was furrowed and his gaze distant. Mariyen knew if she were to get anything else out of him, she would have to interrupt this terrible reverie, but luckily, her mother spoke up again.

"It was elder Bolus. I forget what the problem was, but Absoulim and another squirrel, Davos, were in a fight about something, and Bolus tried to interfere. I can remember sitting there with my friends—this was in the great hall, you understand—and witnessing it. Bolus went to reach between them, to settle their argument, and I could hear him talking but I don't remember what he said. What I do remember is how Absoulim grabbed him by the arm. His face was furious and I remember Bolus saying, quite clearly, 'let go'. Others were looking now, and Bolus was about to pull away and give out some sort of fitting punishment when Absoulim started speaking. That would be his prophecy, if you could call it that."

"What did he--?"

"He told Bolus he was going to die."

Mariyen was silent.

"He dismissed it; how could he not? For a couple days, it was the talk of Edgewood, though. I remember everyone being extra scared to be around Absoulim, not that they hadn't before. He had a...quality, I guess. Two weeks later, Bolus fell from the top reaches of Edgewood, and then Absoulim's prediction was the top news again. Needless to say, he was expelled shortly thereafter."

"The point, Mariyen, is that divination has a dark side and a light side. The example of Absoulim—that is its darkest side. And the field of divination is not fully open to us. We did not know, prior to Absoulim, that such a type of divination was possible. It was in none of the books in our vaults, in none of the written records of years past. We don't know to this day whether it was some arcane type of divination Absoulim studied in secret, or whether it came to him naturally, a mutation of the talent many of us are born with."

Horus got up and began to pace the room; Llewellyn and Mariyen watched him from their respective positions, their eyes meeting occasionally over the flutter of the elder's movement. "There is debate among the elders, to this day, on the topic of whether Absoulim was actually the cause of Bolus's death or not. The most concrete evidence we had to work with was the spike I'd sensed. No one else seemed to have picked it up, which made the debate harder. It is still...unclear. We have no proof, it is hard to have any visible proof. All we have to work with are feelings, suspicions, readings. You understand?"

"So you exiled him?"

Horus looked back at her levelly. "Yes. It was the safest thing to do, considering."

There was a long pause, in which Llewellyn stared evenly at Horus's back. Without turning around, he spoke to her. "I'm sorry for what I said to you, earlier. I know it is not true."

"Fine," she said noncommittally, though Mariyen noticed she looked away as she said it. "Can I speak to Mariyen alone?"

"You know the rule about that."

"Can the rule. That's not why you don't want me to anyway."

Horus turned at last and scrutinized Mariyen's mother. "Don't make me say something else I'm going to regret," he said, the old cantankerousness back in his tone. "Now leave, because Mariyen and I need to talk. *Without* interruptions."

For a moment, Llewellyn didn't move, and Mariyen was afraid for her, but Horus spoke again, and there was meaning in his voice that Mariyen did not understand.

"Do not forget all I am doing for you, Llewellyn Edgewood."

Her mother turned and crossed the room abruptly, looking at neither of them, and went silently through a passage Mariyen had overlooked completely, carved as it was to imitate a part of the wall.

"Mariyen."

Mariyen was still staring at the place where her mother had disappeared, again, from her life.

"Mariyen, this is important." His voice had taken on a softer tone, while remaining stern. She wondered what, exactly, this imperturbable thing between her mother and the chief elder was, for she'd sensed it in the room, and felt somehow that it was what kept her mother from going to her, from embracing her, even. It made her angry, a bit, at the older squirrel now standing in front of her, demanding her attention as he had demanded her mother's.

Horus might have seen a bit of what she was feeling in her face, but if he did, he did not comment on it.

"You must go back to the Summer Chambers and pack your things. Now that you are no longer to be a seer, you will need different accommodations. Don't look that way, the life of a server is not the horror you imagine it to be. Come to me once you have packed, and I will show you to your new quarters."

Mariyen couldn't meet his eyes.

"Look, Mariyen," he said, voice so gentle this time that she looked up, startled. "I didn't tell you the story of Absoulim to scare you, but to remind you that the magic of divination is not something to be taken lightly. It is a heavy responsibility, and sometimes even I wish I did not have it. It's a burden, Mariyen." Sensing her critical reaction to this, he said, "I can't convince you, I know. You have no seer-magic, so what you see in it is something untouchable, something vastly desirable. And I won't lie to you: at first it is wonderful, to feel that you have this sort of power within your very paws. But it is *not yours*, and that is something that we forget. The more powerful we are perhaps, the more we forget to be wise. The magic of divination operates through us; we cannot summon it, however much this may seem to be the case, and we do not operate it. It runs through us, when it chooses, like a stream. There are ways to induce it, of course, but we cannot make magic do anything. If we forget…there are ways that any sentient magic has of making you pay for that crime.

'All I mean to say is, perhaps, though you will not see it, it is really for the best that this particular magic has chosen to leave you barren. Now go, and make ready for your new life."

Mariyen got up to go, hesitated, then turned back to Horus.

"When I am a server…" she started. He waited.

"When I am a server, will I be allowed to talk with my mother? I mean, there'd be no reason not to, right?"

Horus's expression was grave. "We'll see," he said.

She could feel his eyes regarding her as she walked out.

CHAPTER IX

"Wait, wait, wait. Tell me again, Camus."

"Cainus."

"Yeah, that. This god thing—they think it lives in the *ground*?"

"Yeah, I mean, that's what I got from the guards when they're around. They take their shifts down here when the hall is in council."

"Hall?" Lute scratched his head behind his left ear. If you could go insane due to someone else's insanity, he was nearly there.

"Up above us. It's where they hold all their important meetings. You can actually hear them sometimes. I don't know how…there's got to be some ventilation somewhere here. Sometimes they talk about the ground up there, too."

Lute attempted to take his mind from how cold he was. If the insanity of his captors didn't do him in, the frigid air was a close second.

"What do they say?" he asked.

"I don't know, I can't hear them perfectly. It's just a bunch of mumbling from down here, but you catch some of the words if you listen hard enough."

"So they feed guests to their underground god?" Kinder's voice came from nowhere—well, the cell next to Lute, he knew, but it might have been nowhere since he hadn't talked in so long. Lute was beginning to be bothered by this, strangely angry with his companion. They were imprisoned together, after all—wasn't that at least a worthy topic for commiseration?

"Yes," Cainus said, not missing a beat. "I get the impression we're their sacrifices, since they don't want to sacrifice one of their own." His teeth clacked together on this last word, and Lute brought up the most practical of his wonderings.

"Why in all rot is it so damned *cold* down here?"

"I was going to say the same thing, except nicer," said Kinder again, from the other side of Lute. Lute turned around and glared at the wall.

"You wouldn't believe me if I told you," Cainus said quietly.

"What?"

"What is it?"

But Cainus had gone silent. Lute lay back on the cold wood floor of his cell and stared up at the ceiling. Which was when he saw it, the small, round knothole in the wood that went clean through to some other space beyond.

Lute scrambled to his feet. Looking to either side of him, though he knew Kinder and Cainus couldn't see, he attempted to climb to reach the knothole. His hope waned when he realized two things: one, the bars placed over the wood on the sides of his room were there for a reason: he couldn't get a grip. And two, even if he were to climb all the way to the knothole, there was no way he could chew it larger. Practically speaking, it would kill his teeth.

But he wanted to have a look all the same, even if all he saw was the ceiling of the council room, or someone's foot. It wasn't like there was anything else to do in here while he was waiting for his death.

"What are you doing over there, Lute?" Kinder's voice broke him out of his sullen thoughts. He turned to the wall separating he and Kinder and grasped the bars.

"I could ask the same of yew, *friend to the end*."

"Actually, the card just said you were my—"

"Whatever. What's wrong with yew?"

There was a silence, and then, "Why would anything be wrong with me?"

Lute was conscious of Cainus listening to their left, but he did not care at this point. Let him listen.

"Oh, give me a rotting break. Yew fox squirrels are all the same. So I killed someone, yeah. I've done it before. I'll probably do it again. It's called survival. Don't waste yer time moping and drowning in yer own judgment, okay? Spare us."

Kinder's voice was hesitant. "But I'm not angry at you!" he said. "I'm not, really. It's just the first time I saw— you know...saw anyone die, I guess." He paused. "What do you mean, 'us fox squirrels?'"

Lute chose to ignore him. "Yew never saw anyone die?"

"I never saw anyone get killed *or* die. I'm not mad at you. I swear...Lute?"

Lute had gone into a silence of his own. He wished he had something to carve here. Hell, even something to carve *with* would suffice. He could write a nice message to their captors on the walls, one they wouldn't forget.

Kinder was still waiting to hear that Lute wasn't upset. Lute found it ridiculous that he was this invested.

"Do yew think he's asleep?" he asked, in the spirit of forgiveness.

"Who?"

"Cainus."

"You could ask him."

A snore arose from Lute's left and answered them both.

It turned out that Cainus was a very fitful sleeper. Lute thought this might be due to his time here, for it was not exactly easy to sleep with the guards coming down every five minutes or so to check on them, opening and slamming the heavy doors, not to mention the light. The room they were in was constantly lit up to a bright glow, so that it was impossible to tell whether it was night or day.

The only good thing about the experience was the food. The first time Lute received food in this prison, he thought it might be a joke. The sturdy gray who came hustling in to open the door to his cell a crack and shove it in brought a plate of spinach and acorn pudding, watercress salad, and pecan pie. It smelled heavenly, and the brief consideration Lute tried to hold for poison vanished immediately—they were being fattened up after all, right? More meat for that insane god of theirs to chew through. Kinder, who kept complaining of being hungry the first few hours they were here, could not have been more pleased if they were released on the spot.

The nights, though, the nights were a problem. Lute was to discover this shortly after he and Kinder found that indeed, Cainus was sleeping. He wondered if the food they'd had was drugged, because it was only shortly after eating that he felt like going to bed, and Kinder yawned loudly beside him, suggesting the same.

A guard opened the door with a loud scraping, poked his head in, looked around and closed it again with a bang. Cainus shifted in his sleep. Lute tried to get comfortable on the wooden floor, scraping all of the dried grass in his cell into one pile and laying on it. It did little for comfort; he could hardly tell the difference between lying on the makeshift pile of grass and lying on the floor. Next he tried to pile the grass on top of himself to keep the cold out. Again, it hadn't done a thing. Kinder, who'd tried to eat most of the grass in his cell during the hours he was convinced they wouldn't be fed, seemed to have just resigned himself to the floor. He was snorting and breathing weird, which Lute knew from his one night at Kinder's home was how Kinder tried to convince himself he was asleep. By convincing himself he was asleep, he was supposed to naturally fall asleep without knowing it. He'd showed Lute a page in a book which said something to that extent, but Lute hadn't paid much attention. Perhaps he should have now. Trying not to stare into the brightness of any of the light fixtures on the walls, Lute kept rearranging himself for sleep, even offering a prayer to Astrippa for good luck. He was almost asleep once, when the door opened and closed as the guard checked on them again. It was a different guard, so Lute assumed it really was night, though it was hard to tell. How long had it been night? Did it matter? He was going to be fed to someone else's crazed god.

No. He shifted again. His bones were aching from being pressed up against the floor, and he envied Kinder his extra padding—the fool was snoring over to the right like a lightning storm. Lute was tempted to shout to wake him up; at this rate, the noise from Kinder was just another distraction. Lute tossed and turned; a guard came to check again, let the door slam, Lute turned around again. It was a tiring cycle, and his eyes were screaming for sleep that wouldn't come.

Which was why when he saw them, he was sure he was hallucinating.

Something stirred in the corner of his vision, and he turned his head. At first all Lute saw was the glare of the lamp across from him. Then something, some undulating quality in the air, passed over the lamp, making it flicker in films of transparent texture. Lute kept watching, vaguely holding onto the idea that this was a dream, albeit a strange one in which he felt everything, smelled everything—the wood, the bars around him—just the same as he would if he were awake. He kept watching the lamp, waiting for the sensation to come back, that odd rippling, the tightening and loosening of the air, as though the air were a veil of cloth someone had upset by setting something down and pushing it too far across the table beneath.

Just when he thought it might not happen again, that perhaps his eyes were playing tricks on him—they kept shutting after all, heavy as they were—the figure appeared in front of him.

If you could call it a figure, that was. Lute rubbed his eyes hard, shut them and then opened them again. The figure was still there, the faint outline of a face and paws and a tail and body all having materialized out of thin air.

Okay, sure, Lute-boy. Yer cracked. What is this, some kind of ghost? Impossible.

Lute's brain scrabbled for an explanation for what he was seeing, but his efforts fell to dust as he looked beyond the thing in front of him and saw that it was not alone.

Several pairs of wounded eyes stared back at him, from the walls and the corners of the room, the silvery faces they belonged to pensive, withdrawn. Lute waited for something to happen, frozen to his spot, but they only stared.

"What—what're yew doing here?" Lute asked, his voice coming out in a squeak. He felt as though he should talk to these things. Perhaps they wanted him to; perhaps they had come to deliver a message. He always heard about that sort of thing in stories. Stories he usually laughed at, but then, this whole situation was something he would have normally laughed at if a storyteller had begun to tell it.

The ghost-things didn't answer. Their stares were unbroken, and their eyes seemed to be looking into Lute, through him. The air, he noticed, was so cold now that frost escaped his mouth when he breathed.

The door came scratching open over the floor and Lute jumped. The ghost-things were gone.

The guard stuck his head in, looked around, and then smiled at Lute in a thoroughly discomforting manner. Did he know?

It's impossible for anyone to know anything because it didn't happen, Lute-boy, Lute thought only a few minutes later as he began to finally, finally drift off to sleep. *I'm imagining it, imagining it…*

He woke again to the sound of a door, and groaned. His eyes felt as though someone had shoved sticks under his eyelids and attempted to pull down. He could not even muster a glare or a curse for the guard, but slumped against the back wall of his cell and sighed heavily.

"Are you up, too?" a voice came from the left of him.

"Cainus?" His own voice sounded cracked in his ears. Great. Cripes, this must be what death of sleep deprivation was like.

"Yes. You didn't have a good one, did you?"

"As in, night? Cainus, I swear…" He was too tired to finish the sentence.

"It gets easier. To sleep on the floors, I mean. I hear your friend isn't having a problem."

Kinder was still snoring away on the opposite side of Lute.

"It's kind of hard not to hear, isn't it?"

"So how are you two together?"

Lute hesitated. "Long story."

"You're not going to tell me."

Lute let the ensuing silence speak for him, feeling the slightest bit mean for it. Then, after a long pause in which he debated with himself what to say, he began, "Do you ever see any…any…Just recently, I saw…" He trailed off, looking around the room as though they would appear again if he so much as spoke the words.

"Oh, the wraiths. Yes. They've been here as long as I've been here, too."

"But...but why?"

"My mother always told me they were dissatisfied, dislocated spirits that inhabit the place where they died. Beyond that, there are only theories, but between me and you, this place is full of them. It's in the air. I've never been in a more haunted place in my life. I think they're the past sacrifices."

"They just stared at me," Lute said. He felt marginally more awake. Finding out he wasn't crazy from sleep deprivation made him realize he could handle the other costs.

"I don't think they can talk," Cainus said. "Usually their appearance is supposed to be a bad omen or something."

"Well, we don't need any bad omens to tell us we're screwed," Lute muttered. "Is it daytime?"

"Impossible to tell," Cainus mourned.

Lute leaned back again and fell to the floor, putting his paws behind his head and staring up at the ceiling, the knothole in it. He thought he caught a flash of movement, a sudden shadow of presence, across the hole. Then another.

Another.

"Hey—" he started to say, but then the voices started.

The meeting upstairs had begun.

CHAPTER X

Mariyen was not alone. Llewellyn dreamed too, and this was the secret she was keeping from her own daughter.

Among other things, she thought as she clasped her stomach briefly. She kept so many secrets that it was sometimes hard to keep track. But she could have at least given the dreams to Mariyen.

She thought about this, drunk as she was on mint tea, lying sideways across her small, narrow bed in the equally drunken light slanting through the window high above her. Her little room, but it felt like a cage. She hoped Mariyen would get something bigger, something more convincing; something that would allow her to believe that her station in life wasn't going to be doomed, as surely as her mother's. Because of her mother's.

The steam from the mint tea always made her drowsy and sweetly intoxicated, but it did nothing to stop the dreams. Nothing would do anything to stop the dreams, and she knew they weren't important, they weren't real seer's dreams. Just images that played round and round her sleeping head. And would not go away.

She knew Mariyen's *were* important, that was one thing. As she lay getting drowsier and drowsier she mourned the death of her daughter's prospects, but couldn't help being secretly elated at her loss of the chance to be a seer. It was tough, but Llewellyn would not have wished her own experience on anyone.

Run while you still can, Mariyen, she thought, sitting up on her bed and staring sightlessly the few paces across the room, devouring every knick-knack, every broken piece of glass across the floor with her eyes. *There be monsters here, and you're innocent and undeserving of every one of them.*

When she dreamt that night, it was as usual. The darkness, the sparkling of lights, laughter of the friends she used to know before they deserted her like old clothing over fear, fear that can do so much to anyone, a fact she knew particularly well.

There was Horus, and then there was *him*, the one who'd messed everything up, but they flashed by like shadows she could not trace the passage of.

Her dreaming mind settled on an image, nearly in black and white, of her childhood, of the only blissfully unaware time in her life. She saw herself at a table in a long hall filled with such tables. Practice tea ceremony, partners. She tried to jerk away, but the memory only enveloped her tighter. Everything around her was buzzing with sound muted by the cloth of nostalgia she'd thrown over it. She poured the tea into two cups, and waited, the steam brushing her nose, for her mate-to-be Genhaw to find her.

Another found her instead, coming through the steam, the whistling from others' tea pots, wandering as though lost. His eyes regarded her, and the Llewellyn floating above it all, looking down at her younger self, saw what he must have seen in her face: confusion, innocence. Kindness.

"May I join you?" the stranger asked in his soft, scratchy voice, though she knew he wasn't a stranger; she'd seen him, in halls and in group disciplines, she was observant of his awkwardness, his strange way of talking and of how others moved away when he came into a room or sat down anywhere, and so she said the only thing she would allow herself to say.

"I suppose."

She watched him pour his tea, watched the clear toffee liquid flood the bottom of the cup, climb upwards, upwards to the rim. Almost spilling, not quite. His movements were jerky yet oddly graceful. There was a spell of silence after he set the tea pot down, then:

"You could make this mint if you wanted to."

The Llewellyn watching this scene was able to withdraw now. She knew what happened next, she knew everything that happened after.

She knew more than anyone needed to know, that a strange alliance was born on that day, amid the steam and the whistling and the beating of her heart.

A knocking on her door woke her from her deep sleep, and she crossed to open it in one step.

It was Horus, and he was looking flustered. When she opened the door inward, a comically surprised expression crossed his face.

"You...you got here quick."

She plastered on a false smile, knowing it unnerved him. "I can nearly *sit* on the bed and open the door at once in this place."

"Well..." he didn't know what to say to this, and for a moment she watched him flounder before blurting out, "Mariyen's gone and made herself a room!"

Llewellyn grinned. "She's part me after all," she said, "*that* is a relief. I thought that snotty Genhaw might have hogged all her genes."

"It's not funny," Horus ground out. "It's Magdala's old room."

"That musty old thing? Really? Well, I can't commend her for taste, but seeing as it's about five of mine stuck together, she's thinking well enough."

"Llewellyn."

"I'm just proud."

"*Please.*"

"What do you want me to do? Talk to her? I thought I wasn't allowed to do that, Horus."

"Try to convince her to move out. I don't know, say there are ghosts there or something."

"You are insane. What is this really about?"

Horus looked down a moment, fidgeting with the door frame. "Records. Okay? There are records in there that I don't want her to find, and I figured..." his voice was crawling to a whisper.

"What?" She arched a brow.

"Did you hear anything?"

"No..."

Horus turned and hurried away as quickly as he'd come.

Llewellyn shut the door again and went back to her tea. It was cold.

"Yugghhh.." she spat some on the ground indiscriminately and sat down again on her bed. Strange creature, Horus. Perhaps she should not have been so uppity. Her hand went unconsciously to her stomach again, stayed there, feeling as though for a pulse. They were in this together, and she wouldn't want for him to change his mind. More than one life depended upon it.

***

Mariyen held the papers up to the light. The lettering on them was small and squashed, and she couldn't read it without squinting. The room she'd chosen was gigantic, and she wanted to explore it thoroughly before Horus or any of the elders came and demanded what she was doing here.

She'd found the room through simple deduction; dragging her few belongings behind her, she'd been on her way to Horus when she took a detour into the tunnel above the summer hallway—the servers' chambers. She wanted to find out for herself what accommodation she might have.

The hall was long and felt as though it were slowly curving in a circle as she walked along—would it come full circle to Horus's chambers? She stared at the doors as she passed, attempting to discern whether each was being used. There were names on the doors set in faded yellow plaques of paper, and they glowed in the dim lighting like names recited from another time, sepia-toned and serene: Willow, Antonette, Darlene, Daviss, Ringer…

She stopped at a room on the left. The door was open a crack and it was dark inside. She could see part of the bed and a chest of drawers, pushed up against the far wall. The surface of everything was bare, the bed stripped. The name holder in the door was empty, and Mariyen pushed her way in, putting her bag down silently and going to find a light.

There was a globe-shaped lamp sitting on a small table set under a window she could not have seen from her former position. She crossed over to it and turned it on, went to the chest of drawers, and began to open each one, looking for some hint maybe of the server who'd lived here, how he or she had felt about their lot, whether he or she might be a failed seer, too.

That was when she found the pile of papers, stuffed into the corner of the right top drawer, as though someone had put them there for safe-keeping and forgot about them. Gathering them up excitedly, she jumped when she saw something move out of the corner of her eye, but it was only the curtains on the window moving with the cold air coming in. Why was the window open at such a time of year? To air things out? Mariyen went over to shut it, then thought better of it. Best to leave things as they were for now. She brought the papers to the lamp and stared at that small, squished handwriting, trying to make sense of it. The top paper was dated a couple of weeks ago:

Magdala Edgewood: went to get ragwort. Autumn. Found in woods.

Mariyen stared at this simple statement. Flipping forward a bit, she found that the other pages were similarly written, a list of squirrels, times of the year, and the places they were found when, Mariyen presumed, they had died. When she got a couple pages in, the font and the color of the paper changed, signifying something older. It was the same thing. Name, date, place found. Very succinct. Very strange.

"Mariyen."

Mariyen jumped, heart coming up into her throat. She turned and found Horus in the doorway.

"It's so nice to know you're planning on listening to what I say," he said, coming over to stand behind her. "And nicer to know you're willing to look through others' things. You are turning out to be a great server." He took the papers from her paw neatly.

Mariyen could feel herself flush under her fur, but she couldn't restrain herself. "What *is* that?" she asked, pointing to the papers.

"What do they look like to you?" Horus asked, but she thought she caught a glimpse of discomfort in his face.

"They look like a list of the dead to me," Mariyen said matter-of-factly. "Is that what they are then?" She observed him with wide eyes.

Horus sighed in exasperation and sat down on the stripped bed. "Fine. You've heard, I assume, of the deaths that have been occurring recently due to someone going out for a walk or any other such innocent activities, all of which only seem to have in common the act of traversing the ground?"

Mariyen nodded. She had.

"This is our way of keeping track of them. They're all found the same way, all skin and no insides left to speak of anymore. I'm sure you're smart enough to realize that the papers are older at the bottom of the pile. We have record of this happening at one other point in time, several seasons ago when Elder Branwell was the chief elder. It's not a new phenomenon, though we don't know what's causing it any more now than we did then."

"Why did you want this hidden, then?" Mariyen asked, secretly rejoicing at all the information she'd just been given. She'd heard about the squirrels who'd died supposedly 'due to the ground', but she'd never known any of them, and, safely ensconced as she was in Edgewood all the time, she tended to forget such things happened just outside of its walls.

"Because," Horus said, fixing her suddenly with his intense eyes, "If everyone knew that we didn't know…"

"Are you serious?" She couldn't believe it. "The only reason this is a secret is because you want to pretend you know what's happening?"

"It halts fear, Mariyen," Horus said sternly. "Never underestimate the power of fear to destroy an individual, even a colony. It's funny, I admit, as long as the rest of the colony just assumes the elders know what the situation is, that it's under control, they don't spend too much thought on it. Let them know you haven't got a clue, and they start to panic, start to devise their own solutions or to hide in fear, become dysfunctional. We can't have that in a colony so dedicated to the birthing of seers and the silence of deep meditation."

"So you don't have any ideas about what *is* happening?" Mariyen had been one of the many, she supposed, who just assumed the elders knew all the important things: who to select as seers, who was a danger to the colony, the future…

"We have ideas," Horus said, giving her a smile she didn't quite like. "But ideas are not concrete, and even the ideas of elders are often wrong." He stacked the papers more neatly using the small table under the window and said, "Now. This room belonged to Magdala Edgewood. I believe you will have read her name by now."

Mariyen started. She was unsuccessful in hiding her flush this time, and Horus said, "I am going to make you a deal. You don't tell anyone what you read here," he gestured to the papers, "and you may keep this room."

Mariyen opened her mouth, but Horus held up a paw, forestalling her. "That is not all. The reason this room is so large is that the inhabitant had a special job, one unlike the other servers. If Magdala were still here, she might be able to give you a more accurate account than I, but I am sure she would agree that it is a better position than any of the other servers hold. The server who lives in this room is responsible for serving the elders during meetings."

Horus waited, giving Mariyen time to realize the impact of what he had just said. He was sure she would get it; she was a smart one, as was her mother.

He saw the moment it hit her.

"Oh," Her eyes widened.

"Do we have a deal, then?"

She paused, but he knew there was no consideration in it. She was his.

"Yes."

"Excellent. I will leave you to unpack, then."

Horus stepped outside and closed the door nearly all the way before turning in the direction of his chambers. He could see Mariyen's face through the partial crack of the doorway as she bent to unpack her things. Staring down at the papers in his paws, he rifled through them until he came to the page he knew best, scanned to the place right below Paril Edgewood, then Genhaw Edgewood.

Sarina Edgewood. Tending garden. Spring. Body not found.

He could pretend to the others that he had a solution, but not to himself. He could hem and haw with the other elders who had no real inclination to figure things out, but to him there was an urgency. An anger, even.

To him it was personal.

CHAPTER XI

In the next few days, the knothole in the top of his cell (along with the food, which got curiously more gourmet each day) became the best distraction possible for Lute.

Meetings took place on a fairly regular basis, and a gathering of a different sort happened every dawn and night. Cainus told him that this was their worship service, and Lute could hear strains of something like music drifting through during these meetings, along with occasional vocals which echoed clearly down. If he closed his eyes laying down when he heard it, he could imagine it was the celebration of something beautiful and not the worship of some mad god who would chew on his bones.

They took Cainus one morning, coming to the door in a clatter and leading him roughly from his cell. Lute saw him as they left with him gripped between them, not even struggling for the futility of it all, saw that his coat had gotten glossy and he'd put on weight. He also saw the look Cainus flashed back at him, would remember it for a long time to come. That look was part terrible fear, part resignation, and part sadness. *Do what you need to do so this isn't you,* Cainus seemed to be saying to them.

I'll try, Lute thought, but the truth was, he had been doing the opposite over the last few days. Kinder kept referring to how he was thinking of plans of escape, coming right up to the divide between them to talk to Lute, even though Lute had told him again and again that this only made his voice sound more muffled. Lute had always answered that he was thinking on it, or would think on it, if Kinder didn't buy that. The reality was that he had done nothing of the sort.

Being in prison threw him into a funk, he realized, possibly because he'd only been imprisoned once before, and then…those dark stairs winding down into eternity, the complete blackness, making it impossible to do anything but feel her in his arms that time. She'd been crying. *This is so different,* he chided himself, disgusted. *Get yerself together. This needs to be done.* Besides, that mission was over. This was a new day, a new time, a new mission, and whatever he wished about the other part of his life, it was dead and this one could not afford to become merely its mourning.

"Lute," Kinder said, pressing himself against the barrier again once the door had closed heavily behind the guards and Cainus. "Lute, we need to do something."

"Well, that's brilliant," Lute couldn't help but say.

"I have an idea," Kinder said.

He hadn't expected that. "Well?"

It…it involves you. You know the hole in the top of your cell? The one you listen to things through?"

"I can't get through it, Kinder. It's not that big."

"I know. That's not what I was going to say. But…we can hear things in the meeting room clearly if they're loud, right?"

Lute didn't answer. He had no idea where this was going, but something in Kinder's voice made him want to hear the rest badly.

"Well, there's no reason the squirrels in the meeting room couldn't hear *us* if we spoke really loud."

Lute smacked the wall in annoyance, hurting his paw against the cold metal bars and sucking in air through his teeth. "Ahhhh…Kinder, really? What are we going to say to them? 'Let us out?' Have yew lost it?"

"No!" Kinder said, his voice going suddenly all hushed and shy, as though he were about to release a genius plan into the limelight.

Lute pulled strands of dried grass apart as he waited for the explanation. When it didn't seem like it would come, he said, "So?"

"So, they believe in this mad god thing that lives in the ground, right? They feel like they have to sacrifice other squirrels for it, right? That must mean they're afraid of it. We could pretend to be this god while they're in a worship meeting of some sort—tonight would be good. And we could give them orders. Tell them to release us, for one."

"Kinder...I don't think that will work. They weren't born yesterday. They'll know it's our voices coming from the hole."

"Since when can't gods speak through mortals?"

Lute shook his head, then, realizing Kinder couldn't see the action, said, "There has to be more to this. Even yew know this won't work as yew described it."

"Well, yes. There is one more piece of information I forgot to mention."

Lute waited for it, but was not prepared for what he heard.

"We enlist the wraiths."

Later that night, Lute was pacing the sides of his cell instead of lying on the floor as usual. Nervous, wondering. How the hell did one talk to wraiths? He'd tried, but he'd never been sure, the entire time, whether any of them were actually in the room with him, or if he was wasting his words. Judging by the cold, though, they were everywhere in this forsaken place, even if he couldn't always see them.

The sounds of the worship service started up above them, the strains of odd yet hauntingly beautiful music, the passing of shadows over the hole in the ceiling, the sound of talking, and then singing, and then silence. Lute positioned himself beside the far wall from the door, clutching the bars and trying not to think too hard about what he was about to do. He found it funny that he was the one who ended up enacting Kinder's brilliant plan, when Kinder had been the one to think of it. But it made sense: he'd been the one to see the wraiths, so he should talk to them; he had the knothole in his cell, so he should talk to the assembly above.

In the silence that spread after the music above ceased, Lute nudged himself up the wall as far as he could, holding the bars and trying to get a grip on the wood beyond with his back paws. When he spoke, he didn't realize it was his voice doing the speaking, so hollow and terrified it sounded. He could only hope terror sounded like anger to the squirrels above, but at the thought of anger, he remembered how he'd felt at their capture, and no longer had to pretend. His voice strengthened as he continued to speak; he imagined it coiling up through the hole and around them all like a giant snake, chilling them to the bone.

"YEW ARE DISPLEASING ME."

Whoever was talking above stopped, and then another voice said something and it started up again. Lute would not be discouraged.

"YEW ARE DISPLEASING ME. WOULD YEW IGNORE YER OWN GOD?"

The service, which was apparently about to start up some music, let it die down and someone who sounded suspiciously like Engelwaithe said haughtily, and loud enough for both Lute and Kinder to hear, "Shut your mouth, prisoner."

Lute heard breathing near the knothole and knew someone was trying to look through it. A murmur went through the congregation above. Quite a few of them laughed.

"YEW THINK THIS IS FUNNY? I AM NO PRISONER. DO NOT BE DECEIVED BY APPEARANCES. YEW WOULD DO WELL TO LISTEN, FOR I AM GIVING YEW ONLY ONE CHANCE. YER SACRIFICES OVER THE PAST SEASONS HAVE BEEN UNSATISFACTORY. WHY IS IT, THOUGH I AM YER GOD, THAT YEW WILL NOT MOVE TO SACRIFICE YOUR OWN BLOOD?"

There was an uncomfortable stir from up above. The voice that sounded like Engelwaithe kept telling everyone to calm down, and he seemed to be succeeding, as someone yelled, "Nice trick, prisoner!" It was followed by uncertain, straggling laughter.

"Lute!" Kinder hissed.

Lute kept right on going. "IT IS UP TO YEW WHETHER YEW BELIEVE ME. BUT KNOW THIS: I ISSUE YEW A TEST. IF YEW DO NOT PASS, YEW WILL ALL SUFFER FOR MANY YEARS TO COME. LET YER CURRENT PRISONERS GO, AND SACRIFICE TWO OF YER OWN IN PLACE. YEW HAVE BEEN LIVING ON THIS LAND FOR SO LONG; THE GROUND GROWS HUNGRY. THIS ARTIFICIAL BLOOD MAKES ME ANGRY; IT SHOWS A LACK OF DEDICATION ON YER PART. YEW CAN WORSHIP ALL YEW LIKE, BUT IF YEW WILL NOT SPILL YER OWN BLOOD FOR ME, I WILL DISOWN YEW, AND YEW WILL FACE THE CONSEQUENCES." Without a pause, Lute said the most important part of all, "WITNESS MY WITNESSES."

He did not know if it would work at first, had no way of knowing whether his pleas had been heard, but then he realized the room behind him had grown a lot warmer, and he knew.

One of the squirrels above them screamed. Another followed suit and soon the room above Lute was a mess of noise and confusion; he could see shadows crossing quickly back and forth over the opening of the knothole.

Someone banged into their chambers and Lute slid bonelessly down the bars to the floor. The squirrel who'd come in was wild-eyed and breathing hard. Lute tried to make a quick decision on whether to appear possessed or not. As it turned out, he didn't need to worry. To the sounds of Engelwaithe trying and failing to speak upstairs, the gray came over to Kinder's cell, then Lute's, opening them in a state of wild abandon, trying not to look too hard at either of them. He stood back when he'd finished, and said, "Go go go! He's still talking, but damn if I don't need those things staring at me for the rest of my life, I'm saving us all! Get out of here, get—"

When Lute started to move, he flinched backwards, stumbling into the wall. He didn't waste any time saying anything, though there were about a thousand tempting parting words at the tip of his tongue. This squirrel would be a waste of them anyway, trembling and muttering under his breath. Lute wasn't sure he was sane anymore.

"Should we get our stuff?" Kinder asked as they bulleted up the stairs and through the trap door that housed the prison. Lute only gave him a quick glance of incredulity.

"It's just...the food," Kinder panted, but Lute didn't reply. They'd reached the upstairs region. Those in the meeting hall were spilling out of its doors, and they had to push and claw their way through a group of about thirty grays to break free. It was bone-chillingly cold up here, but

Lute didn't turn to see the wraiths, where he was sure they were back in the meeting room. Squirrels turned to look at them occasionally, or shouted out for them to be captured, but the halls were in such a state of disarray that no one could hear well and in any case, no one was working together. It was a much easier task, once breaking through the main crowds, to get to the entrance hall and then the opening, fresh air streaming in at them, and then into the night, a haven at last.

They were in luck—sitting on the branch outside were their things, where they'd seemingly been discarded and forgotten by their captors. Lute shouldered his pack and started down the tree, Kinder panting behind him.

"Do you think they'll come after us?"

"I think they're too scared now," Lute answered, feeling satisfaction course through him at the thought.

"I didn't know you would add that part about sacrificing their own squirrels."

"Don't tell me yer going to have a problem with that, now." Lute stopped short and spun around, his pack hitting him in the back with a hard-angled edge as he did so.

Kinder looked over Lute's face in the pale wash of moonlight. "No," he said, after a time. "I guess not. I mean, it worked."

Lute kept walking, but when he didn't speak again, Kinder began to worry that he was angry with him. "I mean, thanks for talking to the wraiths and—

"Shhhh," Lute threw a paw out in front of Kinder, who almost tripped over it in his preoccupation.

"What?"

The night was silent except for a few cracking branches and the sound of a frog somewhere off to their right.

"Just listen, okay?"

Kinder listened.

At first he didn't hear anything out of the ordinary; then it hit him. There were sounds coming from behind a tree right in front of them, a thrashing around and a clinking as though someone were tied up...

"Cainus?" Lute took a step forward. The thrashing stopped, and the sound of panicked breathing, heavy and uncontrolled, came to them. The location was unmistakable now. Halfway to the tree, a voice spoke, or tried to.

"Heehhhhhhh, heeeeeeee."

The sound put a chill into Kinder's fur, and he looked at Lute, who was still inching forwards, knife out. He was about to suggest that they go no further when a sound, a dry, tearing, sucking sound, came from the area behind the tree. There was a strangled scream mixed in with the disgusting, stomach-turning slurping and then all was silent again. Too silent.

Kinder surprised himself then; without giving any thought to what he was doing, he ran full speed to the tree they'd heard the noises from and went around it until he came to the place it happened. The chains Cainus was tied up in were cast loosely to the ground. Cainus himself was an unrecognizable lump of black skin and fur, ghastly to look at, though it registered as only a flash of surreality on Kinder's radar. His real attention was on the ground a few paces away from where Cainus lay. It was moving.

Or part of it was, anyway. What looked like it had been a perfectly round hole about as wide as Kinder was on all fours was slowly *filling itself in* in front of his eyes.

Lute had come around the tree after him and Kinder heard him exclaim as he saw first what had been Cainus, and then the chains, and then— his eyes snagged on the moving soil just for a moment before the hole was filled in entirely.

"What..." Lute muttered, fumbling with the knife in his paws in a shaky attempt to pocket it.

"Exactly," Kinder said, staring fixedly at the spot where he could have sworn a minute ago, the earth had shifted, seemingly of its own free will. He had his senses, and his senses never lied.

The feeling in the ground was bad tonight.

CHAPTER XII

They decided to sleep that night in a nearly uprooted fir they were sure no one lived in, but only after putting what Kinder judged was a safe distance between themselves and Engelwaithe and his grays. Kinder had fallen asleep immediately, and when he woke again what felt like only a few hours later, he saw Lute sitting nearby continuing to work on the same carving he'd shoved so violently in his pack before. Kinder looked at it through eyes still full of sleep. It was definitely a female squirrel.

"Hey," he said, to let Lute know he was awake. Lute started and stuffed the carving back into his bag again, just as urgently as the first time.

"I thought yew'd never wake up. All that snoring and snuffing. It's a wonder I don't suffocate yew with yer pack."

Kinder was going to ask about the carving, but he was caught off guard. "Am I really that bad?"

"Horrible. Now, we probably ought to get on our way."

"Oh. Oh, yeah." Kinder had the idea Lute was avoiding talking about something, but didn't know how to do anything but leave it be. They started out of the tree, and when Kinder's feet hit the ground, he felt a jolt of fear that the feeling would come racing back, the malevolence of last night traveling up his legs, sending one message: *Not safe. Not safe. Run.*

But it didn't; there were no bad feelings emanating from the ground, and Kinder was initially so happy about this that he didn't notice Lute had stopped again, knife out.

A second later, he heard them, voices coming from not too far ahead, where there was a clearing and what looked like a small field through the trees. Lute wasn't moving, just standing, head cocked to the side, listening. A frown line appeared on his face.

Kinder could see movement now, through the trees. It was coming from the edge of the field; orangey flashes amid the leaves, then some of the raised voices got closer as two of the squirrels, small and ginger colored, burst into the clearing on the fringes of which Kinder and Lute were hiding. They appeared to be fighting each other to the death—kicking and biting hard enough to draw blood, stirring up the leaves around them. In between mauling at each other, the squirrels kept up a steady stream of curses and banter.

"Yew knew I wouldn't git the clock back yew ninny sugarpants rotter!"

"Oh, that's wise, whydincha gimme back my prize, idjit!"

"I don't got it, Hamer has it fer cripes sake. Way to git off topic."

How the squirrels had the energy to keep up this talk while fighting was beyond Kinder. Even though he guessed he and Lute were in plain sight, neither of the tussling squirrels seemed to notice them. He gave Lute a look that he hoped communicated 'let's just go around them' without words, but Lute was transfixed on the clearing, where something else was happening.

Another of what Kinder realized must be chickarees was emerging through the trees on the far side of the clearing. She was older than the two doing the fighting, seemingly more mature, but there was something about her, her sharp gaze, the dangling amulet around her neck, her sinuous way of moving that made Kinder's insides shrink to a decimal. She drew a knife at her side and walked calmly into the midst of the two fighting.

"Hipnik, Jenner, *really*," she said. Her voice was like gravel and smoke, and Kinder wanted to leave now, but Lute was still staring at the interactions as though he was doomed for all eternity.

The two fighting chickarees had realized they were being apprehended. They broke apart with the reluctance of two mating mayflies and one of them spat on the ground as the other began to lick his wounds.

"He started it," the latter whined between licks. The other just glowered at the female chickaree, but only, Kinder noticed, when her back was turned.

"You really shouldn't misbehave, especially when we have a guest." She looked right up and into Kinder's face, and too late he realized he had inched forward, too close to go undetected. The female chickaree started towards him, amulet switching back and forth, back and forth as she walked.

Lute dropped his knife to the ground. The chickaree turned at the noise when she was almost level with Kinder. Her eyes searched the area, before coming to rest on Lute as well.

"Well, I'll be *damned*," she whispered. "Lute-boy, back from the dead."

Kinder, shocked at the use of Lute's name, looked sideways at his friend. Lute looked less than happy. He kept trying to look away from the chickaree in front of him, and Kinder could not read his face, angled as it was away from him.

"Saecka," Lute said, finally.

"Such a warm reception. It's been so *long*, wouldn't you agree? Who's your fat friend over there?"

"No one yew need to know," Lute said shortly, still not quite meeting her eyes.

Saecka reached out and put a paw on Lute's shoulder. She began to walk around him slowly, and whispered something in his ear that Kinder couldn't make out.

"No," Lute said loudly. The leaves crunched, loud to Kinder's ears, as he shifted around, trying to find his knife. The two chickarees who'd been fighting were transfixed on this interaction, while Kinder could hear their brothers and sisters in the background, squabbling over something beyond the clearing.

Saecka appraised Lute with her cold gaze. "Well, think about. You were always like a son to me. You never were a hero, Lute-boy."

In the pause that followed, she moved quickly, like a snake taking its strike, and Kinder thought it was over for them when she came up with Lute's knife in her paws. But she only handed it over to Lute, hilt-end pointing front, and said, "If you change your mind, you know where to find me."

With that she turned, and Kinder saw that her tail was shot with several white furs. The amulet, which he recognized now as a small timepiece, ticked back and forth, back and forth. When she reached a certain place, she turned, and said, "That's nice handiwork there, Lute-boy. Is that gray still thrashing you?"

Lute closed his mouth firmly. Saecka shrugged, a hidden grin on her face, and turned back to her accomplices.

"Jenner, still upset about the clock, are we?" she asked the chickaree who'd been glowering at her earlier.

Jenner opened his mouth, and Saecka thrust her knife into it. Blood gushed everywhere, out of Jenner's open jaw and the back of his neck, dribbling down quick into the leaves, staining them darker colors. Jenner fell down after them, gasping and gurgling for a scant few seconds until he went silent for good.

Saecka was already gone from the clearing, the one called Hipnik following her at a safe distance. Kinder tried to keep his gag reflex down, and eventually the sounds of the gang of chickarees in the field began to lessen, and he knew they were moving on.

Lute was the first to speak. "Sorry about that, I guess. Though I saved us, probably." His voice sounded rusty, too little used, though Kinder knew that was not true, and it made him give another look to his friend.

"I won't ask," he said, then on second thought, "Unless you want to tell...?"

"There's nothing to tell," Lute said roughly. "I was raised by...that. If yew could call it being raised. For the first several seasons of my life I lived with them, ate with them, stole with them— He broke off and Kinder expected him to say more, but it was a long time in coming. "I killed with them."

Kinder remained silent. He didn't know what to say to this, to the way Lute's face looked to him in the light, tough yet twisted inward. He used the first thing that came to his mind.

"We should go see what they were up to, don't you think?"

He could have sworn Lute looked at him with gratitude then, but it was so quick he couldn't be sure. "Yeah," he said. "Yeah, that's a good place to start."

They crept through the clearing, though no one was there anymore to their knowledge, and out into the field beyond, covered in wilting grass and fallen leaves along the perimeter of the woods. Lute saw it first.

"It's another one," he said, beckoning Kinder over to where he was standing. "Like Cainus."

He was right. The body—or rather, the skin—was laid out in exactly the same crumpled manner as the pelt that had belonged to Cainus. This one, older it seemed, was gray-furred and had begun to stink, and Kinder clapped a paw over his nose as he stared down at it, horror transfixing him.

"What were they doing here?" Kinder asked in honest puzzlement, daring to breathe for a moment.

But Lute had already bent down and was examining the torn fabric lying around the discarded carcass. He picked up a shard of what looked like a sack or a tunic--it was hard to tell now— and let it fall to the ground again.

"They were looking for loot," Lute said simply. "His things. Looks like they found them."

"They took a dead squirrel's things?" Kinder gasped before he could stop himself. Everyone knew that was bad luck, he'd thought—he had a charm for it and everything.

Lute, who no doubt thought he was talking more about common decency, shrugged.

"That's chickarees for ya," he muttered. "No wonder Saecka was in such a good mood. They're getting profit out of this whole evil-in-the-ground trend."

That was a good mood? Kinder would have hated to see her in a bad one. "Profit..." he repeated weakly. He needed to get away from the stench of the unfortunate squirrel's body. It was making him ill.

Lute turned from examining the body and seemed to realize Kinder's discomfort.

"Yew know what I think?" he said. "I think the Aspen Forest that creepy rotter told us about is not far from here."

"Why?"

"Take a look." He held out a piece of paper, torn and flapping in the slight breeze. Kinder leaned in to read it.

Gustafok,

Do well at your job today! I know baking pies isn't very interesting, but the children would love for you to bring back an acorn one. Please try and make it back to the Aspen Woods earlier rather than later; we have a surprise for you!

Much love,

Arienne

As Kinder read the note, he couldn't help but wonder what the family had been like waiting for Gustafok. When had they realized he wouldn't come back and put whatever surprise they'd made in the back of some seldom used closet? Was the one called Arienne still sitting at home staring out the window, praying fruitlessly? How would she explain to the children, who may not have learned fully to speak yet, how sometimes those we love don't come back?

"Hey," Lute said. He threw the paper to the ground where it drifted listlessly over to lie next to the body of its owner. "Yew okay?"

"Yes, I'm fine," Kinder said rather too quickly, then, "it's just that I can't breathe, really. The stealing, too, it's...it's bad luck. Could we just eat something?"

Lute stared at him for a moment before shrugging. "Sure. We might want to get across this field first. No one wants to be ambushed while eating a sandwich."

Kinder grinned tightly, trying to push away the strange funk he found himself in. It was the body, of course, and the thoughts of Nadra and how similar she must have looked, how there were squirrels missing her, just as somewhere there were squirrels missing Cainus, a whole family in Oakwood, who, if still alive, would never live quite the same. Something needed to be done, but the closer they got to the potential solution, the less Kinder was sure this white squirrel would be able to help them. *Your friend is going to die,* he thought, remembered his charm disappearing in the curling of those long, cold paws and wondered if this was not what he was on: a mission to his death. What if Lute was right with his initial misgivings? What if they were going in circles?

What if there was no white squirrel?

They reached the forest on the other side of the field after what turned out to be a longer walk than either of them expected. Every time they thought they were getting close, they would scamper over a rise in the field and realize that it stretched on for longer than their eyes could detect. When they finally reached the trees on the far side, Lute immediately started up one, heaving his pack behind him in an ungainly manner. Kinder followed, his own pack even heavier, and nearly fell once, but managed to hold on to a thin branch on the tree that bent perilously the harder he struggled to pull himself up. In the end, Lute had to come forward to rescue him, which was no easy task and nearly had both of them falling from the tree.

"Yer going to need to travel lighter," Lute remarked as they ate, resting up against the trunk. "I'm not willing to do that twenty times over."

Kinder frowned. His pack had most of their food inside, but he knew what was really weighing them down, and it was not food. All of his charms were still piled halfway to the top of the sack. Lute seemed to read his mind.

"Yew don't need them," he said. He was aimlessly carving a random design into the trunk of the tree. Kinder would have sworn that if he didn't remind Lute they needed to stop to eat, they would have starved to death long ago. Whenever Lute sat still too long, he took to carving, even when there was a nice pie in front of him, demanding his attention.

Kinder looked down at the pile of charms. He just couldn't. Lute only saw how ridiculous they seemed, with their strange symbols and abstract purposes. He probably thought they did nothing, because it seemed like they did nothing. He did not understand that the charms were there to prevent bad things *before* they happened, that you never noticed what the charms were doing when you had them, but when you *didn't*, you wondered if every bad thing could not have been stopped. They were here in the bottom of his bag for security, for insurance, for the memory of being small and lying in bed, hearing his father close the door for the last time and wondering *why*. Some things weren't preventable. But the hard thing was that you never knew which things they were.

"I'll get better at climbing," Kinder promised aloud, drawing shut his bag. He waited for Lute to argue with him, but he only rolled his eyes and stuck the knife he was using in the tree.

They packed up once more and climbed down, and Kinder noticed that Lute did not retrieve it. When he reminded Lute of his knife, he only said, "That one was poorly carved anyway. I didn't do the grape leaves right." Kinder watched the knife recede into the distance as they left the tree for the forest, and wondered how it seemed so easy for some to leave the past behind, start over.

After they'd walked for some time, the forest became thicker as the trees grew closer together, and a silence pervaded the area that Kinder had been oblivious to if it had existed before. It was then that he noticed the trees were different. Far more of them were leafy and smooth-wooded, and let the sun in more easily through their leaves.

He turned to Lute to point this out to him, and Lute nodded before he said anything.

"Just a guess, but I think we're *in* Aspen Forest, Kinder."

Kinder had already forgotten the name of the squirrel who'd died on the border of the last group of trees, but whoever he was, he'd been closer to his home than wherever he'd come from when he'd been killed. Had his family gone out looking and found his body? Had his wife cried over it, half in fright and half in sadness at the way she couldn't look at him, couldn't accept the empty shell he had become?

"How do we find this white squirrel, eh?" Lute asked. He looked nearly terrified at the thought, and Kinder remembered his angry words in the seer's tree: *I knew them!* He had still never asked Lute about those words, and Lute had kept his silence on the matter, but Kinder got the feeling that whatever it was, it was part to blame for why Lute looked so oddly frightened right now.

"Well," Kinder said, "If he's a messenger of Astrippa, that means he's got to have some powers, right? I have a charm that attracts magic in my bag. Maybe he'll be attracted by that."

Lute stared at him. "Yer kidding," he said. "I'm serious. How do we find him?"

Kinder hadn't been kidding, but he did not press his point. "Well, this forest might not be very large," he suggested reasonably. "Maybe we should ask the first squirrel we run into."

"And if they turn out to be like Engelwaithe and his merry band?"

"We'll just have to make a quick getaway."

Lute groaned. "I don't like it, but—

That was when they saw the white tree.

It was standing alone in the middle of a small clearing, surrounded by a very unmistakably marked out circle of rocks.

"What's that doing here?" Lute asked, his voice thick with premonition.

"I think my charm worked," Kinder whispered.

Lute gave him a long-suffering look.

"We should go pay a visit."

"What if it isn't really him?"

"We'll just have to make a quick getaway," Lute smirked.

The circle of stones reminded Kinder of a circle cast in magic ritual, and he got a fluttering in his stomach when they stepped inside of it. What did it symbolize?

At least the door in this tree was easy to find, Kinder thought as they got closer. It was set square above a long slender white branch that nearly sloped to the ground. The yellow, orange and red leaves the tree was surrounded in made it glow all the more, a practical invitation to passersby.

Lute was pushing forward to this door already, seemingly fearless though Kinder knew by now not to assume this meant he wasn't scared. He followed along, feeling that every leaf he disturbed was an omen, a transgression against the weird sacredness of this place.

Lute knocked right away. The door was simple and wooden and it did not produce a very impressive sound, but all the same, Kinder had the same sensation that something was being disturbed that was perhaps best left alone.

Lute gave the door a second knock when no one responded, and they waited, letting the silence spill out in front of them once again.

"Maybe he's not home."

"Oh, he's home," Lute growled. He gave the door a third knock, a fourth...

The door swung open, and Lute in all his ferocious energy, nearly fell inside. The face that peered out at them was indeed that of a white squirrel. This alone was enough to put Kinder into awe, but more than that, Kinder was surprised to notice that he was rather younger looking than he'd expected. In fact, the white squirrel in the doorway looked no more than ten seasons older than them, though Kinder supposed he could be much older and hiding it well.

Lute, who might have been struck by the same thing, stumbled back, staring with wide eyes at the form in the doorway

The white squirrel, for his part looked, of all things, puzzled. It was not an expression Kinder would have expected to see on the all-knowing. Then he began to speak and even the sound of his voice was not so magical and mystical as Kinder had built it up to be in his mind.

"What?"

It was the first word from his mouth. This was followed by a long uttering of profanities under his breath and then a, "How did you *find* this place?"

"We were wandering around in the forest and we came into a clearing and there it was," Lute said. "It's not exactly secretive. I mean, yew got the white tree, yer a white *squirrel*. Yew got that circle of stones. We can put two and two together."

"Damn it all," the white squirrel blurted out. "You can see the stones?"

"Why wouldn't we?"

"Oh, well, this—this changes everything," he began to mutter under his breath again. "This changes...the implications...conspicuous..." He looked up after a moment and looked surprised to realize that Lute and

Kinder were still there. "Could you two just…leave, or something? I've got something new to worry about now, indeed." He stiffened suddenly and whipped around, staring at them in a way that made it look as though he were staring straight into both of their eyes at once. "Unless you two are some sort of scouts or something? Is that what you do? Are you here to retrieve me? Because I won't go, and I should warn you—"

"We're not scouts of any kind," Lute broke in. "We need to talk to yew about something important, and we won't leave until we get what we want."

"It's about—" Kinder began, and Lute tried to hush him, but he came out with it anyway, like stumbling and falling in the right place. "—the ground. I think you know what we mean."

The white squirrel stared at them for such a long time that Kinder began to feel convinced that he really didn't know what they meant and they ought to shoulder their bags and head back home because the seer was playing a big, fat joke on them. Then, the white squirrel's mouth twitched in a half-smile and he said, "I'm sorry. You can come in if you like."

He moved aside and gestured into the hallway beyond him. The floors were covered in rugs and there were lanterns everywhere—they crowded tables and they lined up along the floor, lighting up the windowless passageway in a warm yellow light. The second thing he noticed, as the white squirrel led them silently down a short hallway and into the tiny room at the end of it, was that there were also a lot of clocks, set in among the lanterns and on the shelves and tables and even the floor. Some of them appeared to be broken, but a good number were working, filling the tree with a constant dry tick-tick-tick-tOck...Everywhere Kinder turned, there were clocks and lanterns and small tables. It was slightly overwhelming.

The room they entered was the same as the hallways in terms of décor, except that it boasted two overstuffed chairs and a sofa. There was a long table shoved up against one wall, on which lay a steaming tea pot, a deck of cards, and a pipe. The white squirrel picked up this last object and took his time inserting a piece of pipe reed inside before sitting in the chair nearest the table and staring at them mildly. It was such a difference from his former behavior that Kinder could not comprehend what type of squirrel this must be. His eyes kept drifting involuntarily back to the white fur, stained in yellow tones by the lighting. That fur was a novelty to him.

The white squirrel must have noticed their confusion, because after leaning back in his chair and blowing smoke out of his mouth, he said, "I'm sorry about earlier, if I seemed...abrupt to you. It's just—no one was supposed to find me, you know. I had everything set up so perfectly, that I thought, *never* again—

"So yew wanted to hide yerself from the world, huh?" There was still a bite to Lute's tone that Kinder didn't understand.

"No," the white squirrel said quietly, collectedly. "Not quite. I wanted to hide the world from myself."

"Why?" Kinder asked. Lute made a silently derisive noise.

"Sometimes, the things one has done with one's life are not things one can be proud of."

"You mean like the pact with Astrippa?" Kinder asked keenly.

The white squirrel jumped up so fast that some of the burning reed from his pipe crumbled and fell in his lap.

He slapped at it quickly with a wince, and said, "How did—how—where did you hear *that?*"

"We have our ways," said Lute, at the same time as Kinder said, "A seer told us."

"A seer?" The white squirrel looked very ill at ease. "What seer is this?"

"Does it matter?" Lute asked, paws crossed, at the same time, again, as Kinder said, "Absoulim."

"*Absoulim,*" the white squirrel muttered, more to himself than anyone else in the room, "*He* knows where I am? Damn that rotter, I swear." He looked up at them as though realizing they were still present. "What did Absoulim tell you about me, exactly? Nothing good, I trust?"

"Well…"

"He said that yew had a pact with Astrippa but yew broke it by being foolish as a mortal is and now the thing with the ground is happening, *yew* know, how squirrels keep dying and no one can explain it. It's punishment for what yer doing."

"Well, I'll be damned." The white squirrel sat back in his chair and brought the pipe to his lips again. "What a story. It makes sense, too. He always was regrettably smart," he muttered to himself, then addressed them, in the pattern that seemed to be habit to him. "I think I will have some tea. Would either of you like some tea?"

Lute shook his head, still staring intently at the other squirrel, as though he was determined not to let him escape his vision. "I think we've had enough of tea for a while," he said.

Kinder, who remembered the twirling, slow turning steam of the last cup he drank, and remembered what came after— the hard claw grabbing his arm, the premonition— felt his stomach rumble.

"As long as it isn't mint," he said, and the white squirrel filled him a cup, then went back to puffing at his pipe. Kinder took a sip. The tea was honey flavored. He could feel Lute giving him a look, but he ignored it.

"Why did yew leave them?" Lute burst out. "Yew left without helping them, yew didn't even mourn…"

"The white squirrels were never the type to do that in the first place." The one he was talking to stared at him through the smoke drifting up from his pipe, half smiling. "They were very secretive, very solitary, even to the point of hiding from one another. It was not the life for me, but then, I fit the bill perfectly in many ways. There is no use, after a while, in hanging around mourning." He studied Lute. "You have been keeping company with ghosts, have you?"

Lute, for once, broke eye contact and looked down, the fight gone out of him.

"Yeah, I guess, but only because the place is near where I live, yew know…"

"They would have done nothing for you were they alive now."

There was a silence after these words, and Lute looked away.

"They didn't do much for me when they were alive then," he said, and when he looked back, he was grinning tentatively.

"Yes," the white squirrel gave a jerky sort of smile, as though he were unaccustomed to showing so much emotion in his face. "I can believe that."

"Well…" Kinder felt awkward in breaking the silence. "If the Astrippa thing is true, why aren't you doing anything to stop whatever forces are in the ground?"

The white squirrel considered him as he inserted more of the scented reed into his pipe.

"Which part do you want to hear, the part where Absoulim is a liar or the part where I may know what's happening?"

"What did Absoulim lie about?" Lute asked. He was lying back in his chair, trying to look as though he was at ease after his blowup, but he leaned forward now. "I *knew* I didn't trust him."

The ticking of the clocks met Kinder's ears once more and he stared at one in front of him on the desk, small and made of dark wood with a silver face in which he could see all the individual gears working. The thing was, Kinder didn't know if he found this white squirrel trustworthy either. He hesitated too long and too often, and his eyes seemed closed in their very depths, silently pushing them towards the door with every other word he said. If only other squirrels could be like this clock, all complicated but understandable gears bared for them to sort through and find the answers they needed, know the truth behind the faces. *If that were true, he'd be able to see into me, too,* Kinder thought. He decided maybe it was a good thing squirrels were not like clear-faced clocks. He'd be too afraid of what he had to face, everywhere.

"Your tea must have gotten cold," the white squirrel observed, and when he stared at Kinder, it seemed he knew exactly what he'd been thinking. He held out a paw for the cup, and refilled it, still keeping eye contact. There was something infinitely wise in those eyes, but also something tormented, breakable, wild. Dangerous.

"You want to know," he said, handing the tea back to Kinder. "What the problem is with the ground, what sort of forces reside there, just as you did when you went to the flyer. But I'm going to tell you the truth about it."

Lute and Kinder waited in the yawning silence, the ticking all around them only adding to the urge to know.

"It is true, somewhat, what he says about me having a special purpose. I am...not meant, really, to be living as I am. I believe that over time I've messed things up, yes. Time itself, for instance...it's starting to show wrinkles."

Kinder's mind ran with disbelief and fear, little rivulets that ran into one stream and coursed their way down his body. Something about the way the white squirrel said this was not right.

"Time has wrinkles? What do you mean?"

"It would be rare and hardly detectable, but sometimes the past and the future and the present become...one. They bunch together, if you will. Unless you're seeing part of the past in the present, you would not recognize it—

Lute rubbed his head. "So yer saying that yer destroying the way time works or whatever by not doing yer job, and yer *fine* with that?!"

"Not fine, no. Not quite. I did not know initially that this would happen, were I to...experiment. And, well, shouldn't I experience what others are experiencing, just once? Be happy you can remember your birth; it's an irreplaceable thing."

He seemed to simmer as he took another draw on his pipe, and Kinder decided he needed to ask.

"But the ground?"

"I have nothing to do whatsoever with the ground," the white squirrel said. The crackling intensity had not left his voice.

"Then...then who does?" The dismay he felt at never seeming to be able to unlock this answer eclipsed his new concern, the thing dancing in the back of his mind, telling him this squirrel wasn't doing an important duty, that eventually they might all be killed as a result of his negligence. How should they trust him?

But he did. The squirrel in front of him may have been purely selfish, but he was telling the truth. Kinder didn't know whether it was the truth charms in his bag or not, but his conviction on the matter could not be any more firm.

"The problems with the ground are because of what lives under the ground," the white squirrel said simply before a wreath of smoke eclipsed his face. Kinder thought briefly that he seemed too young to be smoking pipe reed already, then said, "But what lives under the ground?"

The white squirrel shrugged. "I have not been down there in all my time here, and I don't find it pressing that I go. However, it's no use at all for you to attempt to negotiate with the monsters that are coming up to snatch the essence of the victims."

"Monsters?" Lute said skeptically. "What type of 'monsters' are we talking?"

"They're tunnelers," the white squirrel answered, ignoring his tone. "Believe me or not, I know it's hard for squirrels to conceive of anything beyond the ground—

"It's crazy," Lute said flatly.

"Yes…and no. We live in trees. Who said there can't be someone who lives underground?"

"I'm unsure what it is you're suggesting," Kinder said. He was exasperated with this going around in circles. Why wouldn't the white squirrel hurry up with them already? But his eyes no longer seemed to be willing them away. It seemed almost as though he were sating some selfish need with their company, and this made him even more uncomfortable than the last impression he'd had.

"All I mean to say is that the tunneling beasts who are feeding on your kind are not on their own—and it's a good thing. As it is, they have no actual faculties for thinking or plotting or anything of the sort. They are frightening, they are deadly, but they are driven by their stomachs. There is nothing magical or metaphysical about this. If they are suddenly coming aboveground to feed, they are getting orders from those who own them."

"*Who* owns them?"

The white squirrel smiled. "I like to call them the underground squirrels."

"I thought yew'd never seen them," Lute said.

The white squirrel only smiled. "I may have, briefly. They are not desirable company, so forgive me if I try to forget. Those creatures are in their employment. If they were not, and they ran out of food belowground, they would have died. They did not know there was an aboveground, and they probably forget it each time they sink under the earth again. Why do you think it is so hard to catch them? You would think they'd stay aboveground once they realized how much nourishment they could get—but they're nearly blind aboveground and they are thus afraid of all the different smells and sensations. Have you ever wondered why they disappear as quickly as they do?"

Kinder thought of the dirt moving on its own next to Cainus's crumpled body. It had been exactly what it looked like—a hole filling in, only not by itself. It had been filling in after the large body retreating back under the earth.

"What do they look like?"

"Large worms, in a sense," the white squirrel said. "Only much more terrible to look upon."

"We need to stop it from happening, then!" Kinder said. "If there are squirrels who control these worm-things, we need to talk to them, explain that they're letting those aboveground die!" He paused, had another thought. "Do they know we exist if we don't know they do?"

The white squirrel looked back at them gravely. "They know something's being eaten, don't they?"

Kinder felt a shiver pass through himself. Lute said, "Well, someone needs to talk to them. If *yew* knew all this, why didn't *yew*?"

The white squirrel smiled, and this time it was in a sad way. "I could not have risked myself that way even if I had wanted to. And I was afraid."

"Saving yerself for yer special purpose, I suppose," Lute grumbled, and Kinder expected that the white squirrel would get angry at this. Instead he merely looked put out.

"You musn't think...it wasn't..." but the white squirrel trailed off as if in defeat.

"Well, yer clearly not interested in helping us out here. Yew keep wanting us to leave, cripes, I'm not blind. I think that yew don't like that we called yew out on this, is that right? Hard to face the truth? Yew could put a spell on me or something, but it wouldn't change the fact that yer a regular good-for-nothing. And before we leave yew, we need to know something else, so if yew won't do anything else, please tell us the answer and have done with it."

The white squirrel stared at them as the ticking closed around them. A particularly loud *tock* from one of the clocks scared everyone into jumping.

"Fine," the white squirrel said sulkily, and Kinder was forced to remember, again, how young he actually was. This was not the behavior of a wise older squirrel because he was *not* a wise older squirrel...yet. Kinder thought maybe Lute's lecturing would have made him unwilling to say another thing, but he only shifted in his chair moodily and put down his pipe.

"What question do you want answered?"

"We need to know," Lute asked, "how we can get to these underground squirrels."

The white squirrel's relief at the question was tangible, as though he'd expected they were going to ask him something else he would rather not have answered. Kinder wondered what that would be, exactly, and a question of his own occurred to him. He clamped his jaw shut on it until the appropriate time.

"There is a rocky slope not too far from here. It's very steep, so I would watch yourselves going up. On the top, just as you crest the highest part, there is a dip, and you'll see a hole in the earth between the rocks."

"That's all?"

"There are several entrances to the underground everywhere, but that is the closest one I know of."

Kinder had finished drinking his tea—there was some cold liquid left on the bottom, but he kept it that way. He didn't want the white squirrel to decide he wanted to read his tea leaves or tell his future the way Absoulim had. They got up to leave, Lute first, and Kinder said, on second thought, "What's your name?"

"Does it matter? Aren't I just 'Astrippa's messenger' or whatever to you?"

"Come on, let's just go," Lute muttered. "Thank you for telling us what we need to know."

"Thank you for nothing at all," Kinder swore he thought he heard the white squirrel mutter under his breath, though when he looked back, he was only sitting in the square of light that was the room they were leaving behind, smoking his pipe and letting the smoke billow out in patterns that he wasn't sure you could make without the help of some type of magic.

***

When they left him, the white squirrel called Zirreo continued to smoke his pipeweed, making the twist of the smoke conform with his thoughts. For so long, he'd been able to hold the world off. For so long, he thought he could. How foolish. But the dreams kept coming, and now this. Two squirrels, younger even than himself, finding his hideout even though he knew the circle of rocks were enchanted sufficiently. The tree should be invisible. Was this an effect of the ripple in time? Or was it simpler and more unthinkable?

"Damned bad luck," he spoke to the smoke in front of him, which had taken the form of a female squirrel, turning in the air and beckoning to him. When he realized what it was, he jumped from his chair and brushed it out with several swipes of his paw, and put his pipe down.

He put his head in his paws. They were lucky indeed to remember their births. When you couldn't remember your birth into this world, the world kept reminding you that you didn't belong, kept on pursuing you through every interaction, pushing you towards that finish line of going back. And Zirreo did not want *back*.

He wondered now if it was the white squirrels that had given him away. The two white squirrels out of many who'd died in the burning tree.

He'd been imprisoned in the back room for who knew how long, when he smelled the smoke, then saw it drifting under the door, and he'd thought at the time, *This could be it. This could be the end.* And in that moment, much as he loved life, he thought that would be fine with him, in fact, it would be wonderful, because he would have won. And then they'd come, hours later when the room was on fire around them and he knew they had no hope. He'd only helped them along, but…had it tripped up something somewhere? Or was it after, where he'd gone, what he'd done? He'd been so young, but then, it wasn't so long ago and it turned out the young paid for their mistakes just as much, perhaps extra. Was it any single incident that had made things come to this? He would never know, though somehow he doubted it.

He'd thought…after what had happened at the tree of the white squirrels, after his tangle with their society, the way he riled them up and drove them to imprison him…after the others, and *her*…he thought if he hid himself well enough things would just stop, come to a standstill around him, and he would be forgotten.

All I wanted was a choice.

But it looked like he was beginning to have no choice.

Did I ever?

The thought hung in the air as he went, as though waking from the stagnation of sleep, to roll up the blinds to one of his windows for the first time.

CHAPTER XIII

Lute and Kinder were, as per the white squirrel's instructions, walking straight from where they were to where they hoped to find the slope he was talking about.

"I swear," Lute said, struggling over the leafy ground as he turned and attempted to talk and walk at once. "If he's wrong—"

He tripped over a rock and was down in an instant, in a flurry of autumn red and orange. Kinder tried to stifle the laugh that came to his mouth, but to no avail.

"Fine," Lute snapped, and Kinder went back to wondering, as he had when they started off this trip, what it was that had him in such a foul mood.

"I think I see it," Kinder said, as Lute got up from his fall. At first he said it just to forestall any unpleasantries Lute might have to foist upon him, but then he realized he was right. If you squinted into the distance before them, there was what looked like a rock wall embracing the end of the forest, like a limit declaring finality: *Go no further*. But that was exactly what they'd do.

Lute looked in the same direction as Kinder, and saw that, thank Astrippa, at least the white squirrel was right about this.

"C'mon," he said vaguely to Kinder, and without waiting to see if his companion was keeping pace with him, he began to make for the wall of rock.

When they got up close to it, it was much, much larger than Lute had expected, and there were very few grooves he could see to hang on to. He walked up and down the length of the thing, but couldn't find any real good place to begin climbing, and the slope seemed to stretch on forever.

"All right," he said, standing back. He was so accustomed to climbing trees, with their rough yet pliant, reassuring bark, that such an unforgiving wall of rock posed a problem.

"I'll go up first," Kinder volunteered, and Lute was inexplicably annoyed to find that he did not sound scared at all.

"No, that's fine," Lute said, and began to climb. His paw found a crevice and he clutched his pack in his mouth and began to inch up the rock, body straining and shaking with each new movement. He could hear Kinder behind him after a while, panting heavy and dragging his overlarge pack which made a clinking sound as it hit the rocks behind him.

What? A million charms for rock climbing? Lute thought in an effort to chase his fear with humor. It didn't work as well as he'd hoped. Instead, when he dared to look up and realized that the end was in his sight, he became more relaxed. All he had to do was slide his right foot into the crack a little below the lip of the slope, and then *push* himself up. He'd be fine. No sooner had he thought these things than he'd done them, and, taking the pack from his mouth and setting it onto the blessedly level stone next to him, Lute looked down at Kinder and began to instruct him.

"There's a crack right above yew…yeah, grab that and then put yer paw in the next one and push."

Lute turned to investigate the area behind him, a harsh rocky ground that stretched until it came to another field similar to the one they'd crossed to get to the Aspen forest. A large rock loomed right in front of his face, and when he went around this to explore, he found it. The rock was canted upwards slightly, sitting unevenly on the earth so that under the far side there was a small bank of dirt.

In this bank, there was a hole.

The first thing that struck Lute was how small the hole was. He looked around without much hope for another hole that could possibly be the one the white squirrel was talking about, but of course, there was nothing to be found. He turned his attention back to the narrow tunnel, tried to see down it past all its probable twists and turns, but the brackish dark within would not reveal a thing. He could probably squeeze through, but it would be tight, and his throat contracted at the thought. And what about Kinder?

That was when two things happened at once: Lute lifted his head to call out to Kinder, and Kinder simultaneously made a strangled sound. Lute heard rock shifting, crumbling, and then nothing. He ran to the edge of the rock wall, stared down it desperately, but nothing below seemed to be moving. Some of the shale under his feet crumbled and slipped down the long fall after Kinder, but Lute could not see the fox squirrel, or his pack anywhere in attendance.

*This doesn't happen, this is un*real, Lute told himself.

"Kinder!" he shouted. "Kinder!"

The second time, he thought he heard something, somewhere answer back, but it was snatched by the wind, and before long it became a part of his imagination. If Kinder were here, he was lying somewhere right below, stretched out over the ground, waiting for the worst, because the ground held horrors, they both knew that. That or—

But he refused to think his next thought, trying instead to get enough of a hold on the steep wall to climb down again. After stumbling and nearly falling tail over head twice himself, he realized that this was a one-way path. He could go up, but there was no coming back down, unless he wanted to die as well. *As well?* He wished he could take the thought back. Rain had started to drop from above, spackle-slapping the rocks and landing heavy and cold on Lute's scruffy coat of fur. "Kinder!" he called again, "C'mon yew fat idiot!"

A bit of an echo came back after his voice, mixing with the low tumbling of thunder in the distance, across the field. A swollen stinging rose in Lute's eyes and he blinked furiously, staring down at the mosaic of leaves and rocks on the floor far below him. Every time it started to drift into one big, watery picture, he blinked it away. It was getting dark, he realized. Surely, if anyone was below, they would have moved about by now, to get out of the rain at least. But all he saw through the dimness was the slick of wet leaves—the once bright colors seemed dimmed too, as though they'd only ever been different variations of rust.

Minutes that felt like hours later, Lute got up from his spot on the rocks. He would have to face it sooner or later, that Kinder was no longer...

That he ran away. I'm a bad travelling companion, that's all it is. He was in it for real reasons, and I was in it for the white squirrels. This was Kinder's mission, not mine.

'Yew were never a hero, Lute-boy', Saecka's voice echoed tauntingly in his head. His mind turned again to her words as she'd leaned over, whispering them in a hush so that only he could hear: *Join us.* He had had to try not to drive his knife into her there and then. Had to pretend not to be interested. Well, now he was alone, and he was free to do as he liked.

An unexpectedly loud peal of thunder came crackling in, and in the lightning that lit up the sky for an eerie moment, Lute thought he saw Kinder returning through the silver slices of rain, but it was a mistake; it was in his imagination only, and the shape changed even as he watched. The face that he now imagined smiling in the rain was a different one, female, one from a distant past, a long ago adventure of trekking through snow and chasing legends to their fiery ends.

He turned from the vision like he'd been struck by lightning and found the hole, waiting like an open mouth behind him. Not waiting long enough for his own rational thought to catch up with him, Lute dug around in his pack, hesitating for only a moment before deciding on his best knife. He stuck it in the empty belt around his middle and started towards the hole, only to turn back and retrieve the looking glass from the sack. His own image glinted at him briefly from the mirror as he stuffed it, too, into the belt and turned to enter the ground.

CHAPTER XIV

Mariyen had a lot of free time. It was the first thing she noticed about being a server for the elder's meetings. This was, of course, due to the fact that the elders didn't have meetings on a regular basis. Part of her loved the freeness of the life she was now living, one where she could explore the halls and vacant rooms of the place she'd lived for so long when she knew others were going about their disciplines, scrubbing surfaces, pouring tea. She no longer had to participate in meditations, either, but sometimes she still did, going into her overlarge room and sitting in the middle of the bare wooden floor beyond her bed, imagining herself breathing in sync with all the others she had left behind. Down in the main meditational chamber, was Hontem's heart beating the same rate as hers, her life cascading as it was down such a different track? In the Spring Chambers, was Ruby running late, her energy a separate current in the minds of the elders that would earn her a talking to?

It was a wonder to her how she'd transferred so quickly from one world to another under the branches of the same tree, and yet how, when she wandered down any given hall, trailing her paw over the smooth wood, access to memories that weren't hers, she felt like an outcast in both.

The one meeting she had gone to thus far gave her an idea of the routine she would follow for the next ten, or twenty, or however many the elders needed to have in her time. She stood in front of the door to the meeting room, a short walk from her own, and met Horus when he arrived there, as he'd ordered. He had looked surprised to see her for an instant, then quickly recovered and opened the door for her, crossing to his table at the front of the room, making no attempt to speak to her before the start of the meeting. The other elders trickled in slowly, and she counted them all: there was the old, crippled one who leaned heavily on his cane, the one who owned a cane but didn't seem to need it in the slightest, but swung it around animatedly instead when he spoke. There was the smallest, elderly one who looked as though she had a habit of combing her fur in the opposite direction, and the squint-eyed, twitchy one named Bogus, who always made her laugh upon sight, even though she knew it was rude.

Once they'd all entered and sat down, it was Mariyen's job to bring them drinks from the small adjoining kitchen room, or to bring Horus any papers he'd forgotten, to call the hours as they passed, and to catch Fairel, the touchiest of the elders, when she fainted, which Horus had previously informed her was usually thrice a meeting.

The first meeting was something incredibly boring to begin with, talk on the meditation room and whether to move it to the bottom floor of Edgewood instead of so close to the great hall. She never would have expected so many squirrels could say so much about so small a topic. After the initial anxiety had died down, Mariyen began to get bored, staring into the same dark brown knotting on the wall in back of Graining, who was beginning to look unnerved despite his interest in whatever Fairel, recovered from her third faint, was now saying.

"...problem with the ground, is it?"

Mariyen zoned back in on the conversation so fast that she felt dizzy from it. She looked over to catch Horus looking in succession frightened, then relieved, then thoughtful, staring down at his paws on the tabletop in front of him. Apparently, Fairel's question had been directed at him, because all of the other elders were staring directly to the front of the room, and Fairel looked like she might faint again and make a record for herself. Mariyen wondered if any of them had seen the weird moment of fright in the chief elder.

"You know that I would like to believe that theory more than anything," Horus said. "But how would he be doing it?"

"He's displayed strange magic before, he can do it again. I see no reason to believe there can't be some type of magic we haven't seen before. Unless you're all so full of yourselves you think you know *everything*?" Bogus twitched on this last word as if to emphasize it, and Mariyen had to keep from smiling. She followed the line of the conversation with her eyes, as one elder after another tried to weigh in until one, she could not tell who, said, "Call him back to Edgewood."

A silence settled over the room. Finally, Horus said, "That is not a good idea, Brint." His eyes settled on the small squirrel whose fur looked as though she'd received an electric shock. Mariyen thought it made her look constantly offended, though she was fairly sure the feeling was genuine now.

"I've said all along that the sentence for certain types of crime should be higher—

"Brint," Horus said, and his voice was icy, making her stop short and stare resentfully at him. "Do you not remember the most precious, the most ancient of our rules? We do. Not. Kill."

"Not even when one of our own could be responsible for the deaths of hundreds more?"

Mariyen stared at Horus. His face profiled against the lamplight was harsh and lined as though he'd become older in the past week. "Absoulim is not one of our own," he said. "We have no proof that he's doing this, and even if he is, there's no way to ensure that he would come back if we called him."

"What if we said we'd give him what he wants?"

The crippled elder spoke softly from his chair and everyone turned to look at him. The silence drew out. "This conversation is closed," Horus said. The crippled elder continued to stare hard at him, but he ignored it. "We have other subjects to discuss. Such as…"

Mariyen began to daze out again, and just like that, the meeting was closed.

"You did well," Horus told her afterwards, and looking up into his face, she longed to ask him the questions he'd refused to answer in the meeting. Did he know more about the supposed menace in the ground than he was letting on? But Horus merely touched her on the shoulder and moved on, as though he'd the questions in her mind and was attempting to soften his dismissal of them. Mariyen was left to her own devices in the wake of the outflow of elders. She put a paw on the wall next to her, traced the subtle whorls in the wood, and looked up and down the hall to either side of her. She was as suddenly and completely alone as she felt she was.

Previously, she'd given herself free reign of the passageways, trailing down corridors she'd never seen before and trying doors. A fair few of them were locked, to her disappointment, but it was more common that she found a door that would swing inward, and check to see that she wasn't observed, before slipping inside. Most of the rooms she'd found up until now were unlocked for a reason: they were uninteresting and therefore held nothing worth locking up. All the same, Mariyen found her feet carrying her down the hallway, to a fork, which she took left and upwards, like she'd done the last time she was alone. She retraced her steps past the single, strange window which appeared to look out only onto more wood, the branch of a tree, perhaps which had grown up next to

Edgewood and suffocated the view. Next there was the table with the flickering lantern, set on a lacy cloth, nearly transparent with age. This corridor was different from the others, it was why she kept returning. It smelled somehow of nostalgia for something Mariyen had never known, even though she knew that didn't make sense. Peering down its short length, Mariyen always felt the urge to rip open every single door and have each room disclose its secrets to her; she knew they must have them. Why else would every single door in this hallway be locked?

She padded down the hallway and stopped after passing the table, about halfway down. Something felt different here. She couldn't explain to herself: in a way, the corridor felt just the same as ever, just as dreamy, enticing like a veil waiting to be torn. But there was something *off* about it this time, as though maybe, just maybe a moth had gotten there first and burrowed its way in, leaving the smallest rent. So it was that Mariyen stood, turning from side to side again, looking for whatever was making her feel uneasy. There was nothing there, of course, and she was about to give up, to walk the rest of the length of the hall, when she noticed it.

A soft gust of wind was whistling through the blocked-off window. She hadn't noticed it at first, but every time the vague whistling sounded, there was an answering creak. Mariyen turned to look a bit behind her at the door across from this window. Sure enough, it was open, but so slightly she could see how she might have missed it.

A surge of adrenaline went rippling through her limbs. It looked like the sort of open door that only occurs through happenstance: someone leaving, probably, forgot to close and lock up, and simple as that, it was hers to explore.

Mariyen crossed to the door in one smooth movement, feeling the breeze for an instant at her back, and stopped briefly in front of the door. What if it wasn't something great after all? What if these were merely the elder's bedrooms?

No one locks their bedroom door all day, her inside voice told her, but she was determined not to disappoint herself. Looking around to either side of her—halls empty as usual (it occurred to her then how she'd never seen another squirrel in this hall all the times she'd been up here, wasn't that strange)—she pushed the door open more and stepped inside.

Her fears that the room would be someone's bedroom were groundless, though she couldn't help feeling let down—this seemed to be some mass storage room. Upon entering, she found herself situated between two shelves of scrolls, what seemed like tens of thousands of rolled yellow parchment, piled laboriously in neat pyramid formation on each shelf. Mariyen reached for the shelf nearest her, and touched the top of one of these scrolls gently. It dissolved into dust. She stared, horrified, at what she'd done. What if the scroll had been important? Worse yet, what if Horus or one of the other elders found it missing and knew someone had been in here?

Well then, she might as well touch what she pleased since he'd already know. Satisfied with this reasoning, Mariyen grabbed another scroll, this time abandoning all caution, and was surprised when the paper did not give beneath the clutch of her paw, but remained. It must have been simply age, then, that defeated the other scroll—what a relief! She unrolled the scroll she was clutching and a bunch of strange symbols and lines stared back at her. She couldn't make heads or tails of it. Turning to put the parchment back, she noticed that the other scroll, the first one she'd picked up, was sitting innocently in its place again.

What?

She stared at it for a moment longer, but nothing happened; it did not disappear again, but merely sat there, appearing for all the world as though it had never been gone.

She stuffed the scroll she was carrying into its niche below the reappearing scroll, and left the aisle she was in, moving into an adjacent row of more scrolls. How was it possible for paper to regenerate? It must be a way to keep her from reading whatever was in the scrolls, but in that case, why did the second one not crumble as well? Mariyen tested a theory, running her paw over the ridges of the pile of scrolls closest her. Four out of seven of the scrolls she touched disappeared, or appeared to crumble in front of her. She looked through the remaining three, but two of them only held the meaningless symbols that she could not read.

The third, however, was even more puzzling. It looked as though a child had made it, and Mariyen wondered whether it was placed here accidentally. There was a crudely drawn picture of a flying squirrel at the top of the page, with its paws spread, and below this squirrel were several others, all colored in differently and sketchily, their only commonality being their lack of wings. There was an arrow pointing from the group of non-flying squirrels to the flyer, and one word: AWAY.

Mariyen stared at this drawing for a full minute before rolling it up again and placing it back on the shelf. She found a few other parchments she could read, none of them terribly exciting, and she was beginning to wonder whether this room ever ended when she reached a different world altogether. The things piled up on the shelves when she turned what felt like her fiftieth corner were not scrolls—they were crystal balls. Each bead of crystallic dew trembled along to invisible vibrations in the air, each set in a holder of varying size and gaudiness. Mariyen walked down one isle of these, holding her breath, feeling as though all of these trembling orbs had secret eyes and were watching her watching them. It should have been frightening, she thought, but she found it oddly pleasurable instead.

She soon noticed that each holder had a name etched into it somewhere. Leaning close to read one of them—*Phelmer,* it said—she realized they were *names.*

Mariyen walked along the shelf, reading all the names, until she came to one she recognized and drew in breath sharply. *Ruby,* the name glinted up at her from the silver base of one of the orbs. If her friend was here…Mariyen walked up and down this aisle and the next, all orbs as well, searching, searching, and at once not allowing herself to admit what she was looking for. A clinking sounded from behind the shelf she was searching, and at first she didn't react in her excitement, didn't notice anything off until she bent down to read the base of another bead of dew and her eyes locked with another pair.

She didn't know how she managed to keep from screaming when the sound was crawling desperately up her throat. Against her better judgment, she did not move. She stared, this time with curiosity, as the eyes retreated slowly, watery and glaring, and as they unlocked themselves from hers, she realized who their owner was.

It was the crippled elder she'd seen in the meeting. She watched him back away from the shelf and adjust his spectacles. He stood for a moment as though he trying to make a decision, and she watched him, wondering why she did not run, wondering why he did not turn and tell her off immediately. Surely he *must* have seen her, unless, she supposed, he was terribly farsighted. Whether he had or he hadn't, he did not spare another glance her way; for a moment longer he looked lost in thought, then he left the room through what must have been another door, leaning heavily on his cane.

Mariyen stood, letting fear overcome her for a second. The elder's silence unnerved her more than any stern talking-to would have. What if he brought Horus back here right now? She decided she could not risk lingering longer, even though she still hadn't found what she wanted...

She went quickly down the row of shelves she was sheltered in, skimming the names desperately as she went, though she could not catch them all, and the ones on the very top shelves she could not even see. She came around the corner to where the crippled elder had been standing and sure enough, there was a door set in the wall before her. This shelf looked like the last in the room, and as she went to place herself in the elder's footsteps without realizing what she was doing, she noticed that the segment of shelf she was now standing in front of was different from the others. It was made of a darker wood, and at the top of the shelf, only discernable because of how large and deep they were carved, were letters that formed the word INACTIVE. Innocuous as it was, the word made her cold. She stared down the shelf, this time fearing to find what she'd been looking for here, but instead, about eye level, she noticed a gap, a length of shelf in which only two crystal balls sat, side by side, their holders layered with a film of dust. She stared at the names, covered too in that grey veil: *Absoulim*, and *Llewellyn*.

Her stomach gave a lurch at seeing her mother's name, and here of all places. She had the sensation that she was slipping away somewhere, that the more she saw of her mother imprinted all over this place, the less she knew about her.

Mariyen heard a noise outside, from the sliver of hall beyond the cracked door, and she turned and pushed on the door, coming out of her reverie in a rush. She closed the door tight behind her, wondering if it would lock again automatically or if she would be able to come back. There was no one out here.

It was then that she noticed that the door she'd come out of was the same she'd come in by. Impossible but true, and she felt an extreme disorientation as when she'd stared at the globes of dew belonging to her mother and to the outcast she'd never known. She thought back to the meeting. What if it was possible for a squirrel to have so much power that he could make the very ground unsafe to walk on? The thought made her feel unreal. How did you defend against a threat like that?

Having nothing further to do, and feeling drained as though she'd been awake for hours on end—was the quality of light different out here than inside that long, many-shelved room?—Mariyen made her way back to her room with no event, aiming to take an afternoon nap.

The dreams revisited her again, after what seemed so long.

This time, it was the dream of her mother again. She was standing veiled again on the other side of a long room filled with fallen shelves, the floor wet with dew. Mariyen felt the damp under her feet as she began to run— it was important to catch her mother, to always keep her in sight, but it was getting harder and harder to do so. She knew she would not like what she found, the vague intuition of other dreams past told her that, but still she ran and the faster she did so, the faster her mother disappeared.

"Wait!" someone called to her from behind, and she turned around, exhausted from running. She half expected to find her regular visitor the fox squirrel, hoped to find him, even.

Instead, a white squirrel with pinkish tinted eyes was coming towards her. She watched the sleek nothing-color of his coat under the lights strung from the ceiling. Her senses were telling her to run, but she watched instead as the white squirrel closed the distance between them and held out a paw.

"I'll take that," he said. His face and his eyes were calm, but it was all a show, the face of necessity. Mariyen, as only happens in dreams, suddenly knew exactly what he was talking about and turned to the spot next to her. Once empty, it now held a single unshattered crystal ball, the one with her mother's name on the holder. She held it up to the white squirrel, who smiled at her. "Thank you," he said, and, gripping its metal holder, he raised the quivering ball to his lips and drank.

Mariyen felt an unease spread through her as the white squirrel started to waver before her eyes.

"I must get going," he said, and the glaze of poison was bright in his eyes. He was infected with something, and Mariyen would do anything to rip the crystal ball back out of his grasp, fix the damage she had done.

"There's nothing you can do sometimes," the white squirrel informed her, wobbling away with that fervent, insane light in his eyes. "Learn it before it learns you."

Mariyen watched him disappear helplessly until her attention was diverted by the vibrations in the ground. Small at first, they were growing larger and larger, and she heard something crying, deep underneath the surface. The thing in her mother's arms, the bundle from previous dreams was coming to get her, she was sure of it. A fissure opened up right next to her paw, and she jerked it away, causing bits of rock and soil to fall endlessly toward the thing coming at her with burning eyes, open mouth forever wailing. She could not run, it was everywhere, the whole earth was breaking apart, the cracks were widening, and sooner or later she would fall into one of them, into the gaping maw of the thing that cried up at her, both deceivingly like and not like a child at all. The ground started to pull apart right beneath her, and she knew she was done.

Mariyen awoke thrashing and turning over again and again, flinching in her sleep. Through glazed eyes, she stared around at the cavernous room, its chest of drawers, the small table by the window, which was open, curtains gently blowing in the autumn air, just a touch too chill. There was nothing here to be frightened of, this was her first bleary and relieved conclusion. She sat up clutching the sheets into a ball in her paws and came to the second conclusion: the dreams were back, and they had not made their return a light one.

What would she do now? Could she turn over, go back to sleep again? She was tired, but suddenly very afraid. She did not want to give her nightmares life again.

Without further thought, she got up from her bed, her mind still catching up with her, wondering where she was going even as she went there She let her feet take her without thought until a small doorway appeared before her. Mariyen was surprised; she had no recollection of walking here. The small door was only two doors away from Horus's chambers, but she made no attempt to be discreet. Knocking with a vengeance, Mariyen stood back and waited. The face that showed amid the dim slivered sneak-peek of the other room was more than surprised...and all too familiar.

Mariyen lurched forward, feeling the exhaustion claim her body again. Somehow she ended up falling through the door and onto the silky covers of a bed. Fighting her tiredness, she managed to speak up through the dark that was trying to claim her with its mellow persistence.

"Tell me," she pleaded even as her voice faded, "what is going on."

CHAPTER XV

Kinder was angry. He figured, since he was angry so little, really, he ought to show it.

At first, he'd tried by running around the tunnel, throwing himself against the dirt walls and screaming angry words he'd heard Lute use like 'rotter' and 'thrice-damn-you'. When he realized his tormentor couldn't hear him and his paws were starting to hurt, he stopped, and merely slumped to the ground.

It had all happened so fast, the strange sequence of events that had led to his current, terrible predicament.

He'd been climbing behind Lute up that ledge, he'd lost footing and thought in that moment, *I'm going to die, and there's no charm against that.* But he'd fallen, and fallen, and by some miracle of chance he'd hit what felt like a gigantic pile of leaves. The musty scent of the earth swallowed his senses and he heard, somewhere up above, someone call his name at the same time as someone else grabbed his arm.

"Arrrrrhhhhhhh!" Kinder yelped, but a paw clamped itself over his mouth, stopped him mid-cry. Whoever was holding him was strong, and knew what they were doing. Body still disoriented and aching slightly from the impact—he'd had the wind taken out of him when his pack landed on top of him—he found himself dragged away startlingly quick over the ground. The paw over his mouth was also shielding his eyes, but only partially, so he could still see sticks leap up before him and the horizon of the ground below him flashed in and out of his sight, black then gray then white and back again. *It's the thing in the ground,* his first panicked thought yammered, *the worms, those giant worms, they're going to eat me alive, suck out my insides—*

Kinder wondered what the pain quotient for such a thing was, and felt like throwing up. But whoever his captor was, he seemed unconcerned with eating Kinder, at least not in a timely manner. He *did* drag Kinder underground, and as soon as Kinder realized this, that he was no longer being dragged horizontally, but vertically down, deep underground, he began to try to scream again. He only succeeded in swallowing a chunk of dirt, because after the ground swallowed him up and the sky was only a ring of light turning to dusk, his captor released his mouth.

After he'd been dragged a good length over the ground, and around an unexpected turn, Kinder was dropped unceremoniously.

"Wait here," whoever had abducted him said, and Kinder thought this was strange. Slugs didn't talk, did they?

Grappling around blindly at first, Kinder found his way to his feet. He had to clutch a wall when helping himself up, it was so dark, and his eyes refused to adjust; he couldn't see the way he'd been dragged in here, or the way his captor had left.

A horrid thought occurred to him. He and Lute had seen the dirt filling in the hole the monster had made when it came up to take Cainus. If he was in the clutches of the monster now, wouldn't it make sense for him not to be able to find the tunnel? It had merely filled in behind him, he knew it. He was being stored down here like a light snack for later.

Lying on the floor, exhausted, Kinder stared up at the shifting particles of darkness above him, anger ebbing out of him through sheer expense of energy, and waited for his fate.

The figure that appeared before him minutes later did not resemble a giant slug, or a monster of any sort. It looked rather like another squirrel, and when a sudden light came into being, lighting up the small underground chamber, he found he was correct. But it wasn't just any other squirrel.

It *was* the white squirrel.

This made so little sense to Kinder that for a while he only stared at the other squirrel. The anger started coursing back up through his body, and he started to speak, but the white squirrel only had to raise a paw to his lips, and he was silenced.

"Come on," the white squirrel told him, "I was checking the tunnel up ahead for you. We don't want to be seen."

Kinder followed the white squirrel in silence until they came to a set of stairs. The white squirrel stepped neatly up them and opened a door at the top. A sliver of very bright light came slicing across Kinder's vision, and he stepped backwards, rubbing at his eyes.

"Come on, come on," the white squirrel hissed, voice now issuing from whatever place he'd entered into.

Kinder followed him into a very familiar place. He'd come up through a trap door in the white squirrel's living room, the very spot they had all been conversing only hours ago.

Kinder stood in the room, looked at all the ticking clocks on shelves, the invitingly overstuffed chairs, the tea pot on the table, lying next to the white squirrel's discarded pipe, and said, "I have to ask. What in seven hells is going on here?"

The white squirrel laughed as though he'd just told a particularly amusing joke, then sobered alarmingly quick. "I need you to help me, Kinder," he said.

"What about Lute? He's still back there. We have a goal of our own, or haven't you noticed?"

"You surprise me with your anger, Kinder," the white squirrel told him. "You looked the unassertive type.

It will prove very useful to you, I think, to know how to get upset every now and then."

"Look, I don't know what's going on here," Kinder said, the anger gone now that the white squirrel had pointed it out. "But I'd appreciate you telling me. It's not remotely decent to drag someone off like that. I could have bumped my head on a rock or lost my charms, or thought you were the monster and—"

"What do you do when you meet someone, Kinder?"

"*What?*"

"What do you do?"

He stared at the white squirrel, wondering if he had truly gone mad.

"Just answer the question."

"Well…you wink at them. For luck."

"Well, Kinder," the white squirrel came forward and winked at him. "Perhaps that was what went wrong with our first meeting. My name is Zirreo."

Kinder winked back without thinking about it, and immediately wanted to slap himself for doing it. "I'm Kinder, pronounced like the word 'kind.' But you didn't need to know that."

"No," Zirreo was still smiling. "But at least we know that we know one another."

Kinder couldn't take that last bit in.

"Sure," he said. Then, "I need to go."

"That's right, Kinder," Zirreo said, perching on the edge of his table and picking up his pipe, running it through both paws. "You do need to go. You need to go with me."

Kinder sighed. He strongly doubted that he could trust this squirrel, but there seemed nothing he could do for the time being. What could be more important than putting an end to the monsters in the ground?

"Where am I going with you?" Maybe he could run for it when they got outside again.

Zirreo stared around at the walls of the room as if the answer were hiding right behind Kinder. He looked excitable and somber at once. The ticking of the clocks was like a maniac pulse, supplement to the gleam in Zirreo's eyes.

"I'm going back to a place I should have gone back to a long time ago. I've realized that—that I need to. I've been having these dreams and it all fits. But I've been...Kinder, I've been afraid. The place I'm going—I made a lot of mistakes there and I have reason to suspect there have been consequences since I've left. I've known for a...long time. You woke me up, Kinder. You and your friend, and I thank you for it. I don't know if I would have ever woke up in time if you hadn't come..."

His shame was something Kinder didn't know what to do with. He sat in silence, feeling Zirreo's eyes on him.

"What about this place you need to be?" he asked, after some time. "I mean, I know it's important to you, and I'm not trying to be rude, really, but how is it more important than what Lute and I need to do?"

"Because," Zirreo looked straight at him with those unnerving, intense eyes. "I think whatever I do there is going to make everything I've started unraveling...time, space, the things that haven't been noticed yet but soon will be...I think it will make that stop. The mess I've made. I've been afraid to face it."

The ticking of the clocks filled in the silence that Kinder didn't know how to break. One of them, the closest to him, had an overlong pendulum made to look like a squirrel's tail. The face of the clock was the body. He stared at the ridiculous thing and thought surely a squirrel with this sort of gag clock in his living room couldn't be all that bad, could he?

Yeah, if he hadn't abducted you, a voice that sounded unsettlingly like Lute's said. He shoved it from the back of his mind. It had a point, though.

"If you want me to travel with you wherever you're going," Kinder said, "that must mean you need me for something. But I can't see how I would be of any use helping you...fix time and all that. There's something you're not telling me. Why do you have underground tunnels? That can't be safe. The thing could have got you a million times using that tunnel and it hasn't yet! Are *you* the monster? Have you been lying to us? And if not, *who are you?*"

All of Kinder's questions bubbled out of him at once in a rush. Zirreo seemed a little taken aback for once, and Kinder thought he would not answer, he was sure the white squirrel would only say something mysterious and elusive. He was surprised when Zirreo actually seemed to consider his questions.

"The reason I have that tunnel," Zirreo said at length, "is because I knew one of the so-called underground squirrels. I ran into him underground, because I thought no part of this land could be out of bounds for me. That's a fancy way of saying I went underground when I shouldn't have. Saw a tunnel when I first came to this neck of the woods and investigated. He wanted...to kill me at first, I believe, but I was able to persuade him to make me a tunnel of my own—useful thing it's proved—in turn for my keeping silent about his existence. I've broken it now, you see, by telling you two, but one does what one must. Since it's my tunnel, their beasts don't travel it, so yes, I am safe from the things in the ground. You want to know what I need you for—this is also a fair question. I—

where I am going, you must understand, they may not take kindly to my appearance once again. The first time I left things rather…in an uproar." He grinned unexpectedly, looking shockingly roguish. "I need someone to act as my companion, so that they cannot refuse us hospitality. It's a rule of theirs," he added as an afterthought, at Kinder's confused expression.

"But where—"

"And your last question, I believe," Zirreo continued, "was 'who am I?' Well, Kinder, I think you know the answer to that already."

Kinder started. "All I've ever heard about you is that story where you're the guardian of Astrippa," he protested.

A thin smile cut across Zirreo's face. The intense eyes never left Kinder's own.

"All stories have a grain of truth to them."

Kinder felt frozen by this admission. Almost afraid of the words he was speaking, he said, "Why me? Couldn't you have, I don't know, picked someone else?"

"You are the first squirrels who came upon this place since I arrived here," Zirreo said simply. "It might interest you to know that this tree is protected by a magical ward. It's supposed to keep others from being able to see it. I don't know what made you two different, whether it was a blip in the laws of nature, for which I have myself to blame, or whether the ward is slowly wearing off of its own volition. Whichever it was, you two are the only life I've had contact with for some time. Forgive me if I take it as a sign," he finished, looking anything but apologetic. Kinder hadn't known it was possible for a squirrel to show as little remorse as Zirreo was showing. He had pulled he and Lute apart, upsetting their entire mission to bring attention to his own in place of it. He didn't know if this squirrel was who he claimed to be, but even if he was not, Kinder would have been uncomfortable traveling with him.

"What about Lute?" he blurted. The far end of the room had a window ensconced in the wall, one he hadn't noticed before. Outside it was nearly full dark and raining, judging by the stippling on the windowpane. The barely audible *pat pat pat* of the water on leaves outside closed in around them.

"Lute has surprised me already," Zirreo said with a strange half-smile. "I think he will be fine."

***

It was pitch dark; this was the first thing Lute noticed. The second was that moving forward was frightening and cramped and suffocating and *oh gods* he could not *turn around.* Lute felt trapped between two unyielding walls with nowhere to go but forward, the space directly in front of him a mystery. If someone came along in the other direction, he knew with great confidence that they could kill him and move on.

But could they get me out of the passage, that's the question, his hysterical mind thought in wild humor.

If they have one of their beasts suck out yer organs, yes, his rational forebrain intruded. This indeed, was his greatest fear, and the babbling part of his mind was struck silent at the grim thought.

Lute checked to see if he could reach his knife. He could, but just barely, and if he were to take it out, sheathing it again could result in accidentally gutting himself. He scooted forward, crawling, crawling...

What if this is not anyone's hole after all? What if this is a dead end?

The thought of this, the greatest fear of all, a slow and claustrophobic and more than mildly ridiculous end at the limit of a dead-end tunnel, caused Lute to let loose his panic. He began to claw his way rapidly forward, forward, forward, each inch convinced that he would hit a wall. Then suddenly, the best gift of all came to him: there was light.

It was dim and flickering in quality, but he knew he was not imagining it. Lute edged himself around a particularly tight bend and eased his body out, like a strangled sigh, into yet more tunnel. Here though, he noted, there was more space to breath.

Forward forward forward. The light hovered at the end of this bit of hall. He clawed his way closer, feeling once or twice something slimy and squirming underpaw and passing it off frantically to his imagination. Lute realized that the opening from which the light emitted was in the floor. *Of course. Down further and further, they must like it like that. What is there, a* world *down here?*

He realized as soon as he thought it that that was exactly what there might be. It was a chilling thought, in the choking dark, that while their world was going along its usual patterns above, another was humming along beneath their feet, undetected. It was strange to think that above him right now, someone might be walking to their favorite bar or coming home from somewhere to take shelter from the rain, to go back to the safety of their tree and listen to it pound down, rustle through the leaves, and know they were safe. You couldn't even hear the rain down here; it was as though the whole world above had been erased. Who in their right mind would want such a world, down with the earthworms and the dirt, the smell of decomposition and only artificial light—nothing but that, ever. He could not imagine, and more importantly, he did not really want to, though he was all too aware that he was heading towards this very knowledge now.

At the edge of where the light came up, Lute stopped. Sure enough, it was a hole in the ground, leading down into an underground cavern of sorts. Lute strained his ears but could not hear a thing. Well, this was one area where perhaps he'd gotten lucky. He couldn't see a thing from here, but if he dropped down into this chamber and found that he could move around better down there, in whatever other maze of passages awaited him, he could bring the element of surprise to his side at least. Perhaps he could form a plan, some sort of strategy. Perhaps he could live.

So it was that Lute inched his body over the rim of the opening, towards the light. *Cripes, there's no way to do this gracefully*, he thought as he slipped, grappled for a hold on something that wasn't there, and began to freefall through the opening.

The good news was, he was able to hit the ground without harming himself. The dim lights burst in around his eyes like fire, so accustomed was he to the total insanity-inducing dark of above, and it took him a while to adjust, which was when he noticed the bad news.

He was, beyond the shadow of a doubt, not alone. The place he'd fallen into appeared to be a council room, and council appeared to be in session.

CHAPTER XVI

Llewellyn Edgewood stared down at her daughter, asleep fitfully on her bed and reflected that this was one of the few times her mattress had been laid on the correct way, so bizarre were her own habits of sleep.

She had known Mariyen would come to her eventually, for where else did she have to go? Horus alienated everyone, even when it was the last thing he wanted, and the other elders were completely useless. And Llewellyn knew things. Not the right things, maybe, not the helpful things, but everyone knew more than Mariyen. She was really the innocent here. *Are you willing to sacrifice?* Horus had asked her, and now it seemed like a double-edged sword, the sound of those words, her answer. She went quietly to the cabinet above her cluttered desk and brought out the vial. It seemed so harmless in her paws, the pearly liquid inside slipping easily one way or the other depending on how she tilted her hold.

It was the dreams that this concoction had been meant to stop, and it was the dreams that had driven Mariyen in here, she knew it. Now, looking down at her estranged daughter's sleep-deprived eyes, fluttering even now as they were shut, no doubt locked in the throes of another dream, she felt like a cheap thief. Would it have been so bad, she thought, to let Mariyen keep taking the solution? Would it have harmed anything, really?

She thought of Horus's lies, telling her daughter it did one thing when it was really supposed to do another. Her ear pressed up against the wood of the secret exit, she'd thought, half in fear and half in anticipation, *he'll ask me to talk to her now*, but he never had. He'd told Mariyen the lie, and he'd sent her away, and Llewellyn knew well the reason why. Mariyen was very like her after all: she'd started to get in the way, started to know too much, to see too much. It wasn't the unexpected that Horus was afraid of.

He was afraid of a repetition.

And how that rubbed her the wrong way. Sometimes she swore that if it weren't for the life pulsing inside of her, he would have seen things differently. She would have *made* him. But things weren't different, and this was her daughter. She was a horrible mother, she knew that, but she no longer really wanted to be otherwise. She recognized that her disgust, even now, had more to do with Horus and the way he lied than the fact that the squirrel he was doing it to was her daughter. How surprised he must have been when the potion he gave Mariyen to stop her dreams actually began to make them clearer, just as he told her it would. And then when he'd had to take it away, well, it served him right. Watching him try to create a pretext for that had been rather humorous.

What was less humorous was finding out she would be the one to steal it from Mariyen's bedside table as she slept.

She'd looked peaceful then, a slight smile on her closed lips, savoring whatever dream she was having at the moment. Llewellyn thought she saw a familiar emotion on Mariyen's sleeping face, but when she bent closer, trying to understand, become a part of the young squirrel's life for just a minute, a sigh startled her back to the situation at hand.

One of the other squirrels was getting up for some water. Llewellyn had nowhere to hide herself, so she had froze until the other squirrel had walked out of the room, and then followed, moving soundlessly between the cloud-white beds and their dreaming occupants.

There was only pain now in Mariyen's face as she slept, in the tightening, the quivering of her mouth, and her clenched paws, folded under her. *If I gave this to her again, she might feel better.* But Llewellyn's paw went to her stomach, and she gave up every thought of it. *When did I become this fearful?* But she already knew the answer. When the consequences had begun to outweigh the benefits of risk, that was when. When she had grown colder, less alive, through necessity.

It disgusted her.

Mariyen stirred, and this time her eyelashes parted and she peered at the ceiling above her. In the moments that it took her to sit up and look around, panicked, the bottle of dreamless sleep found its way back into the cupboard and Llewellyn pulled up the only chair and sat at her side.

"What...oh," Mariyen said, rubbing sleep from her eyes. "I—I forgot where I was."

"Are you all right?" Llewellyn asked, merely because she could not think of anything else to say. She wondered if she had a dysfunction, that she could be so uncaring for someone who'd once been part of her. Maybe it was Genhaw. He was always enough to put her off, especially when he brought her things or cornered her in the hallway and said, *it's time we do our duty,* or whatever stupid thing he'd said. It all came down to the same. Mating because it was easy, hating herself because she'd done what was expected for once.

Mariyen seemed to really think about her question. She looked around the room as she considered. She seemed uncomfortable, and once Llewellyn swore her eye caught on her stomach, though it couldn't possibly be visible, it hadn't been to anyone else. But then she looked away without comment and Llewellyn began to breathe normally again.

"Your room is very small," Mariyen said at last.

"It is."

"Do you…look, you won't tell Horus I came here, will you?"

"No." She must have said it with more forcefulness than she meant to, because Mariyen flinched. She still looked drawn and shaken.

"Okay. I just—I've been having dreams again, and they're getting worse, and well…sometimes you're in them."

It was Llewellyn's turn to flinch. "What?"

"There's also this fat fox squirrel who keeps trying to talk to me, but I don't know what he's saying, and then there's a white squirrel—

"A what?"

Mariyen stared at her mother, unbelieving of the words that were spilling from her mouth, unbelieving, still, that this distant being could be her mother. She seemed so untouchable, so like a part of something else. For whatever reason, the mention of the white squirrel seemed to either panic her or excite her, she couldn't tell which.

"The white squirrel is new," she said. "He-he doesn't make me feel comfortable. He always seems to be on his way somewhere, and, in the dream I had before he drank poison. Just-drank it. Bottoms-up, and walked away, still talking to me like he was teaching me a lesson except he was dying as he walked, or he should have been dying. Maybe that's what was freaking me out. He was wobbling but he wouldn't—fall."

"How did he look?" Llewellyn slid closer to Mariyen on her chair, face intense.

"Well…he was younger, but not young. Like he could still be my father. Like you."

She thought she noticed her mother jump out of the corner of her eye at the word 'father', but thought she might have imagined it. "He talked about a *her*, too." A thought occurred to her, and she looked back up at her mother. "Is that you? Because you were in it, too. Did you know him?"

Llewellyn's face looked drained of all color, and Mariyen didn't think she would answer, but a slight shiver went through her and she nodded.

"You...you did?"

"Yes," her mother said. "He came to us one autumn, much like this one."

And with that, she set into something very like what they described in the nursery rhymes Mariyen used to hear—a story a hundred years old, a secret never been told.

***

If Kinder was having a hard time traveling, it was only because of his companion. All that very night they had sloshed their way through the rain, stopping every now and then for Zirreo to get his bearings. He knew it was unfair for Kinder, but so was the fact that the young squirrel had to come with him in the first place. When he turned once to look over his shoulder and told Kinder to make sure that the bad feeling in the ground didn't get too bad while they were traveling, Kinder had given him an inquisitive look.

"You can't...?" he asked, sopping with rainwater but somehow managing not to look entirely hateful. He was very angry but he was keeping it in. There was something both admirable and sad, Zirreo mused, about someone who kept their own disappointments and complaints so close under cover

"No, I can't feel the badness there," he told Kinder. "That is only you. So you see, you are needed for this just as much as you think you are needed elsewhere."

He could tell from Kinder's silence that he didn't know what to say to this. He'd already prompted Kinder on what to do when they ran into other squirrels. The rule about this was that they could not run into other squirrels.

"What you must do," he'd said, "Is create a distraction so that I can hide." He could not risk anyone seeing him, asking questions, or following their trail. Zirreo was aware that a white squirrel in the middle of the forest anywhere was a rare sight, and thus, would draw the curious and the unsavory to them as surely as treasure drew a chickaree. Kinder didn't question this order, nor did he seem very enthused by it. Zirreo didn't know what he had expected. You couldn't kidnap someone and then expect them to be excited about anything you proposed. Still, he was disappointed in the fact that Kinder didn't really talk to him all night. It was his lack of social contact over the past several seasons that made him crave interaction, no doubt, and he found the need slightly humiliating. When the travelling pair finally set up camp in an abandoned hole at the bottom of a twisty hickory, Kinder rolled over and fell asleep without a word, and Zirreo took out his pipe and a fresh bag of pipe reed, expecting that he wouldn't follow along for a while. He was wrong; almost as soon as he lit up, he became uncontrollably sleepy and only had time to extinguish his pipe—what a waste—before sleep claimed him.

In the dream he knew he'd have, he was staring up at the behemoth of a tree, all twisted and bleached-white in color, terrible and beautiful at once. The rain continued to pour down around him, even though the sound was muted and it appeared to be daylight. He'd sworn he'd never go back, and here he was. But he was not alone; she was there too.

"Zirreo," Llewellyn said, and he turned to find her behind him, also staring up at the tree. He had a mind to ask her what she was doing outside in this weather, before remembering it was only a dream. They were so real, these, that waking was sometimes downright painful and always left something to be desired.

"Mariyen knows," Llewellyn told him, and before Zirreo could open his mouth to ask her how, "She dreams about you too."

Zirreo looked at Llewellyn, her fur illuminated by this dream-sunlight. He could have said many things then, some of which he should have said long ago. But the time was past.

"How can another share the same dreams as you?" he asked. He meant it. As much knowledge as he had about other sorts of magic, dreams were an uncharted territory to him.

"They're not the same," Llewellyn explained. "She's told me how one of them usually goes. You drink poison. Please tell me that's not in your future." Her mouth quirked upwards in a half-smile, but he could see there was strain underlying it.

"How much does she know?" he asked. "She's your daughter, right?" He grinned a little. "Sure you can trust her to keep a secret?"

Llewellyn did not smile. "I've kept plenty of secrets in my time," she said. "And we don't have any choice but to trust her. You don't, anyway. I trust her, because she doesn't owe Horus anything anymore, and she knows it."

"What about her friends?"

"She's not really one of them anymore, is she?"

He didn't know what to say to this.

"Llewellyn, I..."

Something switched in her; he could see it move across her face. She looked slightly away from him, above his head a little. "You weren't going to come for a while, were you?"

"I think I was always going to come. I was just afraid for a while."

"A while might have been too long."

"Well, I'm coming." He wanted her to look at him again. "Do you have them anymore, aside from our dreams?"

She didn't answer immediately, and he had begun to fade out of the dream-reality as she finally turned to speak. He woke suddenly, rain still pouring down around him. The wind was gusting something awful now, so that occasionally a draft of wind would blow some rain into the hollow, coating him with droplets and making Kinder shiver. Speaking of Kinder, did he snore! Zirreo was a bit concerned someone would find them due to the racket, but he hesitated to wake him, and finally decided just to lay back with his pipe and watch the rain fall.

He might not know how to have unselfish relations with anyone, but he knew when to let things alone. If there was one lesson he'd learned in his seasons of mortal life, it was this one, and Zirreo had learned it the hard way.

CHAPTER XVII

At this moment, Lute would rather have been anywhere else. He kept his eyes trained down, getting up swiftly after his fall and dusting himself off.

Maybe if I don't look at them, they'll ignore me. I could say, "oh, I've made a mistake, terribly sorry," and get the blazing rot out of here.

"And who would you be?" a voice challenged Lute as he stood quaking on the underground floor.

No such luck. Lute looked up at last and saw that everything was just as bad as he had imagined. There were tens upon tens, likely bordering on a hundred, of the underground squirrels—in most ways, at least, they *did* resemble squirrels—and they were all looking directly at him. The room was deadly silent, and he knew they'd been talking only moments before, it was *that* type of silence, and he thought, *this tunnel thing has got to be the stupidest thing I've ever done.*

"I asked who you were," the same voice as before said sharply. "Now either you're deaf or you're dumb enough not to fear. Either way, trespassers die."

Lute's attention flickered to the speaker, his paw clenched tight on the hilt of his knife, nearly killing his circulation.

The speaker was very small for a squirrel, but then, so were the others. Lute wouldn't have even hesitated to take on one of them alone, but there was strength in numbers, and against this many of them he didn't stand a chance.

At first he might have mistaken them for chickarees. They were small and a burnt orange in color, but they were different. It was in the shape of the ears, the eyes, the tail, and most of all in their stripes. Lute had never seen such markings on another squirrel before, and they seemed primitive in this setting, more proof that he wouldn't be let out of here alive. The stripes were black and white layered one on top of another, and snaked from beside the squirrels' eyes all the way down their sides. To complete the chilling image, several of the strange squirrels had daubed some odd paint that looked as though it were made from clay over their eyes or elsewhere on their faces. Sometimes the clay was fixed in patterns, like the spiky lines drawn around one female squirrel's eyes. It gave them a fierce, unyielding look at the same time as it made Lute feel terribly foreign and out of place. How could he hope to communicate with these creatures?

The speaker from before interrupted the stream of Lute's thoughts. Lute took him to be the leader. He had yellow markings painted above his eyes in a manner that made it look as though he were narrowing an extra set of eyebrows.

"Speak up already," he said, "or forever hold your peace. Has a beetle crawled into your mouth? Does standing there perhaps make you feel invisible?" He laughed, and his laugh, like his voice, was both caustic and high-pitched and made Lute want to be sick all over the floor.

"What *is* it?" asked another squirrel, leaning forward out of her place on the layered dirt seating. She had red circles painted around her eyes, giving her a constant look of shock.

"It's really ugly," chimed in another squirrel, though Lute privately thought he shouldn't be one to talk: his own face was severely twisted, as though someone had grabbed it once and tried to rip it off.

"What should we do with it?" asked another of the squirrels.

"Quiet!" barked their leader, looking ruffled. "It's clear that either it can't speak, which I doubt," he gave Lute a nasty look, "Or it can, and it's just being dense. Either way, it's armed, which means we must *dis*arm it—"

A squirrel stood up in the back row of seats and cocked an odd looking sling at Lute. "I'll take it from him!" he cried in an excitable tone.

"For crying out loud, Francesci, not *now*." The leader clasped his head in a dramatic pose of long-suffering. "We've got to take him to Chamblis, of course."

"No," breathed a random squirrel Lute couldn't locate.

"Oh yes," the leader said, apparently very proud of his ability to engender such fear in so few words. Indeed, the whole audience of squirrels was looking nervous now, shifting around and nudging one another. One of them finally raised his paw up high.

"*Yes*, Gontesti?"

"He's certifiably crazy," Gontesti said, giving the leader a look that signified he wished he would show some sense. "It's probably not the best idea."

The leader grinned in a way that made Lute think this Chamblis figure was not the only one missing a few nuts and bolts. "Well, the best ideas never win out. You of all chipmunks should know that."

Lute didn't know what a chipmunk was, but he supposed it was the name this type of squirrel had given itself. He was also getting impatient with their talking about things he could not understand, deciding his fate in a language apart from his own, almost. He had considered, for a moment, letting these 'chipmunks' think he was dumb and deaf, and that was probably the smarter choice, but Lute could feel his temper working against him.

"Come on and hurry up, will yew?" he snapped, fear giving way to impatience. "Are yew going to kill me or are yew going to hear me out? I swear I'll go right back where I came from, because I can assure yew, I don't want any of this," he gestured around at the dirt walls. For the first time, he noticed the thin tendril-like roots poking through everywhere, and suppressed a shudder. This whole place, no matter how large, felt claustrophobic to him.

The group of chipmunks had ceased their chatter at his words. They all commenced to stare at him, the various styles of paint around their eyes giving them an intensity he could have done without. Slowly, he felt his cargo of fear climbing back inside of him, and his insides shrunk up to make room. He decided to get right to the point.

"Yer doing something that's causing deaths where I come from," he said. "Apparently none of yew've been above the surface, and I guess that just figures, since I've never been down *here*, but in case yew didn't know, yer monsters—"

"Did he call us monsters?" one of the chipmunks, the one with the spikes drawn around her eyes, asked indignantly.

"I did not. I—"

"Enough of this!" roared the leader, and though his roar sounded more like a high-pitched squeal, everyone turned their full attention to him for once.

"It has been decided. We will take him to Chamblis."

No sooner had he spoken then a tide of chipmunks came sweeping across the floor towards Lute. Swinging out, he caught one of them in the eye and jabbed out at another with his knife. Everyone backed up upon noticing the dully gleaming weapon in his paws, and the leader screeched, "Disarm!"

Lute reflected that perhaps it would have been better for his case if he'd pretended at pacifism, but it was really too late for that. A stinging something hit him in the arm, and he leaned over, feeling ill, like something had just bit him. His arm was completely numb, all the way down to the paw.

"*What...?*" he began angrily, and noticed the slingshot-bearing chipmunk grinning at him from his place back on the stands.

"Rot you all," he muttered, as a multitude of paws muffled his mouth and began to drag him down a passage which, being dark and smelling of dirt, could not promise anything good at its end.

The dank smell increased as they took a downward turn. The chipmunks all pushed and shoved at one another, and their paws on Lute's mouth became more a humiliation than a necessity; he was so squashed by the mass of bodies around him that there was nowhere he could escape to if he wanted to. Besides, if this Chamblis was their leader, he was Lute's only chance, although he was beginning to think that it wasn't a big one, as no one here seemed willing to hear him out, and now he wanted to bite off everyone's head.

Calm down, Lute-boy, he thought to himself, *Yew can't accomplish anything like this.*

It occurred to him that if Kinder were here, he would have been the peacemaker in the situation; he might have even won the chipmunks' audience in the end. The thought made Lute's eyes sting uncomfortably, but he'd be damned if he was going to cry in front of these little savages.

"Inside, inside," he heard the leader of the council room say from somewhere up ahead, just as the pressing throng slowed to a stop. Lute heard a knock, and then an answering voice, muffled and distant. A murmur spread through the group of chipmunks in front of him, but he couldn't hear exactly what anyone was saying; a couple of them looked over at him with beady, gleaming eyes. Lute was feeling his claustrophobia coming back. He tried to block the moldy, dank scent out of his nostrils, but could not, any more than he could ignore the ceiling of the tunnel, so close above his head that he was scraping it even leaning down. There was a jolt in the line of chipmunks and then they started moving again, pulling him along into whatever room lay beyond.

It was more impressive by far than he expected. The cavern he found himself shoved bodily into was twice the size of the one he'd been in before, which was especially startling when you noticed there was only one chipmunk to occupy this place, making the difference seem more vast. He could see this other chipmunk, the one he assumed was Chamblis, seated somewhere back against the far wall, the rocks jutting out all around him curiously shaved off, smoothed in the places they protruded. Aside from the chair the figure appeared to be sitting on, there was nothing else in the room. It was a wide expanse of dirt walls and shaved rocks, and, as Lute's eyes lifted to the ceiling, he noticed the most chilling thing of all.

They must have been directly below some tree or other, because the roots that came through the soil above his head were thick and twisted, like grotesque creatures with a life of their own. While the chipmunks cleared them fine, the roots hung so close to Lute's head that he shuddered as he walked, trying to avoid their touch. The thought that a tree was such an earthly thing, so easily uprooted, when they had always seemed to him so solid and so eternal...it made him shiver.

He cast a glance back at the door and noticed that it was equipped with about a dozen locks, some even placed with chains and deadbolts. He turned away and surveyed the chipmunks closest to him. They kept turning when he looked at them, feeling his eyes quicker than he could look away, and one of them spat on him in irritation. It took all of Lute's powers of restraint not to leap at the little rotter and do him in right then and there. Of course, the thought of leaping was degraded by the heaviness sinking into his gut. What sort of room would this need to be for it to be guarded and locked so thoroughly? Or, what sort of thing within warranted so much caution?

"What is it *now*?" someone said from the far end of the room, and Lute rested his eyes upon the answer to his questions.

The chipmunk before him, if he could call it a chipmunk, was so hideously large he would have made Kinder look downright starved. The thought of Kinder passed through him like the ghost of a pang, he was so caught up in abhorrent awe at the sight in front of him.

The chair upon which the large chipmunk sat was also large, though even this was not quite enough to contain him: rolls of fur covered flesh hung out under the arms of the chair, which looked more like a throne than anything else. Chamblis also had paint on his face, though it was smudged and the patterns of upward running spikes from his eyes made him look deranged. Which, Lute thought, remembering the words of Gontesti, could very well be the case.

A chipmunk with stripes painted on his cheeks moved towards Lute, pushing him forward so that he was standing in front of Chamblis, who squinted angrily at him. Lute lost all doubt when that gaze hit him. Those eyes were frightening, but they were also blank and glassy, like the mind behind them was elsewhere entirely.

"Who is this?" the monstrosity of a chipmunk asked, moving his gaze from Lute to all the chipmunks packed behind him. "Why is he here? I wanted beetles, not this—"

"I thought you wanted us to bring you the king of the underground," the leader chipmunk sneered.

Chamblis glared at him. "You can't fool me. This is no king. He doesn't even have stripes."

"Can you be so sure?" the other asked him. Lute wasn't sure himself where this was going, and normally he would have interjected with something of his own, most likely a *damn all you rotters to hell*, but he didn't like the light he saw in the mad chipmunk's eyes and all his energies were concentrated on not looking up at the ceiling, those horrible tangled roots like snakes, not paying attention to the fact that the earth might eat him up any moment. It was closing around him now. As the walls got smaller and closer, he heard the leader chipmunk say something to Chamblis, who leaned forward and stared at him again.

Finally, the chipmunks behind Lute started to leave. He didn't notice it at first, in his daze, but when he did he started after them immediately. The leader said, "Block the door! Don't let him out!" and suddenly the world came slamming back to him in a surge of panic.

He rushed forward. "Wait!" he yelled, whipping out his knife and heading for the leader. He had no plan at that moment, and he thought, *Kinder might have*, and then the knife was swiped out of his paw and it didn't matter anyway. Lute looked up, stunned, to see the chipmunk leader smiling smugly.

"Enjoy your meeting," he said nastily, "Chamblis doesn't appreciate intruders very much."

With that, the door scraped closed, making a groaning, rocky sound against the hard clay floor. The sound of all the locks snaking back into place echoed in the new hollow forming in Lute's gut.

"How are we?" said a voice behind him, and he turned to face the insanity that claimed this room as its own.

CHAPTER XVIII

Mariyen woke up in an unfamiliar place. Sitting up too suddenly, she felt the room spin around her. And what a curious room it was at that: so small, and cluttered with papers and bottles and odd knick knacks. Mariyen felt a draft against her back and went to close the window she found directly behind her; the weather was getting unnaturally cold lately. That was when she remembered.

Before she'd gone off to sleep to have her strange dreams, or perhaps, indeed, in the middle of them, her mother had been here, and her mother had told her many interesting things.

That white squirrel, the one who was appearing in so many of her most disturbing dreams, her mother had known him. This came as a shock. She thought white squirrels no longer existed—she, and everyone else for that matter, had heard the story about how the last colony of white squirrels had a mishap which burned their great tree in Pinewood to the ground. No one got out alive, or so she'd been told.

"He survived," her mother had told her, in the chair next to her bed that night. "He would have survived anything."

"So you…" Mariyen began, "So he came here?"

"Yes," Llewellyn told her, then, "Maybe not at first. There's a lot I don't know about him. A lot I should have bothered to find out."

She appeared distant for a moment, staring at the wall behind Mariyen, but when Mariyen cleared her throat she came to again with a startling quickness.

"Sorry. Yes, he came here. I don't know what he was looking for. I was actually the first to see him arrive. He was carrying a bag that turned out to be filled with nothing more than a pipe and some bread. I thought he was very young to smoke, especially pipe reed, even though I'd done it before myself. He said he wanted to have his fortune told. I think he knew that wasn't what we did, even then. He could have merely wanted some adventure, I don't know. All I know is that one of the elders, Araccus, disliked him at the outset. Didn't want to have anything to do with him. Told him to turn around and go packing back the way he had come. But he kept pretending at innocence, and asking for his fortune told, and then Camus, the wisest of the elders, reminded Araccus of the hospitality rule. So Araccus was shamed in front of the rest of the elders and had to let Zirreo in."

"That's his name? Zirreo?" Mariyen tried it on her tongue. It was a bit of a silly name, she thought; she'd expected something much more impressive, somehow.

"Yes, that's what he said he was called. He turned out to be a perfect guest. He did everything anyone asked him to do and always obeyed the customs, even though they had to have been different from his own. He was curious, and I don't think he was faking that, at least. He seemed genuinely in love with knowledge: he liked maps and reading and all of that, but his favorite type of learning was about other squirrels. I used to think it was the weirdest thing, but he would stand around the halls listening to others talk and picking up random conversations with those who would talk to him. Some of us were afraid of him at first, because he was a different sort, and we never, well you know, we *never* have anyone who's not a flyer in here."

Mariyen realized it was true. She hadn't considered how closed off they truly were from the rest of the world, even from the rest of Maplewood all around them. There could be different sorts of squirrels just outside of their door, but no one ever ventured even that far.

"I was one of the few who was completely unafraid of him, I guess," Llewellyn said. "My friends gave it up for a hopeless cause when I kept following him around despite their best advice. I was...enamored, I suppose you would say. He was charming. He was new. He was decidedly *not* one of us."

"You were in love with him?"

Llewellyn shrugged, but her eyes moved from Mariyen's for a slight second, and Mariyen knew it was true.

"My first mate, my husband, was supposed to be your father, Genhaw. Everyone knew that; it was simply decided. No one asked me. Zirreo and I spent a lot of time together, all my free time between disciplines in fact. Everyone knew there was something between us but no one, again, mentioned anything. Because that's just how we are. They didn't know what to do with it, so they kept quiet about it. All my friends started treating me differently. They weren't mean, exactly, but they grew very distant; no one would act like they knew me anymore. I used to think maybe I was to blame; I didn't seek them out, after all. I was too tied up in what Zirreo and I were going to do on any given day. Well, they started talking to me again after *it* happened, and that made me wonder whether they weren't fakes all along."

"What happened?" Mariyen was all ears. Sitting up against the wall the bed was shoved against, she waited. She could imagine her mother's life now, imagine her as a young squirrel, only the picture in her mind looked curiously like herself. She could see Zirreo, like in the dreams but younger, in her mind's eye, and she could imagine the hostility and the fear of those around them. She needed to know more. There were so many things she needed to know.

"I told a prophecy," Llewellyn said. "It was my first and it came when I least expected. It was about Zirreo being our downfall, and about the evil product of our union. I didn't know what that meant; then, I was not carrying children. For seasons I was not carrying children."

She paused, shakily, in thought, and Mariyen waited for her to go on.

"Another part of the prophecy was that only he would be able to undo his mistakes. He started showing up in my dreams recently, and I've been talking to him, and he's coming here, because I am with child, and I don't know how it's possible but it's his and I know it. He needs to end it. Mariyen, you cannot tell anyone."

"I won't."

"I mean *anyone.*" Her mother's face was strained with urgency. "It's just that if he's appearing in your dreams too, I want you to know what has to happen. So that when he comes you won't believe what others might say."

So I won't get in the way, Mariyen thought, but she didn't say anything, only nodded.

"Horus knows about it," Llewellyn said. "He knows, but he doesn't want me to tell you or anyone else. It's important that he doesn't know you know. I-I'm afraid he won't help me otherwise."

"Help you?"

"He knows ways of getting into Edgewood unseen, but he holds the knowledge a secret. It's very important that no one sees him, because if he came back…well, after the prophecy, no one was too happy with him. He has a death sentence on his head if he's seen around here again. None of the other elders know. They would get rid of Horus if they knew what he was doing, and whatever he may seem to you sometimes, he is really very kind. He knows things that I've...well, he's willing to give us a chance to do what we need to do."

The words were stuck to the roof of Mariyen's mouth. She knew what she wanted to ask, but she kept staring at her mother's stomach, trying to discern any hint of pregnancy.

"You...what you have to do is..."

"Kill it, yes." The way Llewellyn said these words made something curl, freeze up inside of Mariyen. She opened her mouth, but her mind suddenly filled with the image of the bundle in her dream-mother's arms, the screaming ghastly white thing, its red eyes, the feeling of dread that accompanied it, her mother's empty eye sockets, its endless squalling, the ground breaking up all around—

"Is it responsible for the ground? I mean, all the deaths—"

"I cannot know that," Llewellyn almost snapped. "But it has been suspected. They don't think it's the child though; they don't know about the child. They think it's Zirreo. Or they did, at first. Horus knows it's not true, so he kept them at bay there, until they moved on to other suspicions. All I know is that Zirreo had...talents. There was something about him that was different from all the others, and it wasn't just the color of his fur."

Mariyen thought back to the convention of elders, and to Horus's tentative behavior, to the tension in the room as the topic of the ground was breached.

"Now they—they think it's the exile. Absoulim."

At the name, Llewellyn flinched. "They what?"

Mariyen shrugged. "I was in the meeting they had a while ago, to give everyone drinks and just sort of hang about, and the topic of the ground came up. Some of the elders were saying they thought it was him, using magic from far away or something."

Llewellyn was looking rather faint. "And Horus?" she asked, "Does he think so?"

"No," Mariyen said. "He didn't think there was a type of magic strong enough to do something so widespread. But, I mean—" she bit off the rest of the thought. Her mother was talking to her for once, telling her things she never thought anyone would willingly disclose to her. She was breaking Horus's rules for *her* and she didn't want to make her upset. Her mother was looking at her, waiting for her to speak. She decided to take the chance.

"You knew him, didn't you?"

"For a time," Llewellyn said tightly. "I do not feel that anyone, including him, could have done this. It is, as Horus said, beyond us to cause such widespread occurrences."

"They were talking about calling him back."

"What?"

This time Llewellyn was indefinitely panicked. Her already large dark eyes had widened to an unnatural degree, shining like black pools of anxiety, twin screams. "Mariyen, who said that?" In her agitation, she leaned forward and grabbed the front of Mariyen's robe.

"Just-just one of them, I think. But Horus said no."

Llewellyn let go of her robe and took a while to compose herself. She drew in a long, shaky breath, and spoke on the exhale. "We can't have that happen," she said. "We can't."

Well, that's what Horus said too, but he wasn't quite so frightened by the idea.

Llewellyn looked like she might have heard Mariyen's thought; she looked at her sharply and suddenly, but when she spoke her voice was heavy and tired.

"Just be glad that you haven't made any mistakes you can't erase."

"But I have," Mariyen said, with a sinking feeling at remembering. "The potion. I lost it, and now I can't be a seer anymore."

Llewellyn only gave her a sad half-smile. Getting up, she went over to a cabinet in the far corner by the window. Mariyen couldn't see what she was doing, but when she turned around there it was, smaller than she remembered, a bottle filled with pearlescent liquid. Her mother walked back over to her and placed it in her paws. It was just as cool and heavy as she remembered it.

"Why...?" Mariyen was speechless. Her own mother, take her clarity concoction?

"Horus asked me to take it from you. It—I suppose he just changed his mind about encouraging you to have visions through your dreams. You see, not only was my prophecy terrible, but it nearly killed me. I too was like you in the beginning, having oddly prophetic dreams that no one counted as the real thing. They were encouraged by Camus, the chief elder at the time, but he got a bad rap for it afterward, once things happened so...unconventionally for me."

"Is that why you became a server?" Mariyen asked.

"No. I became a server because it was that or be exiled. The council's decisions came very close to the latter. You see, I helped Zirreo escape when they were after him. After the prophecy. They felt they needed to have him killed, both for mingling with me and for being the source of the bad news in the prophecy. They were trying to save their own necks. I think Camus was able to sway them in the end, though I marvel at how he managed it. The only squirrels who would talk to me for a while were my friends who hadn't had their first vision yet. They kept wanting to know how it felt, though only a few of them were brave enough to ask. I became sort of an oddity, a sideshow attraction. A freak."

Mariyen thought of the long room with all the shelves and the crystal balls of dew at the far end, the shelf collecting dust, the stand with her mother's name on it, a quivering bead held aloft above it. Was it a token she'd never been given, or something that had been taken away from her? Despite all her questions, all her interest, her eyes were slipping shut again. Llewellyn noticed it and gestured toward the bottle in Mariyen's loosening grip.

"Take that," she said, "See if it helps you like it used to. And don't," she laid stress on the word, "Don't ever, ever tell anyone what I just told you."

"Why did you…?"

"Every daughter deserves to have something of her mother," Llewellyn said, and her voice was softer this time. "I know I'm no good at the job, and at some point, perhaps very soon, I could be gone." She reached out and touched Mariyen's paw. "Now I think it's time for you to sleep again."

Mariyen couldn't argue, though she desperately wanted to. There were so many other things she wanted to talk to her mother about, simple things like who she was as a young squirrel. If she had the dreams like Mariyen, how many other things did they have in common? But her body was breath by breath betraying her, and she moved to get up off the bed.

Llewellyn took a hold of her and pushed her back.

"But where will *you* sleep?" she asked. She never got an answer before falling at last to her exhaustion.

Now, in the waking room, the sun coming through the small window and her mind slowly getting its bearings, she still could not find her mother. Mariyen found the clarity concoction sitting on the desk, and was off the bed and to it in two steps, snatching it up. Her eyes roved around the rest of the room, and she thought of exploring while her mother was gone but it made her feel too guilty. She'd explored enough, and her mother had given her so much already.

Just once, she thought, her eyes lingering on the drawer built into the desk. Without letting herself think it over, she eased the thing open. It made a shrill sound as she pulled it out and she froze, thinking that her mother might come back in at any time, or worse: Horus. His room was just a minute's walk down the hall, if that. She was foolish for taking her chances this way. She looked down at the contents of the drawer, feeling rushed, feeling watched. There was surprisingly little inside, given the crowded nature of the room itself. Some mint leaves (for tea, she assumed), and a piece of paper that was torn around the edges were all that she found. Feeling guiltier by the moment, she picked up the note and opened it along the much-folded crease.

The old observatory, the paper said. Nothing more, nothing less.

The old observatory. What did that mean? She couldn't tell whether it was in her mother's script or not, since she'd never seen her mother's writing. Was it a reminder of sorts?

Shrugging it off, Mariyen let the paper fall back into the drawer among the scattered mint leaves and began to push it closed. Halfway through the long squeal the drawer made, she heard something else: footsteps. Turning to the door and noticing it had been left open a crack, she froze. The sound of a somehow familiar voice came drifting to her. The speaker couldn't be far from the door, but she could not see him through the crack.

"You're very fed on the rules of Camus, aren't you, Horus?"

With a shock and a sinking feeling, Mariyen heard Horus reply. He was so close to her that he sounded almost as though he were standing in the room with her.

"Yes, I suppose I am, and I see no reason in changing that. Camus's rules kept us safe—

A snort. "You have got to be kidding. He could come back and—

"From ourselves, Araccus. They kept us safe from ourselves. Now, do you mind doing hall rounds for me?"

There was a moment of silence and then, "Of course not." Resentful.

Mariyen sucked in her breath as someone passed right in front of the door, their shadow filtering into the room for a brief second. She waited. And waited. Finally she heard Horus take his leave, walking in the opposite direction. She let out her breath and shut the drawer the rest of the way, backing up and into the bed again. She felt as though she'd just had a close call. Knowing what she did of Horus now, of her mother, she did not think she could have looked him in the eyes without it showing, like the rockier grains caught in a sieve, seen through the cracks on the other side.

It was time for her to go. Making her way to the door, clarity concoction clasped in one paw, she listened for any sound before peering out. The coast was clear, but it wouldn't be for long; she could hear the footsteps of someone else, probably only a server but a squirrel nonetheless, coming from around the corner. Deciding to take no chances, Mariyen surged out into the hall and fled back to the safety of her own room.

Only later, as she lay on her own bed, staring up at the ceiling and contemplating all she knew, how her life had changed in so many short moments trailing into one, did she realize that she hadn't had any dreams the night she spent in her mother's room. She looked over at her chest of drawers, inside of which she had firmly ensconced the little flask. Had it been the culprit? Her dreams hadn't gotten clearer, they'd merely disappeared. She didn't think too long on it. Inwardly she was just relieved that for once she was well-rested and not covered in sweat from a night hard-won.

There was a scrolling on the ceiling she hadn't noticed before. It was the shape of vines, twisting and curling over one another, overlapping and circling the edges of the room. Tracing this unusually luxurious design, she wondered what her mother's bad dreams had been of, when she had then. Did she too dream of this white squirrel, the one called Zirreo? It was suitable that he was white as a ghost, she thought; he certainly haunted like one.

***

Llewellyn did not sleep at all that night. After watching her daughter fall to sleep on her own tiny bed, she'd left the room as silently as possible, closing the door with a whisper of wood on wood. The halls were lit with a lantern-glow at this time of night, and there was hardly anyone out and about. It was her time to think.

So she'd told some lies to Mariyen. She'd lied about the potion. It was supposed to get rid of the dreams, but Llewellyn didn't tell Mariyen that. She figured now it was up to fate, a plan she was no more comfortable with than sitting on a knotty tree branch for hours; fate had never done anything good for her. She was sick of lying. She figured, *if I am going to despoil everything Horus and I agreed not to say, if I am going to disobey him I might as well do it thoroughly.* And that she had.

She purposefully perused the halls, the object of her search nothing but peace of mind. Every time she crossed a guard or someone else out late, she looked at them long enough so that they looked away first, and did not comment. So it was. She'd learned these things from being young and willful, and they carried her well into the present, which she wasn't sure was much different.

It was all a trap. This place was a trap. She felt as though any moment she might climb out a moonlit window and run away, over the late night dew in the grass to the promise of something other. It didn't even have to be better, so long as it wasn't the same.

The only thing tying her here was Zirreo, the thought of him coming again like that day when all her cells were still alive and dancing with thoughts of how to make this life her own, free from the idea of consequence. Or perhaps she was romanticizing it. If she had lied to Mariyen about anything else, it had been this, the day they met, but then, it was merely a lie of omission.

She'd been sitting on a branch outside, the early autumn day still warm as they all were before the frost hit, and she leaned her back up against the trunk of the tree and blew smoke from her mouth, trying to make it go up in rings. Instead, lopsided circles floated up on the fragrant air.

"Here," Absoulim said, taking the pipe from her and attempting to restock it with pipe reed. His paws trembled too much, something that occasionally happened with him, as though his nerves weren't quite on center. Llewellyn reached out without thought and put her paws over his to steady them. There was a moment of quiet between them then, and Llewellyn still remembered this as much as she remembered what came next.

"I could kill them," Absoulim said. There was no joke to his voice, hardly any emotion in it at all.

The Llewellyn of that time was a free spirit and would not admit to being scared when she was scared, so she only said, "Really? How would you do it?"

It was the elders that she—and she assumed, he too—was talking about. They had been caught that morning shirking their discipline and the elders had pulled them aside for a long talking to. Luckily, old Kantris hadn't seen the bulging in their robes, hadn't found out the real reason they were shirking—to get the pipe they smoked now, right out of elder Bogus's desk drawer.

Absoulim didn't answer her, just put the pipe to his mouth in that jerky way he had and inhaled slowly, before holding it out to her; she didn't think it was out of being rude. Sometimes he legitimately seemed not to understand that some questions warranted an answer. Of course, this was probably her older self reading into the memory. What she did know for sure was that what happened next would change the course of events for good. Her younger self stretched on the branch and took the proffered pipe from her friend.

"Killing's bad," she said, "And we couldn't put watercress in Victus's old trousers if you offed him." She wished the subject hadn't come up. It made him go silent and even though Absoulim had never been one for many words, it was a rare uncomfortable quiet—at least for her.

Llewellyn heard commotion on the branch below them and leaned out of the tree, knowing what she would find and knowing there was a good chance of being caught. She couldn't help herself. The entrance to Edgewood was just below, and two of the elders had made their way to the opening and were peering out, conversing in low tones.

"Someone's coming," said Absoulim from beside her, and she looked. Sure enough, parting with the distance at the horizon was the outline of a squirrel—and he looked like he was heading straight for Edgewood. She had a thought—what if the elders were receiving secret visitors outside of the tree? If they found out about it, she and Absoulim could charge payment for the secret not being released. But when the traveler got to the tree, instead of a welcoming, the elders spoke to him at once, loudly and not exactly friendly. It was clear they did not know him.

"Where do you think you're going?" the one Llewellyn recognized as Araccus said sharply. The squirrel, who was still at the base of the tree—was he *white*? He couldn't possibly be *white*—called up to them, and Llewellyn could tell he was smiling even though she couldn't see it.

"Just coming for a visit, friend."

There was a moment of deliberation among the elders in which they spoke so softly even Llewellyn, in her choice position, could not hear them. Then Camus, the only elder who didn't drive her completely insane, spoke.

"Very well, friend. Come on up here so we can take a look at you."

Araccus hissed something, but Llewellyn was not paying the elders any mind. The squirrel who came up the trunk of Edgewood stopped a few respectful feet away from the two elders ranged there and then took a slight bow. He straightened up again, and Llewellyn got a good look at his face, and in that moment she could have sworn that he looked directly at her. The whole time he talked to the elders,--which was actually not too long, she supposed—she had the sense that he was looking at her, too, even though she was hidden at this angle, and it was the most odd, frightening, wonderful feeling, like those dark eyes had just looked into her and through her and dragged out all her insides in a way, all the way to the front of her chest and body, so thoroughly incapacitating her that it felt like pleasure.

"...because I find your colony very interesting, and I am hoping to learn something from you, in an informal setting, of course," the white squirrel finished explaining himself, and the elders were silent for only a moment afterwards. Llewellyn dimly realized that more elders had come to the door in the meantime--young Horus and Spectus, Victus and Bogus, all peering out at the newcomer, judgment forming in their stares.

"Well, friend, we never keep anyone from coming here, especially to learn, the wisest of pursuits. As I'm sure you know. If we can interest you in something to eat—"

Araccus cut across him, his voice harsh. "On the contrary, Camus, you must remember our policy against strangers. We cannot have someone come in here and stir things up, it's unnatural. Look at him!"

Camus's voice was gentle as always, but he had developed a steely undertone. "Araccus, I urge you to remember that this is not a stranger. This is a guest. Now step aside and let him in."

The voices of the elders receded as they went back down the entrance hall, and the white squirrel followed them, not giving any sign that he'd been looking at Llewellyn, if indeed that had ever been the case. She let out a long-held breath.

"Who do you think that is?" Absoulim's soft voice startled her; she had forgotten for the moment that he was here with her.

"I don't know," she said, still staring after where the white squirrel had disappeared, as though the last vestiges of his aura were still clinging to the outsides of the tree. "But I think he seems very interesting."

The now adult Llewellyn had thought so many times about this moment, about the seeds that seemed to her to be hidden all through it. The white squirrel's eyes on her the whole time he was speaking, the way they came together in the observatory that night, the way it was only natural. Absoulim, saying those words through the smoke of a stolen pipe, *I could kill them,* and then the death of Bolus, much later, falling from such a height, it could have been an accident, but they suspected him. She could remember a team of the elders dragging their culprit up to the second highest branch, strapping his paws to the tendrils of the first highest and taking the thorns in their deliberate paws. They used thorns, long primitive ones, because only a thorn could provoke those types of screams, the ones she heard through her window so loud that all her friends asked her what was the matter, what was the matter, until she told them to get out and just laid on the bed, wishing it would end. In the end they cheered, the sick lot of them watching at the windows. She never saw Absoulim after that, just as she never saw Zirreo after he disappeared from the window of the observatory, waving one last goodbye and going to a place just as mysterious as the one he had come from, the autumn leaves swallowing him up so completely that she was forced to ask herself whether he had been real at all.

Llewellyn had known then, she figured, right about then, that she was completely and irrevocably alone.

No, she hadn't told Mariyen any of that in her need to disclose something, because however great that need was, she thought it would never be great enough to say some things, to say, *I was a fool* and give the explanation that this warranted. Some things were meant for the darkness of one's heart alone.

Llewellyn reached the end of one hall, the one with the dead end and the multitude of windows, all piercing the turnaround with bright, static light. She paused just beyond the part of the floor that was lit up.

It was because Mariyen was from after; she knew that, and she would have to come clean with herself about it. She had always been selfish, and Mariyen was from after. After all hope and options and companionship had been taken from her.

Worse, she was Genhaw's. Genhaw and his good intentions, Genhaw and his overbearing manner, his relentless polite courtship, his fastidious concern for having everything appropriate. Genhaw, sprawled out over the barren ground, divested of his organs, and the horror, both at the sight itself, so clean and unnatural, and at herself, as she thought how appropriate it was that he should finally lose his substance for real.

Mariyen was hers, but she was also his, and good riddance for that—the girl had some logic. She just couldn't love her.

She put a paw to her belly as she was wont to do too often now, and thought, *There will be no one to love at all soon.*

And then, *That doesn't have to be true.*

But it was. She imagined Zirreo's face, his dark eyes, as they appeared to her in her dreams. She loved him as she loved the memory of her younger self, before...all of that happened, before she was forced to hate her selfishness, but worse, her sudden turn to cowardice, perhaps as a result. She knew that when they met again, it wouldn't be the same. It would be about finishing what they started, and nothing more. Taking up the strings of their old collusions, the times they'd whispered forever not knowing what it meant, the times they'd sat in companionable, forbidden silence.

Killing what remained.

At some point she went to the window, and at some point she laid her head against its frame, and at some point she must have drifted off after all, because when she woke, it was to the daylight.

Too soon, she thought, but she got to her feet all the same.

CHAPTER XIX

There was a trail that cut through a forest of close-grown trees—close-grown all except where the trail bisected it, narrow and earthy, and sped off into the distance. It was alarmingly straight, and gave Kinder a queasy feeling if he stared at it too long. The trees went off into the horizon on either side of him, so that it looked as though they had no other option, a fact that Zirreo stated not a moment later.

"We're going to have to go through this mess, Kinder," the white squirrel said; he had taken to calling Kinder by his name whenever possible, as if this alone could establish a bond between them. Just the other day, he'd asked Kinder why he didn't smile so much anymore. Kinder hadn't a clue how Zirreo could know the squirrel he was before Nadra's death, but he did not feel inclined to share.

He did wonder about Lute a lot: where he was, what he was doing, whether he'd found that hole Zirreo told them about and went underground or whether he'd decided he'd been through enough and went back to his normal life.

Lute was his friend to the end, like the card had said. He wasn't sure this meant Lute particularly *liked* him so much as he was bound to him in a way. But if his friend had gone into the darkness, what had he seen and would he ever come out again? 'To the end" seemed so final; he hadn't thought of it like that when he'd read the card depicting the brick wall on a morning that seemed ages ago. In fact, he'd hardly looked at that card; the first one, the one that signified 'friend' was what he had concentrated on with the overzealous enthusiasm of one who has never had such a thing. But now, now the finality of the phrase hit him. What if it was literal? Lute could come to an end doing Astrippa knew what under the ground, because they'd never really had a plan. It was Kinder's mission they were on, wasn't it? If Lute died for it, he didn't know how he would forgive himself.

On his journey with Zirreo thus far, which had spanned a day and involved very little talking on his part, they had been through forests and fields alike, all very short and undisturbed journeys. They didn't use the trees, of course, so this could have had a part in the mysterious isolation that seemed to enwrap he and Zirreo wherever they went, though he suspected it was something the white squirrel did himself. Once, he'd embarrassed himself by letting his guard down and asking excitedly about whether Zirreo could do actual magic or not. That, predictably, was the one thing the white squirrel would not talk to him about, but it stopped Zirreo from attempting to make conversation for a while. So as they went uneventfully along, Kinder preferred to think that they were hiding under some type of spell, an assumption he kept until they reached these trees.

"If we walked around them, we would get off course," Zirreo said, answering a question Kinder hadn't even asked. "I have to warn you, though, these trees are chickaree territory, so don't speak and be as quiet as possible on the ground." His intense eyes roved over Kinder's bag, and Kinder knew what he was thinking before he said anything.

"My charms."

"Yes, Kinder. I know that you're very interested in them, but sometimes there are more important things than luck—living, for instance."

"Don't call me that." Something about hearing his name in the white squirrel's mouth made his blood boil.

Zirreo just turned and set off down the path, leaving Kinder to seethe. Taking his bag, empty of all food by now, in his paws, he turned it upside down and forced himself not to look when the charms flashed in the corner of his eye on the way to the dull ground. Then he reached up to the necklaces around his neck and the bracelets on his wrists and took them off, dropping them onto the pile he knew was collecting. He took out his earring and threw it last of all onto the pile-an offering.

"If you don't hurt us," Kinder whispered so low he could barely hear himself, "This is yours for the taking." *And if,* he thought, on an unrelated note, *if Lute lives.*

It was the last wish he made on the pile at his feet.

Who's the fool now?, he thought as he started off down the path after Zirreo, wondering why, with such a load off of his shoulders, he felt like he wanted to cry.

***

To say that Lute had had better days—a phrase he normally detested since none of his days ever went particularly swimmingly—would be an apt phrase right now.

As soon as the door had closed on he and Chamblis, the grotesquely large chipmunk squirmed out of his seat and plodded heavily over to Lute. Lute, who had no weapon available to him, found himself plastered between the door and Chamblis, and the stench of the latter was not something to write home about, unless you were going for the shock factor.

They locked yew in with their token insane member, Lute thought, *Quite probably, yer going to get out of this scarred at the least, Lute-boy.*

"What are you thinking?" Chamblis's breath was hot upon his face. As with Kinder's wall-chewing mother, he felt frightened out of his mind by the fact that he could not predict what his opponent would do next. This was yet another thing Kinder might be better equipped to handle: his experience with the insane was much more extensive than Lute's.

"Do yew ask all yer prisoners that?" Lute asked, against his better judgment.

Instead of going off on him, as Lute thought might happen, the giant chipmunk only grinned, revealing rotted brown teeth and the remnants of whatever he had eaten last. Lute thought he might gag.

"No, only youuuuu," Chamblis said, drawing out this last word like he was teasing Lute. He began to back away a bit, and Lute thought of making a break for it, maybe running in circles around the room so that Chamblis could never catch him, but he realized he would get tired and then who knew? The chipmunk might eat him. It was not out of the realm of possibility.

Someone should really get his beetles to him. Lute nearly laughed out loud in the throes of his own hysteria. He would rather have been anywhere, truly, even back in Pember's workshop taking the worst beating he'd ever had, the one that caused him to black out and wake up still in perpetual darkness.

Chamblis began digging at the dirt wall next to him, working his grimy claws beyond a thin tendril of tree root, and pulled out a thick pink something. The earthworm thrashed, speared as it was on the end of his claw, and Chamblis watched it for a moment, eyes bright, before bringing it to his mouth and sucking. Lute felt like he would be sick for the hundredth time since he'd been thrust into this chamber. When Chamblis turned back to him, he was grinning larger than ever, and Lute didn't think he was imagining the bit of slimy pink, caught up between Chamblis's front teeth. It was still moving.

Chamblis cleaned the minimal blood off of his lips and said, "Now. Where were we?"

Apparently the question was a real one, because he appeared deep in thought for a second. Lute could tell by the expression that slowly crawled over Chamblis's face that he was not going to like the results. "That's *right*," he said, as though the answer to a question he'd been puzzling over all day had been made painfully obvious, "You're an intruder."

"Um," said Lute. Not a promising start.

"The thing about *intruders* is," Chamblis told him, as though they were sharing a bond of confidentiality, as though he had not just chewed up a whole live earthworm in front of Lute, "I don't have a great *fondness* for them. They make me squirm, in fact. I like it when they're sentenced to death, but I like to have a little *fun* first. Who doesn't like *fun*?"

Lute was willing to bet a lot of squirrels wouldn't like the type of fun Chamblis had in mind.

"We like to keep ourselves *private*," Chamblis continued. Lute had moved along the wall a bit and Chamblis lumbered towards him, breathing heavily through his nose in a way that made him think of a beast getting ready to attack. He looked around the room frantically, and spotted a sort of call bell hanging from the ceiling next to Chamblis's chair. It occurred to Lute that if he could just get over to this bell, he might ring it, and when someone came in, he would rush them and get out.

There were so many problems with this plan—not least of all, the one where Lute rushed out into the open tunnel beyond and into more chipmunks—there was no way he could take all of these awful little creatures. But it was the only plan he had. He had never been so good with the planning, only with the action.

But that wasn't *entirely* true, was it? Lute was a bargainer. He'd had to be, growing up with Saecka and her ilk, though admittedly the things he'd bargained for were all material treasures rather than his own life.

Chamblis was almost upon him, close enough so that he could smell him: the distinct odor of the unwashed, a sour, unpleasant smell.

"Say," Lute broke in, taking a step back despite himself, "Just as a hypothetical question, what are yew going to do with me once yew've had yer fun? Going to chuck me to yer giant worms, have them suck me dry?"

Chamblis squinted at him. "The Gorepedes don't listen to me," he said rather petulantly.

Ah, Lute thought, *but yew know what I'm talking about. I guess that rotter of a white squirrel was right.*

"So these gorepedes, yew think I could see one?" he asked.

Chamblis moved toward him, but Lute backed up again, moving to the side. Chamblis looked angrier than a hungry gorepede must look.

"Stop. *Moving,*" he commanded. Like there was a chance of that.

"Answer the question."

Chamblis glared balefully at him. "You can't see one unless the elders decide to bring one to you. Which they won't. Unless it's time for you to die. But we don't want *that* to come too soon, now do we? Now hold *still.* Perhaps I'll even spare you if you do."

"Oh, I'm not sure you want me to die at all," Lute said casually, edging behind Chamblis's chair now. The stink was even worse over here, and he covered his nose in a dramatic fashion. "Wooo! Yew really should consider bathing more often."

"I'm the king, you know," Chamblis said, switching topics without warning. He then proceeded to run—or perform what looked like an attempt at running—over to his chair. Sweat pouring down his face, he picked up something Lute couldn't see from the other side of chamber. He put it on his head, and Lute thought, *oh gods, it figures.* The nutter had a crown. Chamblis was leering at him now as though the fact that he had a crown on his head now made all the difference in the world to Lute obeying him. *He's going to be very disappointed.*

"So wait," he said, "If yer the king, tell me this: can't yew just make the elders do whatever yew want?"

"Of course I can," Chamblis said, advancing, and before Lute could move away again, he grabbed him, lifting him bodily from the ground—though Chamblis was a head shorter than Lute, he probably weighed ten times more— and put him into the throne. The wooden back of the chair chafed against Lute's skin, and he realized it was not a real throne—real thrones were smoothed over and given intricate carvings. This was nothing like it. Why would the chipmunks be keeping a crazy member of their own colony in a heavily guarded room with a fake, unsanded throne and a crown?

He came to the only possible answer: whoever the real leaders were, they both hated Chamblis and had some sort of superstition built around him.

Chamblis was leaning close to him now, and Lute knew he was going to have to speak, or at least breathe, sometime soon.

"Yew know," he said, "That's not even a real crown."

What in all hells am I doing?

Chamblis took the crown off faster than Lute could think and he felt something cold and angled crack across his jaw. He fell over sideways into the rough arm of the chair, pain shooting through his face like a fire, a million hot pokers. *And now I'm going to pass out.* But, by some stroke of luck, Lute remained conscious. His whole face felt like it was going to fall to pieces if he moved. *Okay, bad idea,* he thought. *Next time I* will *be unconscious and then it's all over.* When he finally straightened up, Chamblis was staring at him with a self-satisfied smile.

"That *feels* pretty real, doesn't it?" the fat chipmunk asked him.

"Yeah, okay, fine," Lute said, trying not to scream as he uttered the words. "So yer crown might be real, but listen. The chipmunks who put yew in here already knew what decision they were going to make. They want me dead. I think that whatever yew say, they're still going to want me dead. They're going to feed me to those gorepedes of yers, even if yew tell them not to."

Chamblis frowned at him, digging in his ear with one long, dirty claw as he did so. "Why would I *say* not to? You're just trying to get out of it. Do I look stupid to you?"

"Exactly," Lute said, biting his lip and, in so doing, bypassing a fractured skull. "They know yer going to want me to die for trespassing, so they're not too concerned. It's not a real choice. I bet if yew said otherwise, they wouldn't do what yew wanted."

Chamblis stared at him. For a second, Lute thought he might be in for another whack from that crown, and if he was, so long to any chances he had of getting out of here.

"If I let you go," Chamblis said slowly, "You would tell everyone aboveground about us. I'm not *stupid.* I'm *king.* It's my *duty* to know these things."

"I might," Lute agreed, "or I might not." On sudden inspiration, he reached for the mirror hanging at his side, ignoring the throbbing in his face. He had quite forgotten it was there until Chamblis had hit him and he'd felt it smash up against his body.

"This," he said, "Is how I contact those aboveground. I could tell them about yew right now, if I wanted to. Or I could let yer *society*, if that's what yew call it, go on in peace."

Chamblis was staring at the mirror through his squinted eyes. Lute was beginning to recognize this expression as one of intense thoughtfulness, or rather, the face Chamblis made when trying to hold his garbled mind together for longer than a minute.

"So," the chipmunk 'king' said, finally, triumphantly. "How come you haven't called them yet?"

"What d'yew mean?"

Chamblis snatched for the mirror nearly faster than Lute could pull away. "I wouldn't do that," he said, heart pounding. "It knows my voice, and I can tell it to tell everyone."

"You can*not*," Chamblis literally slobbered. Drool slowly coursed its way down his lower lip.

Lute raised his eyebrows. "Can't I?" he asked. He turned to the mirror and cleared his throat.

"Wait!" Chamblis shouted, showering him in wet. His eyes were wide, and the paint around them was crusty and cracked. He could be *loud* when he wanted to. Lute took a moment to recover, staring into the mirror all the while.

"Whatever is yer problem?" he said finally, turning to Chamblis. "I thought yew told me my mirror wasn't *real*."

Chamblis looked around wildly, as though he expected other squirrels like Lute to start appearing out of nowhere. "Don't call them…yet."

Oh, thank Astrippa for the superstitious. Maybe I should tell Kinder about this as a cautionary tale, get him to reconsider his lifestyle choices. Then he remembered there was no Kinder to tell if he ever got out of this forsaken place. That was all it took to sober, compose himself. He waited.

"What do you want?" Chamblis said, just as surely as he had predicted. He wiped at his lower lip unconsciously, attempting to glare at Lute as he did so, but the distance between them remained mercifully wide. *He's scared,* thought Lute. *Gods, this is wonderful.*

"I actually want very little," Lute said modestly. "I want yew to stop sending yer creatures, the gorepedes or whatever yew call 'em, to feed on us."

"Actually, we only send them aboveground," said Chamblis sourly. "We don't make them *get* anyone. The elders don't , at least. They're the ones who do the *sending.* They need to *eat.*"

"So are yew telling me that yew don't even have control over that?"

Chamblis's brow darkened. Lute was counting on this. For a second he looked like he was going to hit Lute again, but thought better of it—his eyes went nervously to the mirror and back to his prisoner again.

"I…am…king," he finally said, biting the words out and grabbing onto his crown as he said so.

"Well, I'll believe it when I see it," Lute said calmly.

"And if we decide to *kill* you?" Chamblis's voice went up a good five notches in volume.

Lute shrugged. "If yew decide to kill me, I'll die, but don't expect yer little hideout to remain so secret. Yer going to really get it, yew and all yer other chipmunks. I'm rather important myself, up there. Yew could say I'm a king, too."

Lute gloated inwardly over this next concession. He hadn't planned to say that bit about being king; today was an inspired day.

"Either way," he said, because Chamblis, amazingly enough, seemed to be losing concentration, staring around at the walls and muttering words Lute couldn't quite make out. "I can make them come down here. And there's more of them than there is of yew."

"What?" Chamblis snapped, turning his attention back to Lute.

"I said, I can make them come down here. I'm not even confident yew can make yer subjects do anything."

The large chipmunk jerked towards him, and Lute thought, *oh gods, what if I've gone too far. I'm going to be crushed to death!* But Chamblis reached past him and rang the bell hanging from the ceiling. He kept ringing and ringing it until the din began to give Lute a headache and when the first chipmunk walked in the door, he was so disoriented he thought he was hallucinating.

It was the lead chipmunk from the council hall, and he did not look happy.

"*What* is it?" he asked testily, but Lute did not fail to notice he was keeping cautiously close to the door.

"Call me king, *will* you?"

"You're not—"

But the lead chipmunk decided not to say anything else, a decision Lute thought was wise considering the growing anger on Chamblis's face.

"I have a crown," Chamblis said, his voice a slobbering growl.

"Okay," the lead chipmunk said, "Yeah. I know." He muttered something that contained a curse and what sounded like someone's name. "Have you—" He looked at Lute for the first time, as though he was just realizing he was there. His eyes seemed to widen, making the markings around them appear less threatening, somehow.

"Chamblis—*king*—have you had your time with the intruder yet?"

Chamblis fixed the leader with the same grotesque leer Lute was becoming accustomed to being on the receiving end of.

"Yes, I'm done and I've come to the conclusion that we are doing things *unsatisfactorily.*" He drawled out this last word and gave the leader a meaningful look. The leader looked nonplussed. Lute ventured a guess that he was one of the elders.

"Unsatisfactorily how?" The elder looked nervous, there was no mistaking it. Interesting. Lute's suspicions were proving plausible thus far.

"The gorepedes have to feed elsewhere," Chamblis said, going to sit in his chair. As he fell backwards, Lute scrambled out of the way just in time, launching himself over the arm of the chair and sitting at its side, clasping the mirror and waiting for the verdict.

The elder was looking at Chamblis like he had three heads. "The gorepedes need to feed aboveground. Their source of food down here is limited, and we need to give it time to restock. Is there any, uh, *reason* for this idea, king?"

On saying this, he looked directly at Lute, right into his eyes, and for a stunning moment Lute felt as though the elder could see right through him, before he turned to Chamblis again.

"I see," he said. "Is he of importance up there?"

"He's like a king," Chamblis said, "though not as powerful as I am."

Lute nodded once to this statement and fixed the elder with a level stare. The elder returned it, his hot black eyes seeming to sift through the contents of Lute's mind as he did so.

"That mirror he has can see into his world or something. He can talk to those aboveground."

"Indeed?" the elder asked. His eyebrows lifted. "Well, we can consider an alternative…"

"No," Chamblis cut in vehemently, and the violence in his voice made the elder jump and eye him warily.

"Look, king, it's not as though I doubt your judgment…"

"If you don't doubt it, act on it. You don't need to deliberate. Feed them worms, feed them beetles. If they're not satisfied with that, feed them wrongdoers. I'm sure we can find them."

He gave a toothy smile to the elder, and said, "I have made my decision."

The elder nodded. "Yes, king," he said, then beckoned to Lute.

Unbelieving of his luck, Lute got up and headed for the door. As he went, his paws began to itch for his dagger once again. The elder made no comment when Lute reached him, only continued to beckon him forward until they were standing just outside the door. Lute stared at the chains and the locks and prepared himself to fight if need be. The elder, however, only continued on, with the indication that Lute should follow.

They went down one tunnel that Lute could barely stand up in and down another that was slightly larger. At the end of this one was a door, smaller and much less impressive than the one to Chamblis's room. The elder opened it and Lute detected a sound, a curious smooth hissing that moved unsettlingly along on the air like a slow-moving, viscous fluid.

The elder was standing in the doorway waiting for him.

"What—what's...?" Lute licked his lips. "There's something behind there, isn't there?"

It's them.

"Maybe," the elder said, giving him a look that said, *you know.* The hissing sound was steady, never altering and never-ending. Lute took a step toward the door.

"Well, if I'm going to die, I guess that makes up yer fate for yew," he said, trying to clamp down on his own fear, hold it in place.

"We're not going to kill you," the chipmunk said bluntly, staring at Lute haughtily like if he hadn't figured this out, maybe he *should* have died.

Lute stepped into the room—except it wasn't a room. Instead, he found himself standing on a balcony of sorts, a steep, earthy incline with a thin line of rocks, three tall, curving around as a sort of ineffective guard rail. Beyond the wall, the ground plunged downwards in a drop that Lute was sure would hurt, if not kill any unlucky rotter who was pushed over. Not that this was his only motive for staying away from the edge; *they* were down there.

They were gigantic. Lute had pictured them larger, of course; in his mind's eye, they were huge, fierce beasts like you'd cast for a frightening bedtime story, but these were living creatures and conveyed a terror to him that only came from that which was real, refined in proportion but tangibly *there.*

In a way, they were really only very large worms. Their backs glistened an off-white with a greenish tint to it as they moved smoothly along. They didn't seem to possess legs at all; instead, their bodies undulated like a rippling something was rattling them from inside, trying to force its way out. The long, sinuous hiss was coming from their progress over the dirt below, Lute realized. And they never, never stopped moving—this he also noticed.

The room the gorepedes were incased in was large enough, but still they moved as though by magic across its length, making that hissing sound, before turning sharply and passing each other on the way back. *They look like they're guarding something*, Lute thought. The faces—when Lute first saw their faces—made his heart stick in his chest before it went back to pumping.

They had no eyes. Instead, there was only a gaping hole, always open, that appeared to be the mouth, with two long, green tendrils protruding out of it, twitching and lashing in the air in front of them as the gorepedes moved. It looked almost like...

"Do they have *plants* growing on them?" Lute heard his own voice ask. Eyeless as the creatures were, every time one turned and began to start its circuit back to the other side of the room below, he felt as though it was looking directly at him, and had to contain his urge to bolt.

"They do indeed," the elder said to him. He had closed the door behind them, Lute noticed, and he thought, *well, time to get fed to these things, right?* But the elder continued to unnerve him by not moving forward, by instead only eyeing Lute as though he were an interesting specimen. It was not a look of like, but it was not openly hateful either. The outward flowing lines from his eyes, painted blue, gave him a look of extreme intensity.

"I have a deal to make with you," he said, not bothering to explain the plants further.

"Well, it's good to see you've...er..."

"I know you're not a king."

Lute blinked, his heart sinking again. "Then why...?"

"We have to do what Chamblis says, because if we don't, the real power behind him is going to speak up. And we don't want that."

"The real...?" All Lute could do was dumbly repeat the words handed to him as he stared down at the gorepedes. He did not want to have his back to them. Any minute one of them could come crawling up the side of the incline and into him, and judging from the pace they *slithered* at, he would have no chance if taken by surprise.

"His mother," the elder said, and it took Lute a moment to remember he was talking about Chamblis. "She's in control for real. The queen that never dies. She tried to have a son so many times over the years, and she was never successful until him. She worships him, and if we don't, too...we get brought here. But not simply to talk as we're doing. Do you understand?"

"Yes," Lute said, trying to process this information. The hissing noise, silent as it was, was becoming distracting to him, closing in about him. He suspected it was only the echoes on the walls, but it made him paranoid. He had heard all right, though. The thought of Chamblis having a mother was somehow very grotesque. What would such a chipmunk look like?

"Yew said she never dies?" Lute asked, "What's that mean?"

The elder ignored the question. "So, you see," he continued. "We have to do whatever Chamblis wants, because in a sense, he *is* the king. It's a horrible thing. We've had to make some decisions that are better off not made at all. Some of us have even suggested poisoning him with the beetles he likes so much...but we'd be caught. I know it. And to take another's life, even that of one who is insane…is to die forever when you go, as I'm sure you know." He looked sideways at Lute, and Lute began to realize something: he was frightening to these creatures, as they were frightening to him. He was the new, the unexplored, this strange being from a land they'd possibly never ventured into. The elder was feeling him out, trying to get a sense of a common bond. It made Lute feel strangely guilty. But then…

"Why do you have them?" Lute asked. He meant the gorepedes, and he could see that the elder knew immediately where he was going, because his eyes hardened again.

"We have a reciprocal relationship with them," he said, as though daring Lute to argue this fact. "At the very beginning, the story goes that we saved the last nest of gorepedes—they nest in the roots of plants, and they start out incredibly small---and they repaid us by making our tunnels for us, faster and better than we could have ever done. We used to be diggers. Now we don't need to be."

Something suddenly made sense to Lute: the fact that the chipmunks had holes leading up to aboveground, yet seemed to have no knowledge of the upper world. Were all of these tunnels from some older time, a time when chipmunks might have roamed the earth side by side with squirrels?

The tunnels down here were larger and completely round, in contrast with the tunnel he'd gone down to get here, which had been chokingly small and anything but perfectly shaped. Almost as though someone like him had dug it. That was it, then: holes from antiquity, like the one the white squirrel had found were meant to be forgotten.

"Do you ever go…aboveground?" Lute asked, testing his theory.

The elder immediately shook his head. "It's horrible up there," he said blankly by way of explanation. Lute found himself feeling oddly offended.

"How would yew know?" he couldn't help asking.

"There are stories," the elder said. "I don't know if they're real and I don't care to find out. This is our home, and we—unlike you, perhaps—are content."

"Well, in that case, if yer content," Lute snapped, temper surging up. "Yew think I wanted to come down here? I hate it down here! If yer gorepedes weren't *killing* my friends up there, it would be wonderful. I would like nothing more than to crawl up there again and forget this place even exists!"

In the heated second after he'd finished his rant, Lute thought maybe he'd offended the elder too much, pushed him too far. Maybe he would change his mind, despite his fearsome queen and her mad son. But when the elder looked at him, it was with something much subtler, a fleeting emotion that Lute couldn't pin down, until he realized: it was hope he was seeing in the other's eyes.

"Would you?" he asked.

For the first time, Lute did not hear the hissing of the creatures behind him. The chipmunk's fierce eyes were on him; he could feel their intensity.

"I would," he said, staring levelly back at the elder. "When I get aboveground, yew don't exist."

The elder stared at him a moment longer. "We'd kill you if we could," he said.

"I know."

They waited in the silence that had become uncomfortably equitable. There was an odd sort of squelching sound from behind Lute, and he turned to see one of the gorepedes had stopped its circuit for a while. What passed for its face was pointed toward Lute, and the strange, waving green tentacles that protruded from its empty maw waved about. Lute feared one would shoot out and enwrap his neck, but nothing happened. The other gorepedes were stopping now too, and they all turned to look at him. He didn't know if he could call it looking, since they had no eyes, but they were all facing him, green plant-like growths waving rapidly in the air in front of them— trying to sniff him out? Was it possible they hadn't detected his presence until now?

The elder looked completely unconcerned with this development. His eyes passed over the creatures in their ditch, and as they did so, each gorepede slowly lowered its head again and began, with a sticking, whispering sound, to begin its circuit again.

Lute couldn't quite believe what he'd just seen. Was the elder *communicating* with the gorepedes? For he felt that something had passed between them on the air, something of which he was not part. The elder turned and motioned to him to follow.

When they were back out in the passageway again, the elder closed the door, though Lute could still hear the gliding, insidious sound of the gorepedes on their circuitous journey if he listened hard.

"Come," the elder said, and he followed; there were no more words exchanged between them the whole way back to their destination, the meeting chamber he'd fallen into at the beginning. He didn't allow himself to think as they went, didn't allow himself to get too excited over the fact that he'd somehow managed to stop this, to do what he'd come to do, for fear it would come crashing down around him at the last moment.

Even though hours must have passed, at least (it was so hard to tell down here in the unnatural dark), several of the same chipmunks that had occupied this chamber when Lute had come crashing down in their midst were still there, talking away at one another. When the elder escorting Lute entered, everyone went silent.

The chipmunk Lute remembered as Gontesti stood up.

"So, how did the meeting with Chamblis go?" he said, a smirk starting to spread over his features. The leader must have stopped it with a look, because all of a sudden, Gontesti did not look too confident.

"What? What happened?"

"We're to let him go," the leader said. Lute could suddenly feel all of the eyes in the room on him, as even the last of the muttering died down. The chipmunk with the slingshot stood up.

"Do you want me to hit him one anyway?" he asked, voice shrill with anticipation.

"Sit *down*, Francesci. You all know what we must do now." There was much grave nodding of heads and shifting around among the chipmunks. A couple of whispers escaped from the crowd. Lute started to feel anxious standing awkwardly at the center of their attention.

"Loreni," the leader said, and a small chipmunk Lute hadn't noticed before—probably due to the fact that she could hardly see over the heads of those in front of her—stepped to the front.

"I can trust you to do the deed?" he asked.

Loreni nodded her head. Her face was covered in a brilliant green paint, several dots of it around her eyes and down her cheeks.

"All right," the leader said simply. Turning to Lute, he said, "Remember your promise."

There was warning in his eyes. Lute nodded, and felt a paw on his arm, pulling him away towards the door. He wanted to ask where he was going, but the leader had already turned back to the rest of his audience and was speaking to them.

"Now, my friends, I have some bad news. The gorepedes will not be able to feed aboveground anymore, which means we need to find as much food within..."

As Lute was pulled back down the tunnel behind Loreni, the leader's voice faded from a clear intonation to an echo, to nothing. He was in the dark again, in more ways than one. As he followed Loreni, who made no attempt at conversation at all, he wondered what the 'deed' the leader had talked about was. He was feeling unusually reticent, and did not want to ask Loreni for fear of the answer. Would he have to make some sort of blood pact with them? He supposed he'd do it if it came to that, even though the thought made him queasy. Loreni had a knife at her waist; he could see the unsheathed blade glinting in the dark, and he thought, *if I had a route of escape, I could take that out and get her with it, I could take it and plunge it into her and run.* Of course, he would be a fool to do such a thing and ruin all his work, but it was laughable all the same. Never keep a knife unattended at your waist with an enemy at your back: such a beginner's rule. The chipmunks were clearly not accustomed to violence, just as the elder had claimed.

Lute followed Loreni for so long that he soon felt his feet wearing on him. They went down one passage, through one door, up another passage. Sometimes he felt like they were going up, other times down. Most of the tunnels they went through were large and perfectly round, a sign that the gorepedes had crafted them, though a few of the tunnels were bumpy, rocky and small, hard to squeeze through and smelling of neglect. Loreni navigated these without issue, of course, her size allowing her to practically scamper through, while Lute felt his bones being jolted and jostled, his back scraped until he estimated he had no fur left there. Was this the deed? Getting him as lost and as angry as possible? *Well, yer doing* splendidly, *keep at it*, Lute thought, just as something scrambled under his feet.

"Aaaauuughhh!" he shouted. Loreni hardly batted an eye. "Beetle," she said, in a tone that made Lute think she was privately laughing at him.

Beetle my tail, he grumped to himself, and still they went on. There came a point when Lute was sure they'd walked for at least an hour. He'd finally asked Loreni's back where they were going, and all she'd had to say was, "away." That one cryptic word hung in space in front of him, in the deafening silence, the stumbling darkness, until he began to think 'away' the most obnoxious word any dumb sod had ever created.

The whole time they were in the tunnels, they never passed another chipmunk, something Lute noticed when he was trying to distract his brain from getting too imaginative. He'd had unpleasant things move under his feet, and once a gorepede had even passed them, but the chipmunks were nowhere in sight.

The gorepede was the most frightening. They were approaching an intersection of tunnels when it happened. All of a sudden, Lute felt the ground vibrate a little, and he nearly ran into Loreni—Loreni and that damned knife—as she stopped without warning. Flinging out a paw, she signaled for him to wait, though Lute wouldn't have gone on if his life depended on it. He recognized that hissing sound, like the release of steam from an unseen source. It amazed him, how silent the thing's passage was—first he saw the tendrils of green, waving slowly, the gaping maw, then the bulk of the body, that eerie green color, passing in front of them, headed somewhere to their left. This was a creature that could sneak up on anyone, take anything by surprise. In the rumbling minutes of its passing, he thought, *oh god, it will turn our way,* and he could even smell its smell, it passed so close to him. It was a damp, earthy smell, like the inside of a cavern, or the way the earth must feel around you, he thought, when you were lying long dead and forgotten. One of the waving tendrils of green reached out and, passing dangerously close to them, flicked Lute's cheek. The touch was foreign, like a plant had come alive and touched him, with sinister purpose in mind. He drew back, shivering, and when the creature had passed, he let out the breath he hadn't known he'd been holding and continued after Loreni shakily; she had started again without hesitation and was already farther up the tunnel across from him.

What kind of society used creatures like this, had *deals* with them? What kind of squirrels allowed other squirrels to be murdered for a deal?

They're the kings of out of sight, out of mind, Lute thought, *but like it or not, I'm going to have to do the same thing when I get out of here.*

Well, who would he tell? He supposed he'd have to backtrack and go to the white squirrel, tell him his damned mission was successful. The white squirrel was the only one he knew who already knew the chipmunks existed, though he didn't know what good telling him would be. He still wasn't entirely convinced the chipmunks would keep their word, but if they were faking, they were doing it convincingly.

Loreni was leading him so far and so long that he thought it ought to be nighttime by now. He went to share this acid piece of observation with her, but she held up a paw and gestured upwards at some older looking tunnel cut into the ceiling. It looked slightly bigger than the other archaic tunnels she'd led him through, for which Lute praised Astrippa or whoever the spotty guardian of miscreant squirrels happened to be. Lute could see the dots painted onto Loreni's face very clearly now, savagely bright on one cheek and dull where she was bathed in shadow on the other, and he realized—*sun*—just as he looked up and saw it, a circle of glowing yellow coolness that said to him quite clearly, *you are free.*

Loreni reached to her side, and Lute jumped back, ready for anything now, anything she might throw his way. But nothing happened, and when Lute looked back at her, Loreni had taken the knife from her side—*his* knife, he realized—and was holding it out to him.

"Here," she said. "Take it and don't come back. Forget that this place exists, as you promised. I'm going to close this tunnel after you come up. Keep your part of the deal."

She didn't need to say *or else*, but she didn't need to. He met her gaze and nodded.

"That, I can assure yew, I will do," he said, and putting his knife to his side once more like sliding a puzzle piece into its correct place, Lute fit his paws around some of the rocky soil in the tunnel above and began to climb.

CHAPTER XX

Mariyen stared out the one window of her room. It was snowing, and the small flecks of cold touching the autumn air seemed so strange and out of place. Days had passed since her talk with her mother, and their conversation had attained an unreal quality in her head. Whenever she saw Llewellyn now, it was a quick brushing-past in a dimly lit hall. There were usually more squirrels around them when they crossed paths, and Mariyen used this as an excuse for why she hadn't said a word to her mother since that night.

She'd gone back to her regular schedule, if you could call it a schedule. She slept often, because now she had no dreams, and their absence hurt her, she thought, almost more than the nightmares had. She'd finished the clarity potion, but it hadn't helped; it had seemed to make things worse, in fact.

Mariyen listened to the increasingly rapid tick of the fat flakes against her windowpane. It looked like it might be a legitimate snow, and she wondered about the white squirrel. Was he on his way now? Did her mother know such things? She'd said she talked to him in his dreams, and this must mean the white squirrel knew about Mariyen, too. She didn't know why this excited her, why the idea made her feel special, although the thought *she loves him* crossed her mind as suddenly as any other lazy afternoon thought, and made her think. *Is this what I've come to?*

The snow was sticking now, and she wanted to run out on a branch and stick her feet in it like she used to do when she was a child. She was not a child anymore, though, so she stayed behind her window and only thought.

Snow falling in fall, she thought, her cup of mint tea clutched between her paws, warming them. *And we're expecting the fallen. So many different kinds of fall.*

She smiled at this and balanced her tea on the windowsill. Stepping back, she eyed the picture she'd created. The steam from the cup wafted up, curling in on itself, while beyond the glass the snow fell, a juxtaposition of heat and cold. The flakes were sticking to the window. Mariyen yawned and went to her bed, ready for another nap, another blissful whiting out, when she remembered something.

She remembered the day she'd gone to the long room with the shelves and the scrolls and the crystal balls. She remembered walking to the end, exploring, and then she remembered seeing the elder. The one with the cane. The one who'd left after seeing her; he had not said a word since, and Mariyen had mostly been relieved. She'd even given a private thank you in her mind to the elder that she hadn't known then, the elder whose voice and manner she suddenly recognized now from a few close calls and a chain of stories.

Araccus.

The realization made her sick. She couldn't believe how stupid she'd been. He'd had a reason, of course he'd had a reason.

That time when she'd heard he and Horus outside of her mother's room, talking in hushed tones, the resentment she'd sensed from Araccus, coupled with the story of how he was embarrassed by Camus in days long gone. And that time, in their meeting, when he'd raised a paw, wanting to have the exile Absoulim come back and be sentenced to death, what had he said?

Horus had been angry, and reinforced Camus's policies. *We can't get him back even if we wanted to.* And Araccus had replied, *What if we said we could give him what he wants?*

What did Absoulim want? What was Araccus all the way down in the scroll room for? He'd been hanging out by the shelf of crystal balls labelled 'inactive.' Her mother's name had been on one of the only two balls on that shelf. And whose ball was next to her mother's, in the very spot Araccus was standing when he spotted her through the shelf?

Of course. The only reason Araccus hadn't ratted her out was because he hadn't wanted her to rat him out.

It was wrong, so terribly, terribly wrong. She remembered her mother's panic when she'd mentioned Absoulim coming back. Did Araccus, at this very moment, have what he wanted, what Absoulim wanted? Had he managed to contact the seer in some way only seers could communicate?

Mariyen took a deep breath, her heart now pumping rapidly, staring down at her crisp white bedspread, a terrain that stretched on for longer than was comfortable. White space, so much white space. And then:

White noise: a tapping at the window.

Mariyen turned, feeling like her feet were not her own, and saw, through a patina of white, a skeletal face that could have, for all the dread she felt, been the reincarnation of her nightmares. She blinked, she stared: all she saw was the tea, where she'd left it on the windowsill, the steam still visible, the falling snow outside. Nothing else.

Then she saw it, the pawprint, long and horrible, fading even now as she stared…and then the glass broke, exploding inward and scattering across the floor, the bedspread, some landing in the cup of tea, which toppled and then fell, shattering and splattering its contents everywhere. Mariyen screamed.

***

Kinder had had a restless few nights. He was pacing around in the nearest grove of trees to where he and Zirreo had stopped for the night, when the white squirrel came to him.

He could sense Zirreo looking at him before he said anything.

"What?" he asked, his back to the white squirrel.

"There's a fire," Zirreo said, and Kinder walked into the grove they shared to find that there was. It was a small thing, crackling in place, completely in control and throwing off more heat than its size warranted. Kinder looked back at the white squirrel.

"You did this?" he asked.

Zirreo shrugged. "Yes." There were sticks nearby he could have used. He was admitting to nothing.

It made Kinder nervous. What kind of squirrel could seem to make himself invisible and light fires on his own? He never did these things around Kinder. Kinder used to think it was because he had ulterior motives, but now he was starting to subscribe to a stranger theory despite himself: Zirreo was ashamed of his magic.

Because magic was what it was, what it had to be, but every time he asked, Zirreo would only smile or change the subject. It wouldn't have bothered him so much if Zirreo didn't bother *him* on several points, the first of which had become the ground.

"You haven't felt anything for days," Zirreo said as he sat down at the fire, and Kinder knew they were onto it again.

"That's right," he said, giving the white squirrel a strained smile. "Maybe the menace is gone."

"Or your sensation."

He stared at the white squirrel across the flames. "No. My sensation is not gone. I can feel a lot of things intuitively, and that's one of them. There's just no danger there right now."

"Well, if you didn't lose your sensation..."

Kinder realized suddenly what it was he was getting at.

"Lute," he said. "Do you really think he did it?"

"I don't know either way," Zirreo told him, getting out his pipe reed. Kinder had to bite back on telling him that it was unlucky to smoke pipe reed in front of a fire.

"We're close," Zirreo said, inhaling on his pipe.

That was the other thing. He never told Kinder where they were going, except to say that it was somewhere he'd been before and somewhere he would not be welcome back. But the dreams Kinder had been having when he actually managed to get to sleep, were very confused. All he knew for sure was that there was someone, young, a flyer, who appeared in each one. She seemed to need his help or to want to tell him something, one or the other. She kept reaching out to him, her lips moving in the mass of destruction that sometimes occurred around her, meaningless destruction. There was the crying of a child somewhere in the last dream, and when he woke, he remembered feeling disappointed and afraid. It was like the flyer was a long-lost friend of his and they needed desperately to talk. Now, staring at Zirreo across the fire, he wondered if the white squirrel had anything to do with his dreams.

"I see things at night," he said coolly, testing the waters.

"Nothing lives in these woods." Zirreo was looking off into the distance distractedly, pipe hanging from his mouth. "You have no reason to be afraid."

"That's not what I'm talking about," Kinder said, patiently. He was getting into this. "I have dreams."

He was pleased to note that now the white squirrel was giving him his full attention, and now he even looked a little scared. A bit of ash from his pipe fell into the flames and hissed as it disintegrated.

"Dreams," Zirreo repeated like he had a hearing impairment. Kinder thought this was quite fun.

"Yes, and they tell me things," he said. "There's a flying squirrel in this one. Does the place we're going have any flying squirrels?"

Zirreo just looked at him for a while, then nodded once, slowly. "What else do your dreams tell you?"

Kinder thought of saying he knew but couldn't tell the white squirrel—that would be a way to get him back!—but his capacity for malice only went so far and he frowned as he considered the question.

"I don't know, actually. One of them just tries to tell me something and I don't know what it is because there's all this stuff going on in the background, only I can't tell what it is, and there's a child somewhere—"

"Kinder, listen to me," Zirreo interrupted. He looked more alarmed than ever. "I've never told you what you need to do, but you need to know. When you get to the tree with me, don't stick around. Introduce yourself as a traveler, a stranger stopping by who's injured and in need of rest and healing. The elders will come to the door, and they might seem intimidating, but they'll take you in."

"Wait," Kinder said, alarmed. This was *not* what they'd said before, the last time they'd talked about this. "Where will you be?"

"I will be entering by the back," Zirreo said. "I am going to complete what I started, and I would like you to be around for as little of it as possible, just in case."

Which Kinder understood meant, *I am using you for a distraction and if you are hurt as a result of what I do, I'd have to face the fact that what I'm doing is wrong.* He didn't even ask what Zirreo needed to do; he knew he'd get no answers for his trouble.

Well, fine. He'd do what he needed to do. It was too late to change anything and like it or not, he realized he would be completely lost now without Zirreo. His only hope was to wait until Zirreo had done whatever it was he wanted to do so that he could go back to where they had started and find Lute.

"You need to leave shortly after they show you to wherever you're staying. Once you're inside, it should be easy to get back out. They don't really ask many questions, but you'll probably have to find the door. They don't have a lot of windows."

Kinder was beginning to feel nervous. "What if I forget what to say?" he asked. "What if they don't believe me?"

Zirreo only smiled at him. "They have to believe you." The fire leaped and crackled between them, casting a strange light on him, making him seem older, his smile almost grotesque.

The next afternoon found them standing on the borders of their destination. It was an extraordinarily large, startlingly pale maple tree which looked like it was actually five trees grown together. Somehow the trunk appeared fused of several smaller trunks, wound together and clinging so close to one another that it was optical bewilderment to stare for too long. The other trees around it, much smaller maples that looked like they could be its children, were standing just out of the range of its reach, giving Kinder the impression that if they got too close, they too would be swallowed up and become one with their behemoth mother. Despite the size of the tree, the atmosphere in this clearing was calm, oddly healing in nature, even with the sun behind a cloud and the sky raining soft flakes of snow of all things. It was snowing already? Kinder brushed some off of his shoulder and the cold prickle of the flakes dissolving at his touch made him feel surreal, as though he'd walked into some part of someone's else's life and everything he did from here on out would be fuzzy, seen through tunnel vision, as though he were watching someone else take his own steps for him.

Zirreo nudged him on the shoulder. "Do you see the entrance?" he asked softly. They were standing just beyond the closest trees to the monstrosity Zirreo called Edgewood. Kinder nodded, not taking his eyes off of it, that little pocket of darkness above one of the gently sloping branches. The strange feeling did not leave him.

"Well," Zirreo said, patting him on the back. "You know what to do." When Kinder didn't move, he said, "Go, now. I'll come after."

So it was that Kinder started off towards the tree, counting his steps internally, that heavy calm of indistinctness still blanketed over him as surely as the steady falling snow. He imagined he could feel their eyes on him, those who waited up in the very top of this tree. Maybe even the one from his dream. Here I am, his steps said as he came forward. Here I am, look at me; I am not afraid.

CHAPTER XXI

Horus heard the knock at the door loud and clear, though he was a thousand paces away from the door. He and the other elders had been in a meeting, but when Fairel spotted someone coming outside of the window, everyone stopped to stare.

"Who is that?" Brint asked, coming up beside Horus and peering through.

"They're headed straight for here!" someone chirped behind him.

"Should we go open the door?"

Horus stared down at the small dot making its way over the white-dusted ground. This could mean everything or it could mean nothing at all.

He wouldn't be so stupid as to use the front door, would he?

"Stay here," he said, knowing they wouldn't. As he hurried through the door, he heard Bogus's wavery voice raised in a question.

"Where's Araccus?"

***

Llewellyn was pacing the upstairs hallways when she heard a noise downstairs, through a network of cracks that led to the hole she used to use to spy on the elders when they received someone at the door. Freezing, she put her paw on her stomach and remained that way for two beats, wondering. Then she hurried off in the direction of the place that was waiting for her, just in case.

Just in case this was it.

***

Kinder stood back when the door came open unexpectedly fast. Peering out at him was a younger squirrel than he'd expected, for an elder. As soon as the other squirrel saw Kinder, his eyes softened and his mouth relaxed. He looked rather as though he'd been expecting to be punched upon opening the door. Quickly, though, his mouth reverted to a stern line and he regarded his visitor suspiciously.

"What is it you want?" he asked.

Kinder had thought it through as much as he could with this queer feeling of calm that had come over him, and now he held out his paw. He noticed that a bunch of others had come up behind the young elder, all straining to see him, round eyes curious and wary by turns.

"I..." he stopped. Everyone looked at him. The squirrel in front narrowed his eyes a little. He knew what he was supposed to say, but he'd noticed their wings, that inexplicable flap of velvety skin between their arms and legs, and it made him think of his dreams, of the name he could finally remember from them, so clear, so ready on the tip of his tongue. It was a good name, he thought.

"I would like to see—a healer," he said at last. He couldn't say it yet. It wasn't time.

The lead flyer continued to look stern. "What's wrong with you?" he asked.

Kinder shook his head. "I really don't know," he said. "You see, I used to know when things were going to happen, to others I love, and I used to know when the ground felt ominous," he saw one of the squirrels jump a little at this, "and when I had to take a pee."

"Everyone knows that," said one of the other elders.

"Look," the leader told him. "I don't know what you're doing, but that's not a legitimate sickness, and we cannot help you." He started to close the door but Kinder stuck out both of his paws just in time, forcing it open again.

"I thought you were seers," he said serenely. He reached up to toy with his necklaces, but his paw found empty space and he dropped it again, embarrassed. "Couldn't you do *something* for me?"

One of the squirrels behind the leader was looking at him with something approaching extreme disgust. He primly ignored her.

"Yes, some of us are seers, but all seers perform different purposes." The leader paused, his eyes going a bit wide, head tilted upwards as though he'd just heard something or perhaps sensed something alarming. When he looked down again and back at Kinder, he was noticeably distracted.

"All right, come on in and let us show you to a room. Fairel and Brint will stay with you and attend to you there." The leader turned to one of the other elders, one that Kinder assumed was either Fairel or Brint, and whispered something in her ear. Kinder, who prided himself on being able to read lips, among many other things, knew that the first part of whatever he said was 'find out'. It went on for a good few seconds longer, but Kinder was out of practice. He resolved to whisper to himself a lot in mirrors once he got home.

Home? Yew think yer going back there? a voice that sounded suspiciously like Lute's asked in the back of his mind.

Another, quieter voice asked, *Do you think you want to go home?*

He imagined Skellan baking pies, eating for just himself and his mother chewing on the walls until there were no walls, raging during the night and calling him

Torven when Torven was gone, walked out the door ages ago and *he* wasn't coming back.

"Come," the leader squirrel said to him, and he entered the abode of the flyers.

It was a nice place, he thought, dark without being sinister, with wood floors so smooth Kinder thought he might slip on them. A length down the hallway, there was a young flyer leaning over a bucket. When he neared her to pass her, he saw that it was filled with water and suds, and realized she was washing the entire floor. The darkness of freshly washed wood gleamed out before him, and he hesitated to walk over it. The elders in front of him showed no such qualms, and as they passed over, one of them turned and motioned to him impatiently. On his passing, the squirrel doing the cleaning looked up at him and stared openly.

"Sorry," he said, thinking she might be offended about him trampling on her hard work. She flinched when he spoke and her eyes went wide as acorn tops.

"Um," said Kinder, but he felt a paw on his arm, leading him away bodily this time.

"Don't talk to the novices," Fairel or Brint hissed at him. "They'll never get any work done; strangers are like novelties to them."

They swept on by a couple more of these 'novices', all of whom looked up at Kinder as he passed and stared like he had two tails. They led Kinder up a short flight of stairs and to a door labeled 'guest'. Kinder looked off down the hallway. There were only two other doors labeled similarly, and they both stood with their doors agape, unoccupied.

"This is a bad time, I guess?" Kinder asked, and his stomach took this time to make a noise of protest.

"As good as any," the taller squirrel he was privately distinguishing now as Fairel said evenly. She left him to puzzle over that one, walking into the room and shaking a lamp or two aglow. The other elder, Brint, he guessed, was staring just as openly as the novices had, only her stare seemed more rude than curious.

"Are you hungry?" she asked, after a time.

Lute stared at her. Could she hear his belly? Her tight smile suggested she could. He flushed.

"Yes," he said, and walked into the room he had been given. It was small but well cared-for, with one standing table and a bed. Fairel came out after lighting the lamps and turned to him.

"I will go to see what can be done about that," she said. "Wait here."

Kinder was left standing awkwardly in the middle of the room with Brint standing guard outside. He was beginning to think of her as the less pleasant one of his hosts, and luckily she did not start up any conversation with him; she did not even enter the room. Instead she stood outside, looking distracted, and Kinder had the suspicion again that something was going on that he didn't know about, something they were trying to stow him away for. Had Zirreo managed to make it in? What was it he wanted to do? Had he given Zirreo enough time to do it? Those other elders had disappeared so fast.

Most importantly of all, perhaps, how could he make his escape with someone like Brint guarding him?

When Fairel brought back the food, a steaming plate of sugar-coated walnuts, Kinder ceased to worry so much. As he dug in, there was little thought going through his head except one: where was the squirrel in his dreams? He wasn't sure why, but he was beginning to feel like he had to find her before he left. He thought of the name as he chewed the delicious treats he'd been given, the name that had almost slipped off of his tongue in the cold air outside.

Mariyen.

Where was she now?

***

Mariyen backed all the way up against her bed, mind running frantically over possible escape routes. She could get to the door in time, she knew it, but her legs seemed to have been disabled so that she could not lift one foot and put it in front of the other anymore. She watched the window desperately, the figure climbing through. He was a flyer but he hardly looked like one in some aspects—he was strangely angular and his eyes were disconcertingly pale. Those eyes made her grimace as he walked towards her; they were looking at her without focusing, and their milky quality made her unsure of where, exactly, his gaze was falling at any given time. It was unsettling, just like the jerky yet fluid way he moved across the room towards her. He was wearing a tatty seer's robe of a worn red color over his bony shoulders, and when he reached Mariyen, he grinned flickeringly, though his eyes, both focused and unfocused on her, were not affected by the smile. Absoulim put a paw up to his lips.

"Shhh, we wouldn't want to wake anyone," he said, which was strange since it wasn't nighttime. His voice, too, was strange, all raspy like he was losing it; it made her think of soft shadows behind doors and the puke green remnants of tea leaves in a finished cup.

Mariyen stared, wanting but unable to look away from the pale eyes. Absoulim seemed to realize the effect he was having. He grabbed her arm so suddenly that she

jumped and choked out a ragged scream that was stifled by
his other paw coming up, cold and hard, over her mouth.

"Where is it, do you think?" he asked her.

Mariyen shrunk back; he smelled moldy and
unpleasant and she didn't know what he was talking
about—or did she? Either way, she didn't know the answer
to his question. She wanted him to go, and much to her
own disgust, she realized she'd started to cry, her tears
trickling down her cheeks and over Absoulim's paw, which
he jerked back as though he'd been burned. He stood there
for a moment, still holding her arm, looking from her to the
door and back again.

"You are nothing like her," he said, and, releasing
her, left as abruptly as he had come.

Staring around at the broken glass and her cup on
the ground, spilled out over the wooden floor, Mariyen
continued to cry.

She didn't know when she started to run, but at
some point she must have wiped her tears and used her
fright to power her as far as she could go, down hallways,
through doors, never stopping to acknowledge anyone she
ran into or to wonder where she was going. At some point,
she vaguely realized that she wasn't running into anyone
else; she'd somehow gone off the map, off the beaten path.
Still she kept right on running, faster, faster, through one
door, the next, until she stumbled into total darkness.

She stopped, then, holding her sides and staring
around her, she let her eyes adjust to the dark. She quickly
realized that the darkness was not as total as she'd thought;
in fact, the room she was in appeared to be some sort of
storage closet opening up into a larger room. The sound of
voices coming from this other room made her freeze; she
was evidently not alone here. Mariyen turned back towards
the door, thinking to sneak away—what if it was him

again?—when she recognized one of the voices, and froze again, indecisive. They were coming her way; she would have to decide.

Making a split-second decision, Mariyen clattered her way noisily up the shelf furthest from the door, squeezing to the very back, behind something large and soft which her eyes later informed her was a moth-eaten blanket, covering something smaller and harder. She held her breath and waited, craning her head around the bundle in front of her to stare into the room beyond. She had a surprisingly good view of what was a completely round room opening up on one side, shockingly, to the evening sky, fast approaching dark in brilliant reds and oranges. She stared at this balcony of sorts and wondered, briefly, why you could never actually *see* the sky change, even if you watched it all day.

There was a shelf in the middle of the room with the balcony, empty except for a few oblong knickknacks with a dubious purpose—they looked like something you would either shout through or look through. Then, she realized---*this must be the old observatory*—in the same instant that the source of the voices came around the shelf to stand in her range of vision.

"Did you hear something?"

Mariyen's mother looked exhausted. Her face was strained as she searched the shadows in the corners of the room, and once, her eyes flickered to the closet where Mariyen was hiding. For a split second, she was sure her mother stared directly at her and that their eyes met. But a second later, her mother looked away without comment and she began to doubt herself. The moment was over.

The white squirrel who was with her looked a bit older than her, but it couldn't be by much. He glanced around the room more carelessly and shrugged.

"I don't detect anything," he said, and though he did not even glance Mariyen's way, she was suddenly overcome with the sense that he knew she was there.

Mariyen leaned closer to examine them and saw that the white squirrel was holding some type of blade. It was dangling clean and useless by his side, and Mariyen wondered...

"Zirreo, I swear I heard something."

"We shouldn't leave her alone for too long," Zirreo said, and as though his words were magic, Mariyen suddenly heard a soft crying coming from further back in the circular room, somewhere hidden behind the shelf they'd emerged from the other side of.

Llewellyn looked away from Zirreo for a while, staring up at the shelf to their left as though she saw something of great interest up there. Finally she spoke, in a voice barely audible, so that Mariyen had to strain to hear her.

"Are you sure you can't do it?"

"Llewellyn..."

"It was the plan..." she sounded agitated, like she was holding back tears.

"Could you do it?"

There was silence. Then... "No." The crying continued to echo from the place Mariyen couldn't see.

"Very well, then. We'll just have to think of something else."

"Please. You'll just go away again."

"Llewellyn, no. We'll do this together."

"No, we won't," she said, and her voice was so cold it startled Mariyen, who shrank unconsciously further to the back of the shelf; there was real hatred in that voice. Zirreo opened his mouth and then closed it, cocking his head slightly to the side with a frown.

"I heard something this time," he said, and Mariyen watched Llewellyn slowly cave and follow his gaze to what must have been another door beyond her range of vision. After a while, she turned to face him.

"I don't hear anything," she said baldly. "I think you're trying to change the subject on me."

"No," Zirreo said, but his attention shifted to her, and there was a pleading tone in his voice. "What are you going to do?"

Llewellyn laughed, a cracked and unpleasant sound. "I thought you'd say something like that. Not, 'let me take her', or 'I'm sorry'...."

"I *am* sorry."

Llewellyn snorted. "Tell that to some other young flyer desperate to believe you. You'd walk out of this again if you knew how." As she spoke she was making her way toward the other side of the room, towards the sound of the crying.

Zirreo opened his mouth and Mariyen heard the sound of a door swinging inwards and then Zirreo's sharp, "you."

Mariyen decided to take a chance and moved forward slowly on the shelf, holding her breath for fear of making noise. She got to a point where she could see a bit farther, just beyond her former range of vision, and saw a sliver of Horus's face, but the voice that spoke next was not Horus's, and that was when she noticed the paw, long and spidery, laying across Horus's shoulder. She couldn't scoot further anymore, nor did she want to. Her blood went chill.

"Yes, me," Absoulim said. She could see Horus flinching when he spoke, but the expression on the chief elder's face was more disgusted than fearful. Llewellyn, meanwhile, had stopped her progression to the other part of the room and was staring with a look of open faced horror mixed with something else Mariyen couldn't define. It was she who spoke first.

"What do you want here?" Her voice echoed woodenly off of the walls and Absoulim jerked his head towards her and stared, taking her in for so long that the others in the room began to shift uneasily.

"Answer the question!" Zirreo barked, breaking the uncomfortable silence.

Absoulim turned to look at him.

"I am here for something that's been left for me," he said, taking his paw off of Horus's shoulder. Mariyen saw Horus roll his shoulders back and let out a shuddering breath he must have been holding.

"The chief elder kindly showed me here since Araccus wasn't much use after a point," Absoulim explained. "He was tiring; he kept thinking he was going to get more than he did. He started to have second thoughts about putting it aside for me, but the *chief* elders," he drew a claw down one side of Horus's face, "really are the smartest."

Horus, who hadn't said a word since he'd entered the room—Mariyen was beginning to think he was under some spell—was staring at the knife in Zirreo's paw, realization dawning over his face.

"You didn't do it," he said, looking up at Zirreo. "I let you in here, and you didn't do it."

"Of *course* he's inadequate," Absoulim said; his voice ground up against Mariyen, set her on edge, "he always was. The first time he came here, it was so obvious, but then, the elders aren't accustomed to making good decisions, are they?" He directed this last part towards Horus, who didn't say anything, though his face was as stony as Mariyen had ever seen it. He was under a spell for sure. It was in the way he moved, all stilted, and the way he never once looked around at Absoulim. He was very unlike the Horus she remembered; that Horus wouldn't stand for this.

"What have you been doing lately, Absoulim?" Zirreo said; his face was still the only one that did not betray fear, and he took two steps closer to Absoulim as he spoke. Absoulim reached out a paw, displaying one tattered wing as he did so. Mariyen hadn't noticed the state of his wings before; she'd been too afraid. It was not a pretty sight.

Absoulim was staring Zirreo straight in the face with his paw outstretched, and Zirreo stared right back at him, something of a half-grin coming over his own profile, unexpectedly, irrationally.

"Still doing what you do best, then? Ruining the lives of others with your self-fulfilling prophecies? It must get awful lonely. How hard is it to cope with knowing none of them are me, or have your tastes moved on to slaughtering everyone?"

Absoulim lowered his arm slowly, staring at Zirreo the whole time.

"My tastes have always been exactly the same," he said, and his voice was so soft that Mariyen had to strain her ears to hear every word. "Which is more than you can say for yourself."

Zirreo was silent a moment and then moved, but it was only to lay the knife he was carrying on the floor. He raised his paws into the air.

"A fair fight, then? Unless you cannot resist the temptation of the thing that was promised to you?"

"Where is it?" Llewellyn said loudly. She was coming back from behind the shelf on the other side of the room. Her face looked pale beneath her fur. "Where is this thing you want? Take it and go."

Absoulim smiled then, a thin, twisted thing that was truly frightening to behold, his face like a grinning skull and his eyes like twin pale lamps burning on malice alone.

"Why, Llewellyn, it's on the shelf in the closet," he said, "right behind your daughter."

Mariyen felt all the breath go out of her, her throat constricting. She could smell, suddenly, the contents of the closet all around her, a musty, leafy smell, and as she drew herself towards the wall, she felt her body come up against something hard. Turning, she saw something glowing faintly, its light illuminating the fur on her stomach and the wall beside her. It was the quivering, watery glow of something she knew well, remembered well. The crystal ball. Of course.

Someone was coming her way. She didn't turn back to face them until they were right below her. From the hurried breathing she heard, she could tell that it was her mother.

"Mariyen," she hissed up at her. Mariyen felt around for the base of the crystal ball.

We can't give this to him, don't ask me to.

"It's not here," she heard herself say.

"Loyal," Absoulim said," but not very intelligent. You could die, Mariyen, and imminently." He said her name like it was a joke.

"There will be no need for that particular brand of magic here," Zirreo said. As she'd suspected, he'd somehow known she was here from the beginning.

"You *will* die, white squirrel. That I am going to make sure of." His oddly weak, scratchy voice put Mariyen's fur on edge as it had before in her room. She dug around on the shelf again, trying to bide her time by making it look like she was still searching. Her paws brushed against something, and she stopped; it was not what she was looking for, but it might help. From far away, she could hear the crying start up again, forcibly reminding her that there were five lives in this room with her. Finally, after fumbling about for a while, Mariyen sat up, cradling the crystal ball and staring around the room freely now that she'd been found out.

Zirreo smiled at her. Llewellyn was looking like she was going to be sick. Absoulim had an expression of pure what was it—astonishment? greed? on his gaunt face at the sight of the orb Mariyen held aloft.

"Give it to me," he said, pushing forward in that weird, jerky-yet-fluid way of his, and Mariyen pretended to hesitate for a moment before passing the orb on to him.

Once he had it, Absoulim's eyes lit up; they became manic, frenzied in their anticipation.

"Now," he said to Zirreo. "We'll see you go."

CHAPTER XXII

Kinder finished eating his food, wanted more, and got it almost immediately. They were trying to sustain him in this room, he realized. He could probably ask for initiation rites into their clan and they'd pretend they were considering it, anything to keep him from leaving.

"I need to go," he told Fairel, staring past both elders into the hallway beyond. Every now and then someone would walk by on their way somewhere. It seemed perfectly normal. Which was why Kinder was worried. He didn't need his charms to tell him that when things seemed this normal, it was because they weren't.

"I have that feeling," he told the elders, feeling that maybe honesty was the right way to go here.

"The one where you have to pee?" Fairel asked. Framed against the doorway, Brint's lips curled in an unpleasant smirk.

"Yes, that one. Except the feeling is that something horrible is going on here."

"Oh, never fear that. That's why we're keeping you in here, if you must know."

"Me?" Kinder rose to his feet. "You have to be kidding. You think *I'm* the source of the trouble?"

"We don't think there's any trouble," Fairel said. "We're keeping you from starting it."

"*What?*"

"You can't come here and start talking about some weird feeling in the ground without drawing our suspicions. The chief elder was very interested, but we see through that. I think he's gotten a little daft lately, between you and me. Why would you mention the ground? I've been getting bad feelings for weeks, if you want to talk about bad feelings. They were bad feelings about visitors. You. All of the elders agree, even if Horus doesn't." She looked flushed with the knowledge that she was doing something, at this very moment, that the chief elder wouldn't like.

"Can't you just— Kinder tried to say, but it was at that instant that Fairel started to look a little unstable— literally. She wobbled in place for a moment before falling in a dead faint in front of him. Kinder stared. He decided he might as well go for it, and headed for the door. When he was over the threshold and nearly home free, a paw shot out and grabbed him by the shoulder. He spun around. Of course—he'd forgotten Brint.

Something seemed terribly wrong with her. She was shaking a little, sweating a little, and her eyes were so wide that for a while Kinder thought she must have taken ill like Fairel; he hoped she wouldn't faint holding him.

"Where is he?" she asked. "Is he here?"

Kinder's veins felt sluggish. "I don't know what you're talking about."

Her grip went tighter. "Yes, you do. You came with him, didn't you? He said—he said he would reward us, Araccus and I. That's where Araccus went, isn't it? Where is he? Where did he go?"

But Kinder had broken free of her and was running down the hall as fast as his legs could take him.

Already huffing and puffing and short of breath when he rounded the first corner, he stopped when he realized he had no concept of where he was going. Glancing back nervously in the direction he'd come to make sure Brint wasn't hot on his trail, he tried to think, fighting with the blood pounding in his head. He heard footsteps behind him just as he noticed the figure slumped off to the side of the wall, stirring in slow twitches and tremors. It was an older squirrel, he could tell from the stooped shoulders and the walking stick lying useless next to him on the ground.

Kinder didn't know why he went to the old squirrel, though it ended up making all the difference in the world. He could have turned and left the tree, *should* have judging from the pounding steps tracing his way, coming ever closer, but instead he knelt by the old squirrel and watched as the fluttering eyes tried to take him in. A thought hit him, sudden, imparted perhaps from the other's gaze or from some more mystic source.

"You're Araccus."

The old squirrel only looked at him. It was all he needed.

"Where is the chief elder?" Kinder asked. He held his breath, knowing if Araccus asked him anything, he would be lost and he wouldn't have any time besides. But the former elder only pointed to the hall up ahead, his head lolling back against the wall as he spoke, words barely distinguishable.

"You're not...his..."

Kinder didn't know what to say. He didn't know who this *he* was. He'd thought he had, but he was getting more uncertain by the second.

"No," he said, feeling it was the right answer.

Araccus's posture relaxed.

"...observatory..."

It was all he would manage to say before he stopped speaking for good. It was enough for Kinder. He took the direction Araccus had vaguely pointed in, speeding around the corner into the hall the elder had indicated. Only seconds after he made the turn, he could hear his pursuer clatter into the hallway he'd just left. There was a pause and then a cry; they'd found Araccus. Kinder knew he didn't have long before they'd be on his tail again.

The hallway he had entered was darker and gave off a feeling of magic and time waiting with bated breath. Kinder wanted to slow, to stop and bask in it, and he nearly did. He caught himself just in time, but the lull was enough for him to notice he was hungry. Again.

"Now is not the time, okay Kinder?" he said, trying to talk to himself like he'd heard Lute do several times. It came out of his mouth sounding forced and phony, so he let it drop as he searched the hall. There were several doors, but they were all locked. He ran up and down, trying them each more than once, until he was panting again. It was a dead end. Brint didn't seem to have followed him yet, but at this rate it didn't matter. She'd find him eventually, because he had nowhere to go. He leaned against the last door he'd tried in exhaustion.

This can't be it, another voice spoke up in his head, and this time it was not forced; it contained an unexpected power. It was his own.

There's something you're forgetting. Go over what you know.

So Kinder thought about what he knew. "Well," he said to himself. "When there's an even number of doors…no. When there's an odd number of doors? Yes, the odd, I think. When there's an odd number of doors in any hallway, there must be a hidden one."

That one had come out of one of his books, *What Are Your Doors Telling You?!*. He'd bought it for half-price from a less –than-enthused gray back home. Kinder smiled to himself and began to count the doors.

"One, two, three…four…five, six…seven." His grin went even wider. But how to find the eighth door?

"Araccus! He's dead! Araccus is dead!" Several voices took up the shout, and Kinder heard a commotion in the hall. He didn't have much time. A draft of cold air riffled his fur, and he turned to see a window behind him—

or what looked like it had once been a window. It had long been blocked off by a tree branch, or a separate trunk even—Kinder had seen the tree from the outside after all, and remembered how it looked like several trees bound together. If there was a room partitioned behind this window, though, there seemed to be no way of getting to it. And if there was a room behind the window, why did he feel breeze against his face?

Kinder was about to bypass the window and search further, when the sound of many squirrels walking very, very fast began to come his way. They were talking as they went, their chatter sharp on the air, and he heard enough to know they were after him. The word 'he' was used a lot, along with 'Araccus', and, the dead giveaway, 'find him.' Kinder realized maybe enough time had passed so that they no longer knew what passage he'd gone down, but this gave him no comfort; surely they would check all of them just the same. Sure enough, no sooner had he had this thought than he heard one of the voices, an unpleasant female one that he recognized as Brint's say, "Search everywhere! Don't leave any nook or cranny unexamined, if you know what's good for you!"

Kinder really had no choice. At the moment, he wasn't thinking very hard into it, not stopping to consider that his actions could very possibly be the stupidest ones he'd ever taken. He saw a flurry of movement out of the corner of his eye, the start of a rapid succession of events all pasted together in a way he did not understand. Then he jumped towards the window, into the window, using the table below it as a springboard. He heard a crash, indistinctly, somewhere, and thought he must have knocked the lantern off of the table in his haste. The next moment, he didn't hear or feel anything; his paws grappled for the wood he expected to feel, to grip, so that he could pull himself into a hiding position. There was nothing. Kinder fell a short distance to a cold wooden floor of spikes, spikes he quickly realized, in his scramble to get up, were actually only stairs. He fell against them in relief, his head swimming with confusion.

What just happened? How did I get here?

His thoughts dissolved into a mess of panic: the voices were directly in front of him now, and he jumped on hearing them. Staring in front of him in horror, he noticed that he was looking out into the hall and that some of the squirrels he was running from were right in front of him, looking around. He squeezed further up against the stairs, sure one of them would turn and say, "There he is!", that it would be the end of his daring escape. He was in plain sight after all! But nothing happened, and Kinder slowly realized what he was seeing in front of him might not be a two-way deal. Perhaps when the other squirrels looked his way, they only saw the trunk of another tree blocking a window, rendering it defunct, just as Kinder had.

"Where did he go?" one of the flyers was saying.

"Better yet," said another, tracing the handle of one of the doorknobs thoughtfully, "Suppose there *is* no squirrel to find."

"Huh?"

"Oh come on, Pan. Do you really think a guest killed Araccus? Why just Araccus, that's my question? He could have killed plenty of others. Don't you think it more likely that someone closer did? Someone on the *inside*, perhaps?"

Another flyer jerked his head up. "Della, what are you getting at?" he said. "Be careful what you suggest."

The one called Della shrugged. "All I'm saying is that there's been tension between the elders lately. Everyone's noticed it. Well, except perhaps you, Borim."

"I have noticed it," Borim protested. "It's just...you know the law! It's the most sacred—I don't think they would..."

"You never know," Della said ominously. "Are we done with this hall?"

Borim nodded and they moved out, past where Kinder lay huddled against the base of the stairs. The smaller squirrel, the one Della had called Pan, lingered for a while longer. He turned and stared very long at the section of the wall with the window. Kinder thought he recognized his face from somewhere, and then he had it: the novice flyer, the one cleaning the floor, the one who had stared so much when he first entered the tree. He looked like he was deliberating. Kinder held his breath; perhaps his breathing was noisy, maybe he'd given himself away. At last the small flyer spoke, and Kinder flinched at the sound of his voice.

"If there's anyone back there, I'd leave now, because someone's bound to come who knows about that passage and I wouldn't want to be there when they do."

Then, as suddenly as he had spoken, he was gone.

Kinder sat stunned for a moment—had one of the flyers really just helped him? He wasn't going to let the opportunity go. Turning toward the stairs behind him, Kinder wished for his good luck charm despite himself, and hushed his thoughts. He would have to carry the good luck inside for now; he only hoped he had absorbed enough of it from all the years of wearing those charms. He paused a moment, thinking about whether that was possible.

The more important question, Kinder thought, *is whether I can believe it is.*

He decided that he could.

As Kinder climbed, he noticed that the draft of cold air was getting stronger. Somewhere, this opened up on the outside. And suddenly, he understood, remembering Araccus's last words.

The observatory. Of course. He could find the chief elder here and explain himself, maybe even offer his services in making sure the ground was safe.

Or maybe, whispered the dreaming side of his brain, the sly subconscious, *that's not what you're here for after all.* All he knew for sure was that he was being led by some force, the same calm one that had inhabited him outside of Edgewood when he left Zirreo. It had left for a moment, in the heat of the chase, but it was back and it told him that this place was exactly where he needed to be right now. And this feeling was carrying him up one stair, then another, all the way to whatever lay in wait at the top. If this was his intuition at work, it had never been so strong.

Look at me, see me. Here I come.

***

Mariyen stared, along with everyone else in the room, at Absoulim as he cradled the crystal ball in his paws. For the moment after he took it, a deadly silence descended, and then…

"No!"

Mariyen turned in the direction of the noise. Horus was still standing in the same spot as before, that odd blank look in his eyes, but his paws were to his mouth and the look seemed to be leaving, slowly draining from his face until it became more expressive, more urgent. Angry.

"You must take that away from him, Mariyen. He can't have it. You have no idea what it means—"

Absoulim raised a paw toward Horus.

"Be silent," he said, and Horus fell silent, but his eyes kept regarding the rest of them with that painstaking urgency.

"The spell," Absoulim said, "For what is in my heart. Find it."

He was looking at Zirreo. Mariyen noticed that Llewellyn was nowhere to be found, and assumed she'd slipped into the background again, with the wailing child.

"Heart?" Zirreo snorted. "You don't have one. I'm not going to find anything for you."

Absoulim looked, for a second, like he was trying to regain control of some angry impulse. Then the sides of his mouth curled up in a grin again.

"Fine. I will do one I know, then."

Absoulim closed his eyes and started muttering so low under his breath that Mariyen couldn't hear any of the individual words, if they were words at all; they blended together into one sibilant murmur. Zirreo, she noticed, had begun to get nervous for the first time. He betrayed himself by turning in the direction of the open balcony, and then to the space beyond the shelf-divider at what he knew must be Llewellyn and the child. He looked like he was in the throes of an important decision. Absoulim continued murmuring and Mariyen noticed the air start to take form, contorting around him, like it was gaining a life of its own, breaking free from its form of nothingness.

Then Mariyen began to recognize figures taking shape: a head, a body, a tail, slow-blinking eyes, all formed from a pearly translucence. One, then another, then another, they unfolded themselves in the air above Absoulim and waited, misty eyes trained on Zirreo, who for his part, stood and did not look away. His expression was impossible to read.

Absoulim kept muttering, eyes shut still, and Mariyen noticed that his paws were shaking. It was what she had hoped for, what she had noticed in her room when he backed her up against the bed and she had nowhere to go: she'd noticed that he shook sometimes. It was in his arm when he grabbed her for a second, and she didn't think it was intentional, the type of thing that came from effort, because it almost made him drop her. He was shaking now again, but it wasn't so bad, not bad enough to do what she had hoped it would when she'd handed him the crystal ball.

Please, she thought, *please.* Whatever those figures were—and they looked a lot like wraiths to Mariyen, those creatures that remained after untimely deaths—they were not good news. She felt dread in her heart just looking at them, and even as she looked, they stopped unfolding in the air in front of her and collected above Absoulim's head.

This was all of them, Mariyen realized. This was all of them, and all they were doing now was waiting.

They didn't have to wait too long.

Absoulim raised an arm and pointed at Zirreo.

"All those who have been wronged by this squirrel and now lie dead," he intoned, "Get your justice."

The wraiths needed no other bidding. With a hissing fury, they boiled at Zirreo, coming through the air toward his chest. Zirreo seemed frozen to the ground, and now his mask slipped and his expression was perfectly clear: he was terrified. The first wraith reached him, and instead of ripping into him as Mariyen expected, it went *through* him, just eased on up and tore its way through his chest. It was the only appropriate word, for even though the wraiths were made of the silver air and the more metallic tang of magic, it looked as though each time one forced its way through Zirreo's chest, something akin to a physical injury happened. The agony was apparent on the white squirrel's face, and he stumbled backwards as the third one went through.

There were so *many*, Mariyen noticed, so, so many. How could this squirrel, whom her mother had professed to love once, have committed so many wrongs?

When each wraith had finished tearing its way through Zirreo, it came out over the balcony and shimmered for a second in midair before disappearing altogether. Mariyen, watching the white squirrel so intently, did not notice when it happened at first, until she saw one of the approaching stream of wraiths shudder and almost disappear before it reached its victim. When the next wraiths started to disappear entirely, she looked back at Absoulim, and saw that he'd lost grip of the crystal ball. The one paw holding it was trying to reclaim it desperately while his other paw was still raised for the spell; his efforts were complicated both by the fact that his paw was shaking and that now it was covered in slick red blood.

Mariyen held her breath. It was working; the thorns she'd embedded in the bottom of the crystal ball holder. His paw had finally shook them loose, and if he dropped the crystal ball...

But Absoulim was doing an admirable job of holding on, and the wraiths were taking their toll on Zirreo. He stumbled backwards once more, eyes drooping shut, and slipped to the ground, falling hard. He did not rise.

Mariyen knew she had to do something. She stared at Zirreo's unmoving body; the wraiths were now diving at it from above; it was only the fact that they kept attacking that let her know Zirreo was still alive.

Mariyen ran at Absoulim. It was the only thing she could think to do and they didn't have much time. She wondered, in that moment, where her mother was, why *she* hadn't come to the rescue, then decided maybe it was time to stop caring about what her mother did or didn't do. She was not like her mother, as Absoulim had stated to her back in her room, rather strangely, and the only difference now was that she didn't think she wanted to be like her. It didn't matter that this white squirrel had done some bad things, had messed up occasionally; now he was here, and Mariyen knew that if *she* had once loved someone, she thought that she would be there for him in a time like this even if the feeling no longer remained. Love, once, had to count for something.

Absoulim turned when he saw her approaching, and that was all it took. The ball slipped, then its holder, and both plummeted to the ground, the first with no sound at all, the second with a ringing that echoed off of the walls. The crystal ball part, Mariyen noticed, did not spatter all over the floor; it was still alive, pulsing, shimmering. She didn't know how to break it. It felt like a very bad idea to smash her paw through it, knowing what had come out of the thing. Her disruption had done its job though; the remaining wraiths had vanished, and Zirreo was beginning to stir. He looked extremely ill, but he was moving all the same. She watched him lever himself up onto one paw and stare in front of him with haunted eyes.

"Mariyen!"

It was a voice she didn't know that caused her to turn just in time. Absoulim had turned on her with a snarl, and was attempting to grab at her arm. He got hold once, but the covering of blood over his own paw allowed her to struggle free. He came at her again, and this time Mariyen feinted the wrong way and stepped right into his clutches. Absoulim's pale eyes burned like gray-lit firefly lanterns, burning on hate alone. He pulled her closer to himself and Mariyen thought that her time was surely up when Zirreo's voice came floating clearly to them on the air.

"All those who have been wronged by this squirrel and now lie dead, get your justice."

Mariyen turned and stared, and Absoulim's grip loosened for just a second. She took advantage and pulled her arm away, backing up several steps, continuing to stare at the place where Zirreo stood.

The white squirrel's eyes were fixed on Absoulim and his paw was raised in a similar way to how Absoulim's had been before. The wet tracks of tears were glistening on his cheeks, but the haunted eyes were solemn. He had no crystal ball, Mariyen thought; the only crystal ball lay between them on the ground, trembling impassively. At first, nothing happened. Then, just as Mariyen felt her stomach sink, the form of a squirrel separated himself from the air and materialized over Zirreo's head. He was an older looking gray squirrel, and his shade looked around blearily, as if he did not know where he was. The air shimmered again, and another wraith climbed out from behind the same invisible cover.

Absoulim had grabbed his bleeding paw with the other and was staring at Zirreo intently. He turned suddenly and began to lurch off in the direction of the shelf, his tatty robe wafting behind him.

Though Absoulim was heading for the child and Llewellyn to distract Zirreo, the wraiths didn't know that. All they knew was that their former tormentor and death dealer was getting away, out of their range of vision.

The first of the wraiths, the old gray squirrel, attacked. His spirit arched high over the room and plunged down towards Absoulim, who turned away at the last minute, stumbling into the shelf as he did so. The wraith went into his back, and came out the other side. There was that sound of a silent ripping, a sound Mariyen would probably never have been able to describe aloud.

Absoulim's body shuddered, but he held on to the shelf behind him, baring his teeth. His eyes snapped open again, malevolence embodied, and all Mariyen could think was, *it doesn't affect him.*

She was wrong about that, though. When the fourth wraith plunged its cold body into Absoulim's living one, he began to shake again, only this time it was much more violent than anything she'd seen before. This was a tremor that started inside and worked its way outwards, so that Absoulim's body was having convulsions by the time the tenth wraith appeared.

They kept coming.

How many squirrels had the seer wronged? Mariyen remembered the story of the type of magic Absoulim was exiled for, the self-fulfilling prophecy of death and the elder that had died first as a result. Were all these squirrels victims of the same sort?

Zirreo turned his paw up in a 'stop' motion and the remaining wraiths hovered on the air, looking anticipatory and unhappy with the halt. They were still completely focused on Absoulim. Mariyen was, too, until she saw where Zirreo was looking.

The young white squirrel was staring in the direction of Horus, who was curled up on the floor next to a squirrel Mariyen hadn't seen come in. The new squirrel was leaning over Horus anxiously, and Horus was trembling and flinching and it was then that Mariyen realized the awful truth: he was tied somehow to Absoulim. Every time Absoulim was hurt, Horus suffered too.

Zirreo lowered his paw. The wraiths, still staring with burning eyes at their former persecutor, began to dissolve into the air again. The white squirrel turned to Absoulim again. The dried tears on his cheeks somehow only made him look more fierce in the now hazy light coming through where the balcony stood.

"I knew you couldn't," Absoulim said, his lips stretching in a pained grin. "I knew—

His mouth froze in that fearful smirk, his pale eyes bulging, as something forced its way out of the front of his chest, cold and fatalistically solid.

"I can," said Llewellyn, following her voice around the shelf until she was standing in front of the seer. His body slipped the rest of the way down the shelf, his throat making one strangled noise like he was going to talk before he went silent and fell, face-forward, to the floor. The hilt of the long knife Mariyen had seen Zirreo holding when he and Llewellyn had entered the room gleamed with the sweat of effort, protruding from Absoulim's back.

Horus made a sound, and the squirrel kneeling beside him made a move to steady him; the chief elder was attempting to get up. His face was white and strained like he was about to pass out, or die himself. Before any of them could make a move towards him, his eyes had scanned the room and he turned and began to run, wild and stumbling, towards the door. The squirrel next to him cried out in surprise and went after him to the door, but Horus long gone. Mariyen listened to his footsteps trail down the hall, hard and fast.

The squirrel who'd been kneeling next to Horus turned from the door and looked up at them all shyly.

"Sorry," he said, gesturing out into the hall. "I didn't think it was a good idea to go after him. He seemed a little mad, to be honest."

Mariyen thought she heard Zirreo reply over the rushing of recognition in her mind. This squirrel, russet-furred and more than pleasantly plump, was unmistakably the squirrel from her dreams. He didn't have any necklaces on, but she felt she would have recognized him anywhere. She took a step forward. "I'm—"

"Kinder. And I'm Mariyen. Or, I mean...*I'm*—"

"Kinder," she said, contemplating the name.

"That's right. You saved me, didn't you? It was you that called my name, back when Absoulim was trying to—"

Kinder flushed.

Before either of them could say anything else, Zirreo cried out from behind them.

"Llewellyn! Stop!"

Mariyen saw Kinder turn and followed suit just in time to see Llewellyn, a bundle wrapped in her arms just as in all of her dreams, poised on the edge of the balcony, atop the wooden border meant to keep sightseers from falling.

She did stop, but only briefly. Turning about, she regarded them all for a moment and then let her body drop.

Zirreo made a sound like all the wind had gone out of him, and rushed over to the balcony's edge. Swinging himself over in a flash, he began to climb down the tree. Mariyen and Kinder heard his voice drift up to them, calling, "Llewellyn! Llewellyn!" and in the subsequent silence, both squirrels suddenly realized they were alone.

Kinder turned to look at Mariyen shyly, and she let him look. She looked over at Absoulim's body by the shelf, sprawled with his tattered wings to either side of him, his moth-eaten robe covering him as though someone had begun to wrap him up and take him away. The crystal ball, she noticed, was gone, a single wet patch on the floor where it used to be, the holder lying uselessly a few feet away. They died when their owners died, then; somehow that made a lot of sense to Mariyen. Just because others told you you'd lost the privilege to be a seer, didn't mean your seerhood disappeared. She thought of the room with all the crystal balls, their slow quivering glow haunting the cinnamon wood like the dream of purpose, and thought she would return there soon; there was something she needed to know.

CHAPTER XXIII

When Lute emerged into the sunlight again, he stood in shocked reverence. No light had ever been so bright, nor so welcome. He bathed in the warmth for a while, tracing his paw over the hilt of his knife.

Well, Lute-boy, next time yew curse at the morning for coming, remember this. Remember those rotting chipmunks and their insane king. Or better yet, forget 'em all. Forget...where the hell am I?

Lute looked about him. Ash trees stood in a small copse only a few yards from where he stood on the dry autumn ground, crisp leaves scattered about his feet. He decided it didn't matter.

Been homeless for a while, I'm not going to start caring now, he thought with a private smirk.

This must have been the purpose of walking so far and long underground—the chipmunks wanted to make sure he was far away from wherever he came from, so that he'd have to work to find his way back. He guessed it was supposed to be a punishment. Well, that blew up in their faces. What did he have to go back to? A rotten, collapsed log and the memories of those no longer living. It was getting old.

It was perhaps the fluttering of a garment out of the corner of his eye that let him know he was not entirely alone. The form of someone or something awaited him on the gentle rise of land just before the ash grove. He watched it for the span of a minute, but whatever it was, it was completely still, except for the flapping of something it was wearing or carrying in the wind. He cautiously approached it, a sick premonition rising in his stomach as he got closer.

Sure enough, when Lute got close enough he saw the deflated remains of a young fox squirrel, yet another victim of the gorepedes.

Kicking at the ground in front of him, Lute searched around the area for any holes in the ground, any hint at all that the thing had been here. Then he remembered how when Cainus had been killed, the ground had seemed to fill up on its own. Gorepedes left no traces if they didn't want to, apparently. It was a good thing. Lute had half a mind to forget his truce, plunge back into the ground, and beat up a chipmunk or two—but he kept his cool. This kill was obviously days old. They had technically not broken their side of the truce, so he could not break his.

Looking around him, Lute tried to get some sense of where he was so he could decide where he wanted to go from here. Another gust of wind picked up, and blew the young squirrel's clothes up in a flurry of cloth.

Checking briefly to see if anyone was there to observe, Lute bent down over the fox squirrel, trying not to focus on the empty eye sockets staring up at him.

"Out of luck, kid, aren't you?" he said by way of conversation, searching the squirrel's clothes gingerly for a pocket. He seized upon what he was looking for, and had to turn the thing inside out to get at what was inside. Not much. Five rengolds, but he supposed that was enough to start on. His eyes caught unwillingly on the young squirrel's face and he quickly looked away again.

"Thank y—"

He started to speak, rising, and froze. He could not believe what he was looking at, would not.

The other squirrel across from him did not move for a long time, and he thought maybe it was a trick of his mind, maybe he really was going insane. He'd seen her other places, after all, and none of those were real.

When she spoke, she sounded just like he remembered her and not at all like he remembered her, which told him this was real.

"Lute?" Her voice was soft and disbelieving, but there was an edge to it, and he was all too conscious of his paw between them, clasping the rengolds, in the process of bringing them to his chest.

Edelle took a step closer to him, then two. She opened her mouth, and he thought she would address him again—he was preparing himself—she would ask about how he'd been, what he'd been doing, and he'd say he'd been doing anything and everything but it would be understood that all he'd really been doing was waiting for her. Instead, she dropped to her knees on the other side of the young squirrel and began to cry.

"Bench…oh, Bench. I'm sorry, it should have been me. We all knew the danger, I should have gone, forgive me…"

She held on to the young squirrel, rocking back and forth for a moment, heedless of the fact that he had no insides anymore, he was only a shell of whoever he used to be. The staring sockets of his eyes didn't seem to perturb her one bit; when she looked at them, she only cried harder.

Lute was feeling incredibly awkward. How was he to know Edelle knew this squirrel? What were the chances?

"Uhm," he said, and Edelle looked up, dry-eyed, though a tear still ran down one of her cheeks. Her expression told him that in her grief, she'd forgotten he was there. Now her eyes hardened.

"Thief," she hissed.

"The thing is, I didn't know—"

"That I knew him? So you would have done it to someone I *didn't* know, and that would have been all right? Oh, I'm *relieved*. I thought you weren't like that. I really thought you weren't. I should have known. I mean, look at you."

Lute's paw went to smooth his fur before he could think to hold on to his dignity. *I've just been under*ground, he thought of saying.

"I used to think," Edelle said. "That I'd like to meet you again, to talk to you. I used to *miss* you, Astrippa help me."

"Edelle!" A voice shouted, and the sound of cracking twigs and crunching leaves informed Lute that someone else was coming along to bust up their friendly get-together. A gray squirrel about their own age clattered out from the cover of the aspen grove and leaned up against a tree to gain his breath for a moment.

"Edelle, did you find him?" the new squirrel asked. He then straightened up, looking from Lute to Edelle with a sudden gleam in his eye.

"What's this? Who is this? Are you in trouble?"

What a half-witted question, Lute nearly snarled, *If she were in trouble, yew'd know. And she wouldn't need* yew *to help, either.*

Edelle merely smiled, not seeming to share Lute's opinion of the smog of utter idiocy surrounding this squirrel.

"Edgar, I'm fine. It's just a dirty thief. Now go and get the others so we can take Bench away." She shifted her burden into her lap, not seeming to mind at all that Bench had been dead for days. She stroked his brow and waited. After a time, Edgar finally detached himself from the tree he was leaning against and disappeared into the woods again. Lute could hear him shout to someone. He stared down at Edelle.

"We can still...talk," he tried. She looked up at him again, and he could see her annoyance that he had not gone, that he had not turned his dirty hide and left yet. It clawed at him from a place uncomfortably close to his chest.

"You had better go," Edelle said. "The rest of the colony is about to come over here and I can promise you they won't be happy."

Lute looked at her, feeling resentment fill the hollow space in him. He let it; it felt like warmth after that strangeness, the feeling of being scooped out.

"Fine," he snapped. He chucked the coins he was holding at her. Some of them rained down onto Bench's body, and others rolled off and into the grass on either side of him.

"Edelle!" someone shouted from the woods, and Edelle got up, apparently deciding it was safe to leave Lute with Bench's body, and went off in the direction of whoever called her. Edgar, probably.

Edgar.

That name rang a bell. That face...he couldn't be sure, but hadn't he seen it before at his door, begging him for a favor, saying he'd have the money later, he swore? Edgar the drunk.

Edgar the *dead*.

It was impossible. And yet... He recalled the white squirrel, saying to them how he might have messed up in certain ways. Time. There would be wrinkles. Amid the ticking of all those clocks in the white squirrel's haven, it had seemed possible to him. He remembered the curling of the smoke from the white squirrel's pipe, his words: *It would be rare and hardly detectable, but sometimes the past and the future and the present become…one. They bunch together, if you will.*

It couldn't be. He couldn't give himself time to consider it, it was too much, too far out there. Not to mention what it would mean…

Lute looked to the woods. He remembered the face of Edgar's wife and he remembered the feeling he'd drawn from her strength, who she reminded him of. He knew what he needed to do, but he needed to do it quick. He didn't expect to be there when she came back.

Digging in his belt, Lute pulled out the mirror he'd carved what now seemed ages ago. He bent and placed it on Bench's body, so that it balanced evenly across his silent chest. He stopped for a moment, the word *thief* beating its way through his head, and scooped up all the rengolds he'd thrown at the young squirrel's side. He would get something from this, he would.

He didn't feel like he had anything though, running away. The rengolds burned in his pocket, and the more they weighed on him, the more his anger burned. With every step he took they thumped against his body, clinking and sliding around, and he stopped just to rid himself of the sound, whipping around behind the nearest tree violently and standing there for a moment, breathing back his rage, blinking back whatever was in his eyes.

He could only run for so long before he realized afresh he had nowhere to go.

Yes yew do, Lute-boy.

Saecka's voice, in his head again. Hadn't she been in his head all along, telling him when he was being a fool, and then that one day whispering in his ear, with all the delightful ferocity of the wicked who were unashamed, *come back to us.*

He'd said no, then, of course, like he was above it, and Kinder was with him so maybe for the moment he was. But now Lute's mind, so bent on one mission for so long, bent to other things. There was no mission anymore, and there was no Kinder. Edelle's face swam up, mouthing the word 'thief', 'dirty thief'. Well. Wasn't that what he was? Astrippa knew he'd been fighting it for so long, and now he couldn't remember why he'd tried *so hard*. They were his family, and somehow he'd gotten to where he thought he was too good for them. Left them for an old squirrel who taught him how to talk proper and to carve proper and sometimes beat him senseless. Civilized. There were Edelle and Kinder, but they were lost forever; Edelle would marry a drunk who would sell her mirror in a freak flash to the past that she would never be able to reconcile or remember later; Kinder was dead.

He had an open invitation.

He could have despaired because he'd become lost, but if you knew a band of chickarees you could never really lose them. He could ask around—other chickarees were easy to find if you knew where to look— and he was sure that they would be helpful.

Lute put a paw over the hilt of his knife. With the right amount of persuasion, anyone could be helpful.

CHAPTER XXIV

Mariyen took the cup as it was passed to her with a low thank you and took a sip before passing it on. The mood was somber in the hall where all of Edgewood was packed together, waiting.

They were waiting for the white squirrel to come back, and Mariyen wondered if she was the only one waiting for Llewellyn as well. They'd practically camped out here in the observatory, a thick crowd trailing all the way from the door to the closet she'd hidden herself in. The elders were going about with food and drink, and all disciplines for the rest of the day had been called off.

Kinder had a lot to tell them. At first, when the elders caught sight of him, they stiffened and talked together in clipped tones. They wanted to have him out for potentially murdering Elder Araccus. Mariyen had to come to his rescue there, and they explained together what had happened.

"Where's Horus now?" an elder Mariyen didn't recognize asked, eyeing them suspiciously. Elder Bogus whacked her atop the head with a loaf of bread.

"We d-don't need Horus to tell us th-these two are innocent. C-c-come on, who was saying earlier that Araccus and B-Brint were b-being suspicious? No one t-trusted them."

After misinterpreting an offer of bread—he took the whole loaf when he was offered a piece—Kinder had begun to explain to the group of elders how he'd come with the white squirrel. He hadn't known what the mission was, what the white squirrel intended to do, but he told them about Zirreo being the messenger of Astrippa.

Though flyers by nature were skeptical of Astrippa's existence, this created a buzz in the hall by all who heard it.

More and more squirrels who happened to overhear them stopped and listened. On the chance that the white squirrel came back, they wanted to ask him questions.

The elders, by contrast, weren't incredibly surprised. They exchanged glances very quickly and then the elder Mariyen didn't know said, "There was a prophecy years ago about this squirrel, when he stopped by Edgewood. It was about him giving life to some terrible spawn, so we had him leave."

Mariyen exchanged glances with Kinder. They wisely kept silent on the subject of the 'spawn'. Kinder instead began to explain his original mission, and how the white squirrel had told him the cause of the problems with the ground. He told them that he had a friend who at the moment might be fixing that problem for good, and how he hadn't felt anything wrong with it for the last day. This provoked a lot of discussion.

"You can really tell when the ground is dangerous?" one of the elders asked.

"Squirrels live *underground?*" a random squirrel asked.

Kinder nodded yes to both questions just in time before a whole new set came rushing in. Mariyen watched him try to answer what he could between overly ambitious bites of bread, and marveled at the easygoing way he had. Only an hour ago, these squirrels were hunting him down, but he didn't seem to hold any resentment over it.

They hadn't gotten to talk to each other much, and neither felt the pressing need to. There was easiness to being with Kinder, one that seemed to *require* fewer words.

"What I don't understand," said Mariyen, in the first real pause in the chatter directed at Kinder, "is why Absoulim wanted Zirreo dead so badly. He could have just taken the crystal ball and made his getaway. That's what he came for, after all."

There was a silence in their immediate group, and then Bogus cleared his throat before saying, "It's hard to tell, b-but once a squirrel gets to certain heights of p-power—"

"They always want more," the female elder agreed. "And white squirrels, their type of magic is different from that of a flyer. It's more of an inborn thing, an easy energy. They don't have to work so much for it."

"Absoulim was jealous," Kinder said, though the statement sounded more like a question, a private musing.

"I suspect it," Bogus said. "B-but you can never know some things for shu-sure."

Mariyen remembered Zirreo doing the same magic as Absoulim without the aid of the crystal ball. She also remembered the tears on his cheeks, the way he sounded when he screamed her mother's name.

She knew he wouldn't come back, but something kept her from saying this aloud to the waiting crowd. It was like she and Kinder; neither of them knew exactly why they'd appeared to one another in dreams, unless it was simply to foreshadow this coming together, this sure fit of minds and near-reading of thoughts with a mere glance. There were answers somewhere, and white squirrel or no, fallen messenger of Astrippa or no, she was confident that they would find them in time.

And so they waited, in the late end of fall, for something like spring, though everyone knew there was a winter to survive, just as surely as the leaves now fell, outside, all around on the silent ground.

***

If anyone chanced to be up in the chief elder's chambers and happened to look through the window down into the overgrown garden below, they would have seen someone stirring among the weeds and fallen leaves. But no one, of course, was up in the chief elder's chambers, and so no one was there to see Horus move, coming at to life at last after a long, solid unconsciousness.

He wished it was death. For a moment he only lay there, disoriented, unsure of where he was. The ground tilted up at him, the sky down, at two different angles that clashed together and made him feel sick. Crawling forward, retching on the ground as he went, Horus hoisted himself up a little, using the bark of the tree nearest to him to bring himself to a near-sitting position. Was it Edgewood at his back? He thought it was, but it was so hard to remember. The last thing he clearly remembered was that horrible seer, the one they should have had killed when they had the chance, coming to him in a densely crowded hall in which everyone somehow seemed to ignore his presence, telling him he needed a word. He thought he said no but he could not remember. The sky tipped downwards in front of him, the wan clouds shaking in the line of his blurred vision, and he began to laugh.

Never mind that seer, never mind Edgewood. A single memory occupied his mind now.

This place, this garden. Summer. *Her.* Laughing, turning away from him at something he said. Probably something foolish, but she found it funny all the same. Pulling up weeds, trying to nurse her roses back to health while he told her about how he'd been chosen as one of the few who might become chief elder. Her grinning, saying she wished he didn't feel the need. He'd never took that seriously, had he? She always wore that yellow bow, and everyone called it frippery, but he knew her and there was no one less inclined.

Oh, Sarina. He fell forward onto the ground and pulled himself forward, digging his claws into the earth. He hadn't even bothered to care for this garden after she left, he couldn't bring himself to touch it, the last thing they'd both shared before he'd become too great, too busy.

The sky continued its mad tilt, and he continued to crawl along, around weeds, over the remains of plants, the roses now wilted, not pausing to register the thorns which became stuck in his fur, in his skin. If he reached his paws down far enough, he could plunge them into the ground, take back what was his. What was taken from him.

Horus began to laugh again, and it was a frightening sound, a dry rasping. That was the thing, *exactly*. The ground had taken what he wanted, but how did one get back at the ground? There was nothing to fight it with; it did what it wanted. You could grow your flowers, but in the end they either bloomed or failed, but you couldn't blame the ground. The ground was unaccountable.

Horus struggled forward, his mouth becoming full with dirt, with the rich, gritty texture and the earthy taste. He stopped laughing abruptly when his paw disappeared into nothing. Struggling upwards, the squirrel who was once chief elder but now hardly knew right from left stared at the place in front of him.

It was an opening, a hole! He couldn't believe he hadn't looked for it before, it was so simple! He would show them, the ones who got Sarina. He imagined them down there, laughing over it, monsters from the corners of every nightmare he'd had as a child. He would get them.

It didn't take him long to get the fire started. He grabbed two sticks and rubbed with all the madness in him until a flame leaped up between them, flickering weakly, then blazing so suddenly that he nearly dropped them. Edging over the hole, he peered down and then dropped the blazing sticks before they could singe his paws. They plummeted down, down out of his sight, soundlessly falling. Horus strained his ears but could hear nothing, and he began to think maybe that the hole was a part of his imagination. He stared long and hard into it as if to keep it from vanishing, even as a spasm overtook his whole body. The after-effects of a spell he could not remember had come to take their final toll.

Horus twitched only once, and laid still, the garden quieting around him, the sky tilted back into its normal place, his blank eyes still staring into the shifting darkness.

Somewhere below him, another world flexed and functioned, momentarily oblivious to the lone flame that still burned as it fell.